Spotting her friend, Officer Barney Culpepper, Lucy elbowed her way through the crowd and went up to him. "What's going on?" she asked.

Barney considered for a minute, glancing left and right as he removed his cap. Then he brushed his hand through his crew cut and carefully replaced it.

"We've got a homicide."

Lucy gasped in shock. "Who?"

"Curt Nolan."

For an instant, Lucy didn't register the name. Then it hit her. Her hand flew to her mouth. "Oh, no."

"You know him?"

"A little."

Lucy tried to remember when she'd seen Curt last. Of course—it had been yesterday at the pie sale. She could practically see him raising a fork loaded with blueberry pie to his lips, a glint of mischief in his eyes.

"You're sure he's dead?" asked Lucy, unwilling to believe the bad news.

Barney nodded grimly. "Murder weapon was right there beside him. Some sort of Indian club . . ."

Books by Leslie Meier

MISTLETOE MURDER

TIPPY TOE MURDER

TRICK OR TREAT MURDER

BACK TO SCHOOL MURDER

VALENTINE MURDER

CHRISTMAS COOKIE MURDER

TURKEY DAY MURDER

WEDDING DAY MURDER

BIRTHDAY PARTY MURDER

FATHER'S DAY MURDER

STAR SPANGLED MURDER

NEW YEAR'S EVE MURDER

BAKE SALE MURDER

CANDY CANE MURDER

ST. PATRICK'S DAY MURDER

MOTHER'S DAY MURDER

WICKED WITCH MURDER

GINGERBREAD COOKIE MURDER

ENGLISH TEA MURDER

Published by Kensington Publishing Corporation

A Lucy Stone Mystery

TURKEY DAY MURDER

Leslie Meier

KENSINGTON BOOKS
Kensington Publishing Corp.
http://www.kensingtonbooks.com

KENSINGTON BOOKS are published by

Kensington Publishing Corp.
850 Third Avenue
New York, NY 10022

All Kensington Titles, Imprints, and Distributed Lines are available at special quantity discounts for bulk purchases for sales promotion, premiums, fund-raising, and educational or institutional use. Special book excerpts or customized printings can also be created to fit specific needs. For details, write or phone the office of the Kensington special sales manager: Kensington Publishing Corp., 850 Third Avenue, New York, NY 10022, attn: Special Sales Department, Phone: 1-800-221-2647.

Kensington and the K logo Reg. U.S. Pat. & TM Off.

ISBN-13: 978-0-7582-2892-5
ISBN-10: 0-7582-2892-9

First Hardcover Printing: October 2000
First Paperback Printing: October 2001
20 19 18 17 16 15 14 13 12

Printed in the United States of America

CHAPTER 1

"Look at that face. I ask you. Is that the face of a cold-blooded killer?"

In her usual seat in the second row, part-time reporter Lucy Stone perked up. Until now, she'd been having a difficult time paying attention at the Tuesday afternoon meeting of the Tinker's Cove Board of Selectmen, even dozing off for a few moments during the town assessor's presentation of the new valuation formulas.

Lucy studied the face in the photograph Curt Nolan had propped up on an easel in the front of the hearing room, allegedly the face of a multiple killer: big brown eyes; an intelligent expression; a friendly, if somewhat toothy, smile. He didn't look like a mass murderer to her—he looked like a plain old mutt.

"Kadjo's not just some mutt," continued Curt Nolan, his owner and advocate at the dog hearing. "He's a Carolina dog. I went all the way to North Carolina to get him from a breeder there. He's descended from the dogs that accompanied humans across the Bering land bridge from Asia to America thousands of years ago. He's a genuine Native American dog." He paused for emphasis and then concluded, "Why, he's got more right to be here than you do."

That comment was aimed at Howard White, chairman of the board of selectmen, who was chairing the dog hearing. White—a tall, thin, distinguished-looking man in his early sixties—didn't much like it and glared at Nolan from behind the bench where he was sitting with the four other selectmen as judge and jury.

This was more like it, thought Lucy, studying Nolan with interest. Most people, when called before the board for violating the town's bylaws, exhibited a remorseful and humble attitude. Nolan, by contrast, seemed determined to antagonize the board members, especially Howard White.

Even his clothing declared he was different from the majority of people who resided in the little town of Tinker's Cove, Maine. Instead of the usual uniform of khaki slacks, a button-down shirt, and loafers, which was the costume of choice for board meetings, Nolan was wearing a fringed leather jacket, blue jeans, and cowboy boots. His glossy black hair was brushed straight back and tied into a ponytail with a leather thong. A second leather thong, this one decorated with a bear claw, hung from his neck. His face was tanned and deeply creased, as if he spent a lot of time outdoors in the sun.

"We're not interested in the animal's bloodlines," growled White. "We're here to decide if he's a threat to the community. I'd like to hear from the dog officer."

Cathy Anderson stepped to the front of the room and consulted a manila folder containing a few sheets of paper. Lucy had struck up an acquaintance with Cathy over the years and knew she hated speaking in public, even in front of the handful of citizens who regularly attended the selectmen's meetings. Cathy flipped back her long blond hair and nervously smoothed the blue pants of her regulation police uniform. That uniform didn't do a thing for her well-upholstered figure, thought Lucy.

"The way I see it," said Cathy, taking a deep breath, "the problem isn't the dog—it's the owner."

Hearing this, White exchanged a glance with Pete Crowley. Crowley was a heavyset man who tamed his thick white hair with Brylcreem so that the comb marks remained permanently visible. Also a board member, Crowley was Police Chief Oswald Crowley's brother and a strict law-and-order man.

"Mr. Nolan has refused to license the dog," continued Cathy, "in clear violation of state and town regulations. He also lets the dog run free, which is a violation of the town's leash law. If the dog were properly restrained we could avoid a lot of these problems."

Crowley beamed at her and nodded sympathetically.

"Can I say something?" Nolan was on his feet. Without waiting for permission from White, he began defending his pet. "Like I told you before, Kadjo is practically a wild dog. He's closely related to the Dingo dogs of Australia and other wild breeds. He needs to be free—it'd be cruel to tie him up. And licensing him? That's ridiculous! We don't license bear or moose or deer, do we?"

"You're out of order!" White banged his gavel, startling his fellow board member Bud Collier.

Collier, a retired gym teacher, slept through most board meetings, rousing himself only to vote. Lucy often debated with herself whether she should mention this in her stories for the paper, but so far she had refrained. He was such a nice man, and so popular with the townsfolk, that she didn't want to embarrass him. Nevertheless, she wasn't entirely comfortable about covering up the truth.

"Ms. Anderson has the floor," said White, raising a bristly white eyebrow. "Please continue."

"Thank you." Cathy glanced at Nolan and gave him an apologetic little smile. "I'd like to call a witness, if that's all right with the board."

White nodded.

"I'd like to call Ellie Martin, who lives at 2355 Main Street Extension. Ellie, would you please tell the board members what happened last Monday?"

Ellie Martin stood up, but remained by her chair in the rear of the room. She was a pleasant-looking woman in her forties, neatly dressed in a striped turtleneck topped with a loose-fitting denim jumper. She was barely five feet tall.

"We can't hear you from there," said White. "Step down to the front."

Clutching her hands together in front of her, Ellie came forward and stood next to Cathy.

"Just tell them what happened," prompted Cathy.

"I don't want to make trouble," began Ellie, glancing back at Nolan. "I only filed the report because I want to get the state chicken money."

"What state money is this?" demanded board member Joe Marzetti. Owner of the IGA and a stalwart of the town Republican committee, Marzetti was strongly opposed to government spending.

"It's to reimburse people whose livestock has been destroyed by dogs," explained Cathy. "It's actually town money mandated by state law—it comes out of the licensing fees."

"But you said Nolan hasn't licensed the dog."

Lucy resisted the urge to roll her eyes. Trust Marzetti to find an excuse—any excuse—that would save the town a few dollars.

"That doesn't matter," said Cathy. "It's a state law."

"Well if it's a law, how come I never heard of it?" Marzetti had furrowed his forehead, creating a single fierce black line of eyebrow.

"Well, it hasn't come up in a long time. Not many people bother to keep chickens or sheep these days."

"What kind of money are we talking here—how much are the taxpayers going to have to cough up?"

"Thirty dollars."

"Thirty dollars for a chicken!" Marzetti's face was red with outrage. "Why, I sell chickens for a dollar nine a pound in my store! That's ridiculous."

"Thirty dollars total," said Cathy. "Mrs. Martin had a dozen hens and she'll get two dollars and fifty cents for each one."

"Oh, that's more like it," said Marzetti.

"The dog killed the chickens? Is that what this is about?" demanded Pete Crowley, who was growing impatient.

"You'd better tell them," said Cathy, giving Ellie a little nudge.

"Well, it was like this," began Ellie. "I was busy inside the kitchen, cleaning the oven, when I heard an awful commotion in the yard outside. I went to look and saw the dog, Kadjo, chasing the chickens. They're nice little pullets, Rhode Island Reds. I raised them myself from chicks I got last spring. They'd just started laying and I was getting five or six eggs a day. That is, I used to. The dog got every one." Ellie's face paled at the memory. "It was an awful sight."

"Every one?" Sandy Dunlap, the newest board member and the only woman, was clearly shocked at the extent of the carnage. She was also sympathetic. When she'd run for election last May, she'd promised to be sympathetic and she'd stuck to her word. Nobody with a problem got short shrift from Sandy. "That must have been awful. I think the least we can do is vote to reimburse you for the chickens. I'd like to make a motion."

"That's not the question," snapped White. "She'll get the money. What we're here to decide is if the dog should be destroyed or banished or what."

"Hold on a minute," said Nolan, jumping to his feet. "I haven't heard anything here about it being my dog. How can you be sure it was Kadjo?"

White banged down his gavel. "Mr. Nolan, I'm warning you."

Nolan sat down, perching on the edge of his seat.

Lucy gave Nolan points for trying, however. In her opinion, White tended to be something of a small-town dictator.

Ellie smiled apologetically at Nolan. "Curt, you know perfectly well I'd recognize Kadjo anywhere. After he'd finished chasing all the birds, he picked one up in his mouth and brought it over and put it at my feet, like a present. He was real proud of himself. It was Kadjo, all right."

"Well, Ellie, he was just doing what comes naturally," said Nolan in a soft voice that made Lucy wonder exactly what their relationship was. "It's his instinct, you know."

White reached for his gavel, but was interrupted by Crowley.

"Is the dog vicious?" Crowley asked. "That's what we've got to determine. I'd like to hear from the animal control officer."

"Ms. Anderson—come on now. It's about time we had your report," said White.

Cathy Anderson leafed through the thin folder. She gave a big sigh.

"The way I see it, the dog isn't vicious. He isn't a problem dog. This is the first complaint I've had about him. Kadjo needs a little training and he really ought to be neutered. Frankly, I think that would take care of the problem."

"Neutered!" Nolan was back on his feet, his face bright red with anger. "That's outrageous. Besides, he's a pedigreed dog and I plan to breed him."

White banged the gavel and glared at Nolan, who promptly sat down.

Watching Nolan, Lucy saw that he was having a hard time restraining himself. He seemed tightly coiled, like a spring, ready to explode.

"A lot of people feel that way but it's really kinder in the long run. He'll have a longer, healthier life," said Cathy. She turned to White. "That's my recommendation."

"Thank you," said White. "Do I have a motion?"

"You'd like that, wouldn't you?" demanded Nolan, unable to contain himself any longer. "Face it. It's what you've been doing to my people for thousands of years. Trying to wipe us out. It's not enough that the U.S. government has waged a sustained policy of genocide against Native American people for hundreds of years. Now you're after our dogs, too. You can't let wild Native American dogs breed, can you? Nope. All you want are Welsh corgis and Scottish terriers and Irish setters—Old Country breeds."

"Order!" snapped White, banging down his gavel. "You're out of order, Mr. Nolan. That vote isn't until next week."

Suddenly, a little lightbulb went on in Lucy's head and she understood the tension between White and Nolan. Nolan was a Native American, one of the town's few remaining members of the Metinnicut Indian tribe, the original inhabitants of the area before European settlers arrived in the early eighteenth century. The tribe had recently applied to the federal government for recognition and had asked the board to endorse their application. That vote was scheduled for next week, and if Lucy had been asked to predict the outcome, she'd have to say the Metinnicuts' prospects weren't good with this board, especially White.

"Do I hear a motion?"

Bud Collier roused himself from his nap. "The dog's vicious. It's a killer. I move we destroy it."

Lucy snapped to attention, astonished. This was the last thing she had expected. In similar cases up until now the board had always voted to recommend a course of obedience training, perhaps followed with a probationary period. Collier's habit of napping had obviously prevented him from getting the correct information, which happened all too frequently. Usually, however, the board members amended his motion if it seemed inappropriate. In fact, Lucy noticed, Sandy Dunlap and Joe Marzetti were looking rather pointedly at Pete Crowley, as if urging him to amend the motion.

"Do I hear a second?" snapped White.

Crowley nodded his head. "I second the motion."

Lucy's eyes widened in surprise as she hurried to scribble it all down in her notebook. The board usually followed Cathy

Anderson's recommendations, and she'd urged obedience training and neutering. She hadn't even mentioned destroying the dog.

"You can't do this!" shouted Nolan, jumping to his feet. In the front of the room, Ellie Martin was whispering frantically in Cathy's ear.

"Could I add something?" asked Cathy as Ellie placed her hand on Nolan's shoulder to restrain him. He got the message and sat back down, but his knee jumped as he nervously tapped his foot.

"Out of order," said White, shaking his head. "Do we have any discussion?"

"I'll start," said Crowley. "The way I see it, a dog starts with chickens and the next thing you know he's got a taste for blood and he's after everything that moves. Nip it in the bud, before he attacks a little child. We can't have this sort of thing going on in our town—predatory beasts going after our children."

"I think we're jumping the gun just a bit here," said Marzetti. "This is the first time the dog's come to the board's attention, and let's face it: We have plenty of dogs we see three or four times before we vote to have them destroyed. It's always been a last resort. I think we should give the dog another chance. We don't need to go around destroying people's pets. I mean, the dog is his property, after all, and he's got a right to it."

Bravo, thought Lucy, wondering how she'd found herself agreeing with Marzetti's conservative logic. On the margin of her notebook she jotted down *1:1.* So far it looked as if the ayes and nays were tied.

Sandy Dunlap was next.

"I, of course, want to make sure that children are safe in our town, and I did see a special on *60 Minutes* about dog bites.

Did you know it's the second major cause for emergency room visits in the United States for children?" Sandy Dunlap pursed her lips and nodded, making her blond curls bounce. "And of course, I have to agree with Mr. Crowley that an ounce of prevention is worth a pound of cure."

Lucy started to add a second stroke to the ayes.

"But we have no proof that Kadjo is really vicious. I mean, there's a big difference between chickens and people. My old dog, Harold—what a sweetie—why, he'll chase a rabbit or a squirrel but he wouldn't dream of biting a person."

Sandy gave a big sniff and blinked. "I know how awful I'd feel if something happened to Harold—I think we have to give Kadjo another chance."

Lucy added the stroke to the nays instead.

"What about you, Collier?" asked the chairman. "Are you voting to put the dog down?"

"Wh-a?" Bud Collier blinked.

"You moved to put the dog down. Is that how you're voting?"

"I moved to put the dog down?" Collier scratched his head. "I must have been mistaken. She says the dog's an old fellow who wouldn't dream of biting anybody. I don't want to put him down. I vote no."

Lucy let out a big sigh of relief and put another stroke with the nays.

White threw his hands up in the air. "That's three nos. The motion doesn't pass."

Nolan stepped forward to retrieve the photograph of Kadjo.

"Not so fast," said White, shaking a finger at him. "Be warned: The board won't be as lenient next time. You can be sure of that."

Nolan didn't respond, but Lucy noticed he had clenched his fists. Ellie Martin reached out to touch his sleeve and he suddenly grabbed the picture and marched out of the hearing room. Ellie hurried after him.

"Meeting adjourned!" declared White, banging down the gavel.

Adjourned for now, thought Lucy, as she closed her notebook and tucked it into her purse, but she'd be awfully surprised if this was the end of the matter. She had a feeling the board would be seeing a lot more of Curt Nolan.

And maybe, she thought, as she crossed the town hall parking lot to her car, just maybe, it was time *Pennysaver* readers learned exactly how their board of selectmen actually operated.

CHAPTER 2

Next morning, at the *Pennysaver* office, Lucy stared at the blank screen of the computer. Somehow, writing about the dog hearing wasn't as easy as she thought it would be.

Yesterday, as she had driven home in a fury of righteous indignation, the words and phrases had flown through her head and she'd practically had the whole story written when she pulled into the driveway of the restored farmhouse on Red Top Road she shared with her husband, Bill, and their three daughters. Toby, her oldest and the only boy, was a freshman at Coburn University in New Hampshire.

At dinner, Bill and the girls had laughed when she described the meeting.

"You should have seen the look on Howard White's face when Bud Collier changed his mind," she'd told them as she dished out the ravioli. "I've never seen anybody look so furious."

"What does Kadjo look like, Mom?" asked Zoe, who was in first grade and could almost read all by herself, even though it was only November. At the library, she always went for the dog stories.

"Kind of like Old Yeller in the movie," said Lucy.

"Old Yeller died." Zoe sighed and picked up her fork.

"I can't believe they were really going to kill Kadjo," said Sara, who was in fifth grade and was a member of Friends of Animals. Last summer she had volunteered at their shelter, caring for orphaned baby birds and other injured wildlife.

"If you ask me, maybe they should have," declared Elizabeth, who was a senior in high school and a contrarian on principle. She speared a chunk of lettuce with her fork and took a tiny bite. "He killed twelve chickens, after all. What about them?"

"Killing the dog wouldn't bring back the chickens, would it, Mom?" Sara's round face was flushed with the effort of reaching across the table for the breadbasket. "It would just be killing another helpless, innocent animal. And Kadjo is a special dog, an endangered breed."

"I don't know if *endangered* is the right word," said Bill, giving Sara a pointed glance as he passed her the bread. "If they've survived all these years, they're hardly in danger."

"Just because they've done okay up to now doesn't mean they're not endangered," insisted Sara, holding out her plate for seconds. "They're losing habitat. People are building houses where there weren't any—there's less and less room for wild animals."

"There's going to be less and less room for the rest of us if you don't stop eating like that," said Elizabeth, who had limited herself to four raviolis and a large helping of salad. "You're going to get fat, like that man on TV last night."

"He weighed 1100 pounds," said Sara, defending herself. "I only weigh one tenth of that."

"Right," said Elizabeth, rolling her eyes in disbelief.

"That's enough." Lucy then repeated what had become her mealtime mantra: "It doesn't matter how much you weigh— what's important is feeling healthy and having enough energy."

* * *

"Hey, Lucy, how's that story coming?" demanded Ted Stillings, editor and publisher of the *Pennysaver* and her boss, intruding on her thoughts and snapping her back to the present.

Lucy shook her head, to clear her mind, and looked at the computer screen. It was still blank. As much she wanted to write the truth about the meeting, she was finding it hard to overcome her old habit of reticence. "Discretion is the better part of valor" had been one of her mother's favorite expressions, and Lucy had grown up believing that, if you couldn't say something nice about someone, you didn't say anything at all.

But she was a reporter, she reminded herself. She had an obligation to tell the truth. She straightened her back and took a deep breath, as if she were preparing to dive off the high board into a deep pool. Then she began tapping at the keys, picking up speed as she went and quickly filling up the screen.

Kadjo, a Native American dog, narrowly escaped the fate that overtook his human companions when Selectmen voted 3:2 to spare his life.

"Lucy, I think you need to tone this down a little bit," suggested Ted, after she had sent the story to him for editing.

"No way, Ted." Having taken the plunge, Lucy was in no mood to compromise. "I wrote it just the way it happened. Nolan didn't get a fair shake. Listen, I've covered a million dog hearings and they always give everybody a second or even a third chance. I think they were discriminating against Nolan because he's Indian—I really do."

Ted tapped the mouse and scrolled through the story again.

"Look here. You're sure you want to say that Bud Collier 'roused himself from his usual afternoon nap?' Let's cut out that phrase, okay?"

"Ted." Lucy had set her teeth. "He sleeps through every meeting. Every one. People have a right to know."

Ted shrugged. "He's been on the board for twenty years or more and keeps getting reelected. He must be doing something right."

"Ted! People vote for him because they don't know he sleeps through the meetings. How are they going to know if we don't tell them?"

Ted chewed his lip. "Okay. You have a point. I'm just going to cut "usual afternoon nap" and put "brief nap." How's that?"

"It's waffling."

"It's using discretion, and that's the name of the game in community news."

"You sound just like my mother," said Lucy with a shrug. "It's your paper. I'm just the hired help."

"That reminds me. I have a feature for you with a nice Thanksgiving tie-in. And since you're so keen on Native Americans these days, you'll love it. It's about a woman who makes American Indian dolls and won a prize." Ted scrambled through a pile of papers on his cluttered desk. "Here it is. Ellie Martin. Lives on Main Street Extension."

"That's the woman at the hearing last night. You know, whose chickens got killed."

"I thought her name sounded familiar."

"Some coincidence." Lucy took the press release from the

American Dollmakers' Association and studied it. "She seemed real nice. I'll give her a call. When do you want it?"

"To run on Thanksgiving. As soon as you can get it to me. Oh, and Pam asked me to remind you about the pie sale."

Pam was Ted's wife, and this year she was in charge of the pie sale that raised money for the Boot and Mitten Fund. Without the fund, a lot of children in Tinker's Cove wouldn't have warm winter clothing.

"Oh, gosh. I did forget," said Lucy, remembering that in a moment of foolish optimism she'd agreed to bake six pumpkin pies for the sale. "Now, if you don't have anything else, I've got to run. I promised I'd help Sue take the day care kids on a field trip, and I'm late!"

"I was getting nervous," said Sue when Lucy pulled open the door to the recreation center basement where the day care center was housed. "I was afraid you'd forgotten about the field trip."

Sue Finch, Lucy's best friend, had convinced penny-pinching town meeting voters to fund the center several years ago, and it had been such a success that now there was hardly a murmur when the budget item came up every year.

"I got here as soon as I could," said Lucy, smiling at the group of preschoolers who had gathered around her, eager for attention.

"Hi, guys. Who's here?" She went around the group, pointing a finger as she named each child. Harry. Justin. Hillary. "Where's Hunter? There he is, behind Emily. And who's this?"

Lucy had spotted an unfamiliar face: a slight little girl with pale skin and huge black eyes.

"This is Tiffani," said Sue. "Today's her second day with us and I was hoping you'd be her special friend. How does that sound, Tiffani? Will you let Mrs. Stone hold your hand?"

Tiffani didn't answer but studied her shoes. Lucy could see a fine little blue vein throbbing at her temple. She gave a questioning glance to Sue, then reached down and took the little girl's hand. She was surprised when Tiffani didn't snatch it away, but instead gave her a little squeeze.

"Okay, gang. Let's put on those jackets," urged Sue.

Lucy helped the kids zip and button their coats while Sue gave last-minute instructions to Frankie Flaherty, her assistant, who was staying at the center with the three infants. When it was Tiffani's turn, Lucy couldn't help noticing how thin and ragged her lavender hand-me-down jacket was; the quilted lining was worn through at the elbows and shoulders. It could hardly provide much warmth and was much too big, besides. Making a mental note to tell Pam that Tiffani was a prime candidate for the Boot and Mitten Fund's largesse, she once again took the girl's hand and they followed the others out to the minivan Sue had borrowed from the senior center for the trip.

"All aboard," cried Sue, cheerfully. "We're going to see the turkeys!"

"Is that where we're going?" Lucy asked, doubtfully. "Andy Brown's turkey farm?"

"Where else?" replied Sue, sitting down beside her. "It's Thanksgiving."

"I know," said Lucy. She glanced at the kids, who were so small that their legs stuck straight out on the adult-sized van seats. "Turkeys can be a little scary, especially when they're bigger than you are."

"Nonsense," said Sue with a wave of her beautifully manicured hand. "We've been learning all about turkeys. When we get back, we're going to make hand turkeys."

"Hand turkeys?"

"You know. The kids trace their hands on a piece of paper. Then the thumb is the head and they color in the rest of the fingers for the turkey's tail."

"I remember when Toby made one in kindergarten," said Lucy, a tinge of sadness in her voice. "He was so proud of it."

"Do I detect a touch of empty-nest syndrome?" Sue peered at her. "Is Toby coming home for Thanksgiving?"

"He's coming Tuesday, right after classes, and he's bringing his roommate, Matthew. What about Sidra?"

Sue's daughter had graduated from college a few years ago and was living in New York City, where she was the assistant producer of Norah Hemmings's daytime talk show. Her engagement had just been announced.

"Not this year. She's going to *his* folks," Sue snorted, fidgeting with the silk scarf she'd tucked in the neck of her tailored tweed jacket. "They're not even married and it's starting already."

Lucy smiled. "Do I detect a touch of jealous mother-in-law?" she asked.

"Touché," said Sue, smoothing her neat pageboy and staring out the window at the passing fields and trees. "I'm just not used to the idea of her being engaged, much less married."

"It must be hard," acknowledged Lucy. "I can't believe how excited I am that Toby's coming home. I really miss him. It's like there's this big, gaping hole at the dinner table." She laughed.

"Actually, I guess he took the bottomless pit with him. For the first time ever, I have leftovers."

Sue chuckled and turned to check on the kids. "You know," she said as she settled back in her seat, "you have to expect some changes in Toby. You never get back exactly the same kid you sent away."

"Oh, I know," said Lucy. "But that'll be nice: seeing how he's grown and changed."

"Sure," said Sue, giving her hand a little pat. "Okay, kids, we're almost there. Now, who can sing with me? 'Over the river and through the woods,' " she began.

" 'To grandmother's house we go!' " screamed the kids.

They were still singing merrily when they arrived at the turkey farm. When Andy Brown had taken over his father's failing dairy farm, a lot of people in Tinker's Cove had thought he was crazy. He had proved them wrong, however, and had turned the farm into a local attraction. In spring the place was filled with lambs and bunnies and chicks and he held Easter egg hunts. In summer he sold fresh fruit and produce. In September it was apples and cider, and by October the fields were full of pumpkins and a dilapidated old barn had been transformed into a House of Horrors. Now, in November, some of those Easter chicks had matured into a flock of Thanksgiving turkeys.

"Hi, kids, I'm Farmer Brown," said Andy, greeting them at the bus. "Welcome to the farm." As usual, he was dressed in overalls and sported a bright red bandanna.

"Good morning, Farmer Brown," chorused the kids, prompted by Sue.

They all climbed out of the van and gathered in the barnyard, which separated the farmhouse from the barn. A parking lot was off to one side and beyond that stood a cluster of equipment sheds.

"Are you here to see the turkeys?" Andy asked.

"Yeah!" said Harry.

"And what's the noise a turkey makes?" Andy had shown lots of school groups around the farm. He knew the routine.

The kids all began making gobbling sounds, the boys vying to see who could be loudest. Tiffani was the only one who remained quiet, standing silently beside Lucy.

"I guess you all know that turkeys are called *gobblers*," said Andy. "Come on. Follow me!"

Lucy took Tiffani's hand and they followed the rest of the group across the barnyard and around the barn. There, in a huge pen dotted with A-frame shelters, were several hundred white turkeys. It was an awesome sight.

"Wow!" said Sue. "Turkeys are bigger than I thought."

"And noisier," said Lucy, listening to the din. She was aware that Tiffani had slipped behind her, only taking occasional peeks at the turkeys.

"And smellier—phew!" said Harry, making them all laugh.

Studying the turkeys, Lucy decided they were remarkably ugly animals. The males were enormous and sported long, fleshy combs that dangled across their beaks, hanging down one side. Wattles, in lurid shades of blue and pink, dangled from their necks and a large tuft of course black hair sprouted from each male's chest. Their scaly, reptilian feet had sharp spurs in addition to their three-clawed toes.

The females, although smaller than the males, were still

substantial birds. They didn't have combs on the tops of their heads, but they didn't have feathers either. Their bald heads were covered with lumpy, knobby skin.

Oddest of all, thought Lucy, studying the birds with the fascination truly horrible sights seem to require, were their eyes. They had an odd reflective quality, and when they blinked it reminded her of a shutter on a camera lens.

"How do we know turkeys are birds?" asked Sue, who was holding up a large white feather.

Emily knew the answer. "They have feathers."

"That's right," said Sue. "What else makes them different from us? Do they have mouths with lips and teeth?"

The kids studied the birds, trying to decide.

"They have beaks," said Justin.

"Farmer Brown, what do they eat?" asked Sue.

"Mostly corn and grain. See over there?" He pointed to the opposite side of the pen, where a worker was emptying a sack of grain into a metal hopper. "He's feeding the turkeys."

"Isn't that Curt Nolan?" asked Lucy, recognizing him from yesterday's hearing.

"Yup. Curt helps out this time of year."

"Farmer Brown," asked Sue, intent on continuing her lesson, "how big are these turkeys?"

"These turkeys are Nicholas Mammoths. The females dress out to between fifteen and eighteen pounds, the males at twenty to twenty-five pounds."

"What do they wear when they get dressed?" asked Hillary, giggling.

"They don't wear clothes." Farmer Brown scratched his head.

"Oh, I get it. Dressed means something different. It means after they're killed and ready to cook."

"Killed?" Emily's face was white. The kids had suddenly grown very quiet. Behind her, Lucy could feel Tiffani's little body stiffen.

Lucy and Sue exchanged glances. Suddenly the trip didn't seem like such a good idea.

"A lot of food comes from animals," said Sue, using her teacher tone of voice. "Cows give milk and chickens give eggs, but to get meat we have to kill the animals. That's the way it is."

"All of them?" Hillary was horrified.

"All except one," said Farmer Brown. "TomTom Turkey. Want to see him?"

"Sure," said Sue, stooping down and giving Hillary a hug. "Let's go see TomTom Turkey."

"Old TomTom won the blue ribbon at the county fair last summer. He's the biggest turkey you're likely to see."

Andy pulled open the door and they all followed him into the large, airy barn. Lucy inhaled the scent eagerly—a rich mixture that recalled the cows that had once lived there combined with the fresh, sweet smell of hay. She loved the smell of a barn; it reminded her of childhood visits to Uncle Chet and Aunt Elizabeth in Thompson's Ridge, where they had had a dairy farm.

Unlike their barn, which had been filled with cows, Andy's barn was largely empty. Bins and shelves for produce lined the whitewashed walls, and pens were set up for displaying baby animals in the spring, but these were all vacant now. The only inhabitant of the barn was TomTom, who lived in a wire pen in the southwest corner, where sun came through a high window.

"That's some bird," said Lucy, simultaneously appalled and amazed. Tiffani was tugging at her arms, so Lucy lifted her up. She could understand the little girl's desire to be safe in somebody's arms. TomTom didn't seem entirely pleased to have company. After cocking his head to study the group, he'd begun puffing out his chest and spreading his tail, strutting around his pen. The kids were definitely impressed and stood silently, watching warily.

"How big is he?" asked Sue.

"He weighed fifty pounds last summer and he's probably grown some since then. I'd guess close to sixty pounds."

"So he's older than the others?" asked Lucy.

"Yup. I've had him about a year and a half. He's full grown."

"What made you decide to keep him?" she wondered aloud.

"Well, that's a funny story." Farmer Brown was leaning against the wood and wire pen. "First year we raised turkeys we picked him out for our Thanksgiving dinner. But when we got all done and all the turkeys were sold, my wife said she didn't want to have turkey after all. Said it wouldn't hurt her feelings if she never saw another turkey in her entire life, in fact; so we went off to her sister's in New York for the holiday and we took along a ham. And that's what we're going to do this year, too. So it looks like Old TomTom here is safe for a while."

"What's he doing?" asked Justin.

Farmer Brown turned to see. TomTom had suddenly become agitated. His comb had become more erect and his wattles had inflated. He was rocking forward and backward, staring at Farmer Brown.

Brown laughed and removed his bandanna, waving it in

front of the bird. TomTom seemed to puff up even more, if that were possible, and then charged at the bandanna.

The terrified kids ran for cover, cowering behind Lucy and Sue.

Brown laughed and waved the red bandanna again; TomTom went for it, hurling himself against the pen. The children shrieked, and Hillary began to cry. Tiffani buried her head beneath Lucy's chin and clamped her arms firmly around her neck. Lucy knew they should lead the children away, but she was fully occupied with Tiffani, whose body had gone rigid.

Just then, a side door opened and Nolan appeared. He made a sound like a turkey's gobble and waved his red cap; TomTom turned and stood facing him.

Lucy took advantage of the moment and loosened Tiffani's grip, shifting her to her hip. Sue took Emily and Hillary by the hand and started toward the door. The boys followed.

"Thank you for letting us visit," called Sue as they quickly exited the barn and headed for the van. Lucy was bringing up the rear and she turned to give Farmer Brown a good-bye wave.

He didn't notice. He was gesturing angrily at Nolan, who didn't look too happy. To Lucy, in fact, it seemed that the two were engaged in a heated argument. She gave Tiffani a little squeeze and hurried out the door.

CHAPTER 3

Ellie Martin looked at Lucy over the rim of her mug, filled with herbal tea, and chuckled.

"Boy, I've got to hand it to you. You sure like to live dangerously." She glanced at the copy of the *Pennysaver* that was lying on her kitchen table with the rest of the day's mail.

"Oh, I don't know," said Lucy, ready to defend her story. She looked around Ellie's neat kitchen, where the scent of baking filled the air and new loaves of bread sat cooling on the counter. Then she took a bite of warm, buttered anadama bread. "After I saw the way they treated Curt, I decided it was time to tell the awful truth about the board of selectmen. Inquiring minds want to know—at least I hope they do."

Ellie smiled, revealing perfect white teeth. "Don't get me wrong," she said. "I don't have any problem with what you wrote. Frankly, I think it's long overdue. I just hope you know what you're in for."

Lucy experienced a sinking feeling, unrelated to the fresh bread she had eaten. "You think people are going to be upset?"

"Oh, yes," said Ellie.

"Oh, well," said Lucy, with a sigh. "There's nothing I can

do about it now. It'll blow over. In the meantime, tell me about your dolls."

"Come on. I'll show you."

Lucy followed Ellie down the narrow hallway of her ranch-style home into the third and smallest bedroom.

"Now that the kids are grown, I finally have a room just for my dolls," said Ellie. "My husband died a little over two years ago. He made the shelves for me."

"I'm sorry," said Lucy, wondering if a romance was brewing between Ellie and Curt Nolan and trying to figure out how she could ask.

Ellie led the way into the room, pointing out her workbench, complete with sewing machine, set up in front of the single window. The rest of the walls were lined with storage units, cabinets below and shelves above. The shelves were filled with supplies: baskets containing bits of leather, jars containing colored beads, a rack holding every color of thread imaginable. Taking center stage, opposite the window, was a lighted cabinet with glass doors containing the finished dolls. Ellie opened the door and Lucy stepped closer to examine them.

"These are exquisite," Lucy said, genuinely impressed by Ellie's craftsmanship. Each doll was different and each seemed to tell a story. A mother, dressed in a buckskin dress with flowing fringe on the sleeves, sat with her legs tucked beneath her, holding a tiny baby. Two little girls were posed together; they were holding tiny baskets filled with minute blueberries. A little boy with a bow in his hand seemed to be bursting with pride; Lucy guessed it had something to do with the bulging game bag that hung from his shoulder.

Ellie opened it, revealing a tiny, beautifully crafted rabbit, perfect down to its little white cottontail.

"These are incredible," said Lucy. "How do you do it?"

"I start with wire frames," said Ellie, showing Lucy several forms she was experimenting with. "Then I model the bodies using a special resin—the hands and the faces are the hardest. It's important to get them just right.

"Then I paint the features and make the wigs and clothes and accessories. . . ."

"You make everything? Even the baskets?"

Ellie's cheeks flushed. "I make it all. I don't use any findings. Of course, sometimes it takes a bit of thinking. Take the blueberries, for example. What do you think I used?"

"I can't imagine," said Lucy, bending closer to study the baskets.

"If you shake them, they roll around. They're not molded together or anything."

"I give up," said Lucy.

"Tapioca. I painted grains of tapioca with acrylic paint, and it was quite a trick, getting just the right color. In the end, I used several colors, even a few pinks and greens. Makes them look more realistic."

"That's amazing. It's no wonder you win prizes. Let's see," said Lucy, flipping open her notebook. "You won 'Best in Show' and 'Most Authentic Ethnic Doll' at last month's meeting of the American Dollmakers' Association.

"It's kind of like the Oscar of the doll world," said Ellie, a touch of pride in her voice.

"Was the competition stiff?"

"I'll say. Thousands of people enter every year."

"And which doll won?"

"You can't see it. I mean, I don't have the winners here. They're on display at the Smithsonian."

"Wow. That's a real honor," said Lucy, scribbling the information down in her notebook. "Do you ever sell them?"

"You bet. That's what got me started. I needed to make money and I didn't want to leave my girls. Angie's in law school now and Katie's at Dartmouth. So I started making dolls and selling them at craft shows. That's how I got started. I sold the first ones for five dollars each. Can you imagine?"

Something in her tone made Lucy suspect the price had gone up. She had to ask. Maybe she could get one for Zoe. "How much?"

"It depends on the doll. The mother there—she'd go for about twelve hundred."

Lucy gulped and decided Zoe would have to go without an Indian doll.

"That little boy—he's special. He'd probably go for eighteen. I know it sounds like a lot, but people buy them as investments. I've heard of dolls I sold years ago for a few hundred dollars going for thousands at auctions."

"And you make only Indian dolls? How come?"

"Well, I'm part Metinnicut. I guess it's really been a way to affirm my heritage."

Lucy was surprised. She hadn't had the slightest inkling that Ellie was a Native American. Now that she knew that Ellie was Metinnicut, it helped explain her behavior at the dog hearing.

"Is that why you were so reluctant to testify against Curt?" she asked.

"In a way, I guess. I've known him all my life."

Lucy didn't want to blow the interview, but she had to ask. "And you're just friends?"

"Just friends," said Ellie, firmly, changing the subject.

"The dolls are all authentic, you know, in a generic way. I couldn't learn much about the Metinnicuts in particular, so I took patterns from other tribes in the Northeast. I call them 'Eastern Woodland Indian.' That way I can use designs from other tribes that appeal to me. Take the fringed dress, for example. I saw one in the museum in Cooperstown—that's in New York— and modified it. Working on such a small scale I had to simplify it, anyway, but the spirit's there, if you know what I mean."

Lucy studied the expression on the doll's face, which seemed to capture not only maternal love but also the mix of anxiety of hopefulness that all mothers feel for their children. Then she nodded.

"Why couldn't you learn about the Metinnicuts? There's Metinnicut Pond and Metinnicut Road. There's even Metinnicut Island out in the bay. And isn't there a war club in the Winchester College museum?"

"There is, but it's actually the only remaining Metinnicut artifact. Except for the names, I haven't been able to find anything else. It's all disappeared: the language, the culture, everything. The tribe died out in the eighteenth century. A lot of people around here have some Indian blood, but it's mixed in with a lot of other stuff. Frankly"—Ellie gave a little laugh—"I've probably got more Italian genes than anything else."

"But if there's no Metinnicut culture left, why are folks like

Curt Nolan making such a big deal about it? They're even want recognition as a tribe from the federal government—the selectmen are voting on their petition next week."

The question hung between them before Ellie finally spoke. "Because of the casino."

"Casino?" Lucy wondered if those occasional lapses of attention during selectmen's meetings were getting out of control. This was the first she'd heard about a casino.

"That's why they need federal recognition," continued Ellie. "If they get it, they can build a casino. I've heard they even have the plans. They want to put it on Andy Brown's farm."

Lucy remembered the disagreement she had witnessed between Andy Brown and Curt Nolan the day before.

"And how does Andy Brown feel about this?"

"He's all for it. He'll make a lot of money. That's what it's all about: money." Ellie's voice was full of sadness. "It isn't really about Metinnicut heritage at all."

"How come I haven't heard about this before?"

"Because nobody's talking about it. They've kept it pretty quiet. I only know because Bear Sykes—he's the tribal leader—is my uncle. They're going to present the whole plan at the selectmen's meeting next week." Ellie smiled slyly. "I thought inquiring minds would want to know—off the record, of course."

Lucy said her goodbyes quickly, knowing she'd better get back to the *Pennysaver* office as fast as she could to check with Ted. She only hoped he'd be there. Thursday afternoon, after the paper came out, was typically a quiet time when he took care of personal errands like haircuts and dental appointments. When she arrived, however, she found he was still working and so was Phyllis. Both were talking on the telephone.

As Lucy hung up her jacket she wondered if Ellie had been right about her story. Maybe the voters were capable of outrage; maybe there was hope for the democratic system after all.

She sat down at her desk and booted up her computer. While she waited for it to complete whatever it was doing, the phone rang. Ted and Phyllis were still on the other lines, so she answered.

"I'm calling about the dog," said a woman with a quavery voice. "That Kadjo."

"If you have an opinion about that story, we'd welcome a letter to the editor," said Lucy. "That way, we could print it."

"I don't think that dog should be allowed to run around. It's a menace. My sister lived next to a man with a vicious dog, and that dog killed her cat."

"That's very interesting—"

"Not that the cat died right away. She got it to the vet and he did what he could but poor Misty never regained consciousness."

"This was in Tinker's Cove?"

"No, no, no. Maude lives in Chagrin Falls, Ohio."

Lucy was confused. "I thought the cat was named Misty."

"Misty is the cat." The quavery voice was definitely getting a little testy. "Maude's my sister."

"Right. And could I have your name?"

There was no answer.

"Hello? Hello?" said Lucy, finally concluding the line was dead.

"That was funny," she said to Ted and Phyllis. "A woman called about a dog that attacked her sister's cat in Ohio."

"It's been like that all day," said Phyllis, letting the phone ring. "The phones have been ringing off the hook. Everybody's got an opinion about that dog story."

"They're calling about the dog?" Lucy's eyebrows shot up. "What about the selectmen? Aren't people mad that Bud Collier sleeps through the meetings and Howard White is a megalomaniac and Joe Marzetti is practically a fascist?"

Phyllis smiled. "Sorry. They're calling about the dog."

"Yeah?" Lucy was disgusted to find she was relieved. "What do they say?"

"It's been about fifty-fifty," Phyllis continued, ignoring the ringing phone and taking a moment to examine her manicure. Then she sighed and picked up the receiver. "*Pennysaver.*"

A sudden crash—Ted slamming down the receiver—made Lucy jump.

"No more dog stories, okay?" he snarled, glaring at her.

"No problem," said Lucy. "Actually, I think I'm on to something big. Very big. Maybe a scoop."

"Really?" Ted was skeptical.

"Maybe." Lucy was suddenly hesitant. "It's the first I've heard of it."

"Well, what is it?"

"Ellie Martin told me the Metinnicuts want to build a casino on Andy Brown's farm. They even have plans."

Ted stared at her, forgetting the ringing phones. "You're sure about this?"

"I'm not sure. It's just what Ellie said. But she is part Metinnicut."

"Yeah. She's Bear Syke's niece."

"So she said."

"Well, I guess she'd know then." He paused. "I suspected something like this, but I didn't know it had gotten so far."

Lucy shook her head. "I don't know. A casino in Tinker's Cove—it's crazy."

Ted snorted. "Crazy is right. It's madness." He tilted his head toward the still-ringing phone. "This is nothing," he said. "When people in this town find out that the Metinnicuts want a gambling casino, all hell's gonna break loose."

CHAPTER 4

Thin November light filtered through the kitchen windows and fell on the big, round golden oak table in Lucy's kitchen. It wasn't bright enough to allow her to make out the tiny expiration dates on her coupons, so she had also lighted the milk-glass hurricane lamp that hung above the table. Spread out before her were a colorful array of magazines and coupon sections from the Sunday paper, the IGA flyer, and yesterday's food section from the newspaper.

The town might be on the brink of a tremendous furor about the casino, but Lucy had other things on her mind. She stared at the blank sheet of paper in front of her and bravely wrote *Thanksgiving Menu* at the top. This year, she thought, she'd like to try something different. She flipped through the magazines until she found the article she was looking for: "A New-Fashioned Thanksgiving."

Low in fat, rich in flavor, our easy-to-prepare Thanksgiving dinner is sure to please even the pickiest Pilgrims, promised the story, which was accompanied by artfully designed photographs.

She turned to the recipes with interest. Pumpkin soup seved in hollowed-out pumpkin shells? She didn't think so. It looked like something unspeakable to her and the kids would never eat it. Never, ever.

Come to think of it, she decided, there was no point in serving a soup or appetizer course. It would just spoil appetites for the feast to come.

She paused, doing a quick head count. How many would there be? Herself and Bill, the four kids, Toby's roommate Matthew plus her elderly friend, Miss Tilley, who was practically one of the family. That made eight.

She smiled in satisfaction. Eight was a nice number. Her dining room, newly redecorated after a plumbing disaster last Christmas ruined the ceiling, could seat eight very comfortably; she had sterling for eight. There were even eight teacups remaining in the china service for twelve she'd inherited from her mother. Eight would be perfect.

But what to serve them? Turkey and stuffing, of course. Creamed onions—she liked creamed onions and only bothered with them once a year. She glanced at the magazine menu. There were no creamed onions; there were zucchini boats stuffed with corn kernels. What happened to "easy-to-prepare"? She checked out the other vegetable suggestion. Brussels sprouts?

She clucked her tongue and wrote *peas* on her menu. Her picky Pilgrims would never eat Brussels sprouts.

Oops, she forgot mashed potatoes. Bill loved mashed potatoes, especially with plenty of gravy, and there would be plenty of gravy. That reminded her. There had to be sweet potatoes, too, but not with marshmallows. She shuddered. Just a little brown sugar. And of course, cranberry sauce and pickles and celery with olives—really just an excuse to use her grandmother's celery boat shaped like a little canoe.

That should do nicely, she thought, adding nuts to her shopping list. Three kinds of pie: mince, apple, and pumpkin, followed by nuts. It was her favorite part of the meal: that second cup of coffee and the leisurely cracking and dissection of walnuts, pecans, almonds, and filberts. Not hazelnuts—good, old-fashioned filberts—and grapes from the centerpiece.

She put down her pencil and studied the menu. *So much for something new*, she chuckled to herself. It was the same Thanksgiving dinner she served every year—the dinner her mother had made, the same dinner she remembered eating as a little girl perched on a slippery telephone book at her grandmother's long linen-covered table.

At the IGA, Lucy pulled the Subaru into her favorite parking spot and grabbed her coupon wallet and list. She loved grocery shopping; she saw it as a weekly challenge. Getting the most she could for her 120 dollars. To her way of thinking, there was nothing more satisfying than finding a buy-one-get-one-free special and matching it up with a coupon that she could double—or even triple using one of her precious triple coupons—if the deal was sweet enough.

Reminding herself to buy some extra canned goods for the high school food drive, she reached for a cart and tugged it loose from the others. Whirling around, she almost bumped into Franny Small.

"Sorry, Franny. I didn't see you," she apologized.

"No harm done," said Franny, reaching for a cart.

Franny looked remarkably good these days, thought Lucy. The tightly permed gray curls were gone. She now had a sleek frosted do and had replaced her pink plastic glasses with contact lenses. Also gone was the faded pink raincoat she'd worn for years; today she was wearing a sporty golf jacket.

"How's business?" asked Lucy as they pushed their carts into the produce section. Franny had recently landed a contract with a major department store for the hardware jewelry she designed.

"I've got more orders than I can handle," said Franny. "I've got a catalog company that wants ten thousand pieces but I can't find enough pieceworkers. I'm supposed to meet with some community development people from up north next week. I'm hoping I can get them interested in setting up a home industry program with me." She reached for a bag of carrots. "It's kind of frustrating, you know. I've got so many ideas."

"It's marvelous—what you've done for the local economy," said Lucy. "The unemployment rate is under ten percent for the first time I can remember."

"It could go even lower if we get that new casino they're talking about," said Franny. "That'll provide a lot of jobs, not to mention a terrific marketing opportunity for my jewelry. I'm already working up some Indian designs."

So the word was already out, thought Lucy, speculating that the Metinnicuts were carefully leaking news of the casino, hoping to build grass roots support through a word-of-mouth campaign. "You're in favor of the casino? I thought you were a Methodist," teased Lucy.

"I am a Methodist," said Franny. "And I'd never dream of gambling myself. But other people don't see anything wrong with it. The Catholics have bingo, don't they? Who am I to tell other people what they can and can't do?"

"I don't know," said Lucy, adding a bag of apples to her cart. "Somehow it just doesn't seem right."

"You've got to change with the times," said Franny, checking her watch. "I've got to run. If I don't see you before then, have a happy holiday."

"Thanks. Same to you," said Lucy, watching as Franny flew down the aisle, headed for the dairy section. She wasn't through in the produce section, not by a long shot. She still needed potatoes, at least ten pounds, and fruit for lunches, not to mention a holiday centerpiece. And those nuts—where did they hide them?

Almost an hour later, Lucy pushed her heavily laden cart up to the checkout, where she got in line behind Rachel Goodman. The cashier, Dot Kirwan, was busy ringing up another customer, a sixtyish woman with her gray hair cut in a neat sporty style.

"I don't know what the world is coming to," said the woman. "Did you see the paper this week?"

Lucy pricked up her ears.

"You mean that dog? Kadjo?" asked Dot. "I think he deserved a second chance."

"Not the dog. What that reporter wrote about my Bud! Honestly, the man dozes off for a few minutes and she makes it sound like he sleeps through all the meetings or something. It's outrageous. I don't know how they can print lies like that."

"It's not a lie," Lucy found herself saying. The three other women all turned to face her. "I've been covering those meetings for years, and I have to tell you Bud sleeps through all of them."

Mrs. Collier wouldn't hear it. She was so angry that the little wattles under her chin were quivering. "You're Lucy Stone?"

"I am." Lucy braced herself for the attack.

"Well, you ought to be ashamed of yourself! Writing trash like that! And don't think for one minute that I won't be complaining to the publisher."

Taking her bundle from Dot, Mrs. Collier plopped it in her cart and sailed out through the automatic door.

Standing in her place in line, Lucy felt rather sick.

"Well, I guess she told you," observed Dot.

"Don't give it a second thought, Lucy," said Rachel. "It's about time the truth was known." She glanced at Lucy's overflowing cart. "Is Toby coming home for Thanksgiving?"

"Yup. With his roommate Matthew. What about Richie?"

Richie, Rachel's son, had graduated from Tinker's Cove High School with Toby and was a freshman at Harvard.

"He's staying in Cambridge. He says it's a good opportunity to catch up on his work." Rachel furrowed her brow. "I think he feels a little overwhelmed."

"It's a big adjustment," said Lucy. "I can't wait to see Toby. He says everything's okay but I need to see for myself—if you know what I mean."

"I do." Rachel began unloading her groceries onto the conveyer belt. "In fact, Bob and I are driving down and taking him out for Thanksgiving dinner."

"That's a good idea—plus you don't have to cook," said Dot as she began ringing up Rachel's order. "I see you got a turkey anyway."

"For the freezer. At this price, why not?"

"I got two," confessed Lucy. "One for Thanksgiving and one for the freezer."

"So you didn't get the fresh ones from Andy Brown?" Dot was grinning wickedly.

"At $1.69 a pound, I don't think so," said Rachel. "Not with tuition bills to pay."

"When that casino comes, our troubles will be over," said Dot. "We'll all be rolling in money. I went to Atlantic City last fall and won twelve hundred dollars. On the slots. That's the way to pay those bills."

"You were lucky," said Lucy. "I don't think you can count on winning. Most people lose money."

"That's true," conceded Dot. "But think of all the jobs. That casino will be a shot in the arm for the local economy."

"I don't know," said Rachel doubtfully as she began bagging her groceries. "Casinos bring a lot of problems: organized crime, drugs, money laundering. I can't say that I'm for it. In fact, Bob's going to be speaking against it at the meeting next week."

Rachel's husband, Bob, was a lawyer.

"That's good. People ought to speak up," said Lucy. "This is a nice seaside town. What do they want to go and spoil it for?"

"For money," said Dot matter-of-factly. "That'll be $141.38."

"Ouch," said Rachel, pulling out her checkbook. "That hurts."

"I feel your pain," said Lucy, nervously eyeing her own cart.

"Can I sell you a scratch ticket?" asked Dot.

"No!" chorused Lucy and Rachel.

CHAPTER 5

Zoe was excited about being able to read.

"S-T-O-P," she read the letters off the red sign, pronouncing the letters carefully. "Stop! Stop the car, Mom."

Obediently, Lucy braked at the corner and turned onto Main Street, driving a block to the Broadbrooks Free Library, where she pulled into the parking lot.

Lucy had, until recently, been a member of the library's board of directors and was still struggling with the mixed emotions of guilt and relief over her resignation. She had been tempted to avoid the library, but that wouldn't be fair to the kids, especially Zoe. This Saturday morning Lucy had firmly set her emotions aside so Zoe could attend a special program. Dr. Fred Rumford, an archaeology professor at nearby Winchester College, was leading a workshop on flintknapping, teaching the kids how primitive people made weapon points out of rocks.

"P-A-T-R-O-N-S," pronounced Zoe, staring at the PARKING FOR LIBRARY PATRONS ONLY sign. "Pat-rons. Mom, what's a patron?"

"It's *patron*. It means a person who uses something," explained Lucy as they followed the concrete path that led around the library to the front door. When they rounded the corner of the building she noticed Curt Nolan, who was raking the last of the leaves, and she gave him a wave.

"We're going to the library, so that makes us patrons," she continued, as they climbed the front steps, "and we can park here. If we were going to the stores across the street, we couldn't park here."

"But you do park here sometimes when you go shopping. You parked here when I got my school shoes." Zoe pursed her lips primly. "You broke the rule."

"I'm sure we went to the library that day, too," said Lucy so firmly that she almost convinced herself.

"No, we didn't," insisted Zoe. "I'd remember."

"Maybe I meant to, but ran out of time," said Lucy, pulling open the door. "Now remember: It's the library, so you need to use your very best manners."

Zoe nodded solemnly and hoppped over the sill. Passing in front of the glass display case containing a pewter tankard she started reading off the letters: "E-Z-E . . ."

"Ezekiel Hallett," said Lucy, taking Zoe firmly by the hand. "He owned that mug a long time ago."

She pushed open the inner door and glanced at the circulation desk, then felt annoyed with herself for feeling quite so relieved that it was unattended. This was ridiculous, she told herself. People quit jobs, especially volunteer ones, all the time. And she had a good excuse. Her paying job at the *Pennysaver* was taking up more of her time.

"Mrs. Stone, how nice to see you."

Startled, Lucy turned and smiled at the new librarian, Eunice Sparks.

"Well, you know how it is," said Lucy. "Work, kids—there's never enough time."

"Oh, I know," Eunice agreed solemnly. Her brown eyes seemed almost liquid, floating behind her glasses. "And I see your byline *all* the time. Do you know we're having a special children's program this morning. With Fred Rumford from the college. Such a *fascinating* man."

"That's why we're here," said Lucy. "Zoe and I want to learn all about the Indians."

"And Indian dogs," said Zoe.

"The workshop is just starting downstairs in the meeting room," said Eunice.

"Thanks—see you later," said Lucy, leading Zoe through the children's section. "We'll pick out some books afterward, okay?"

As soon as Lucy opened the door to the stairs they heard the voices of the children and parents gathered for the workshop. What Lucy didn't realize until they reached the meeting room was that all the other children, except for Zoe, were boys. They were accompanied mostly by their fathers, but there were a few mothers, too.

"Let's go, Mom," said Zoe, halting in the doorway. "I don't care about Indians."

"Nonsense," said Lucy, heading for the two remaining empty chairs. "Indians are interesting."

"That's right," said Fred Rumford, a tall man with thinning hair who had a pair of wire-rimmed glasses perched on his nose. "Indians are very interesting."

He was standing at the head of a long conference table with a plastic storage box in front of him.

"What I have here," he said, peering down at the group seated at the table, "is the only remaining genuine Metinnicut artifact—at least, it's the only one we know about.

"The Metinnicuts, as you all know, lived here for hundreds of years before the European settlers came. We don't know very much about them or how how they lived. We do know that they hunted for game—deer and rabbits and things like that—and they also ate a lot of shellfish." He paused and looked at the children. "How do we know this?"

"Fossils?" asked a little boy with a fresh haircut.

"Good answer. But the Indians only lived here in the past thousand years or so. Fossils, bones that have turned to rock, are much older than that. But we do have archaeological evidence we've dug up. What do you think it is?"

Lucy knew Zoe knew the answer. They'd read about an archaeological dig in a children's magazine last night. She nudged her, but Zoe remained silent.

"Arrowheads?" asked another boy, who was wearing a cub scout uniform.

"Yup." Rumford nodded. "We have found arrowheads and spear points. What else?"

"Treasure chests?" guessed a boy in a plaid shirt. Lucy heard Zoe give a disgusted snort under her breath.

"No treasure," Rumford shook his head. "What do you think we've found?" He was staring at Zoe.

She hesitated, and Lucy held her breath, willing her to find the confidence to answer. Finally, she did. "Shells and bones."

Predictably, the boys hooted. The answer must be wrong because a girl said it.

"That's right!" exclaimed Rumford, silencing them.

Inwardly, Lucy gave a silent little cheer for Zoe. She hoped her daughter would always be able to summon up the courage to give an answer, even a wrong one, but she knew the odds were stacked against Zoe. The older the little girl got, the harder it would become.

"We can tell a lot about what the Indians ate from their garbage piles. We find bones from animals they ate and big piles of shells. We also know from what's in this box that they didn't just kill animals. Sometimes, they killed people."

He had the boys' undivided attention as he opened the box and lifted out a decorated wooden object for them to see. It seemed to Lucy to be in two parts: a wooden shaft decorated with black designs that held a solid wooden ball.

"It's a Metinnicut war club, used to bash out the brains of their enemies."

"Yeah!" exclaimed the boy with the haircut.

"Yuck!" said Zoe, wrinkling up her nose.

"I'm going to put it back in the box and let you all take a look at it, and while you're doing that, I want each of you to take a pair of these protective goggles. Then we can start making some flints, okay?"

Once Zoe was settled with her safety glasses and chipping away at her piece of flint, Lucy got up and wandered around the room, examining the displays that Rumford had brought from the museum. These were mostly points of all sizes—many of which would seem to be nothing more than bits of rock to untrained eyes. The war club, however, was undoubtedly something remarkable. Examining the workmanship, Lucy knew that it would have been difficult to produce anything like it even with modern woodworking tools. How could a native craftsman, working only with crude stone tools, make such a finely crafted weapon?

As she studied the war club, Lucy wondered about Metinnicut culture and all that had been lost. What had their garments looked like? Their houses? How had they managed to survive in such a hostile climate for hundreds, perhaps thousands, of years? What did their language sound like? What were their songs and dances like? What games did their children play?

It seemed terribly sad to her that nothing remained of the Metinnicuts except for the war club. So much had been lost, impossible to recapture. She couldn't help wondering how different American history might have been if the European settlers hadn't considered themselves superior to the natives and had been willing to learn from them.

"Look, Mom! Look what I made!"

Zoe was standing next to her, holding a crude arrowhead in her small, plump hand.

"Wow! That's neat."

Lucy picked it up and turned it over. "Was it hard?"

"No, Mom. C'mon. I'll show you."

Lucy allowed herself to be led back to the table, where Zoe instructed her in the fine art of flintknapping. When they were through, she, too, had produced a passable arrowhead. When she finally looked up, she realized everyone else had gone.

"I'm sorry," she stammered, blushing. "Are we holding you up?"

"Not a bit," said Rumford. "It's great to see someone take such an interest."

"It's fascinating," said Lucy. "It's amazing when you think about it. We have refrigerators and freezers and cars and TVs and computers, and it's a national emergency when the electricity goes out. These people lived so simply. . . ."

"Exactly," said Rumford, starting to pack up. "And they were successful until disease, brought by the Europeans, wiped them out. They had no immunity to common illnesses like measles and smallpox."

"Can we help you with this stuff?"

"Thanks," he said. "We can go right out to the parking lot through the workroom next door. Saves going up and down the stairs."

In a few minutes they had packed everything into plastic totes and gone out to the parking lot, forming a little parade. Rumford led, carrying a pile of boxes, followed by Lucy, who also had a stack of containers. Zoe was last, proudly carrying the box with the war club.

"It's the gray van. It says *Winchester College* on the side."

"W-I-N . . ." began Zoe, then stopped abruptly as Curt Nolan threw down his rake and approached them. He stopped in front of Zoe, towering over her.

"What you got there?" he demanded.

Zoe didn't answer, but stepped closer to Lucy.

"Is it a war club?" Nolan bent down so his face was level with hers.

Zoe nodded.

"Aren't you awful little to be carrying something so important?"

Nolan was no longer addressing Zoe. He had stood up and was talking over her head to Rumford.

Lucy started to speak, defending her child, but Rumford beat her to it.

"She's a very trustworthy child," said Rumford. "She was doing just fine."

"Well, what's fine to you and what's fine to me are two different things." Nolan glared at him. "Of course, it's only an artifact to you, a curiosity. To me, it's my history and my heritage. It's sacred. And if you can't take proper care of it, you ought to return it to the people who can—the tribe."

"What tribe?" Rumford's voice was contemptuous. "There are no Metinnicuts left. There is no tribe. And that's what I'm going to tell the feds."

Nolan's face flushed purple and he made a move toward Rumford. His hands were clenched, he seemed ready to take a swing at the professor.

Rumford's face was also flushed and he seemed ready to chuck the boxes he was holding in order to defend himself.

Lucy stepped toward him, staggering and causing her boxes to slip. The professor reflexively braced himself, allowing her to steady herself.

"How clumsy of me," she said, chuckling nervously. "We'd better get these things safely in the van."

"Of course," said Rumford, turning and setting his boxes on the curb. Slowly, with shaking hands, he took the keys out of his pocket and unlocked the back door, pulling it open.

"How's your dog?" Lucy had turned to face Nolan and spotted Kadjo, sitting patiently in the cab of Nolan's pickup truck. "Is he staying out of trouble?"

Nolan didn't answer, but stood for a moment glaring at Rumford. He suddenly turned and stalked off, stopping to pick up the rake he had thrown on the grass and tossing it into the bed of his truck. He jumped in the cab beside his dog and drove off, leaving rubber.

"Thanks," said Rumford. "I really didn't want to tangle with him."

"He's not so bad," said Lucy, carefully taking the box with the war club from Zoe and handing it to Rumford. "Emotions are running high these days. The Metinnicuts have a lot at stake." She smiled. "He might have a point, you know. Didn't the Smithsonian recently return some Indian artifacts?"

Rumford's face hardened. "If they get recognition as a tribe, and that's a big if, then we'll have to reconsider." He snorted. "If you ask me, it's just a big bluff. They don't care about the war club or anything else. They only want to be a tribe so they can have a casino." He paused and looked at her. "I mean, if they care so much, how come they've never protested when the football team uses the club at their pep rally every year? I care about that club a hell of a lot more than any of these so-called Metinnicuts—that's for sure. I make the team captain sign a paper saying he understands how valuable it is and that he accepts liability if anything happens to it, but believe me, I'm not happy until the club is safely back in its case."

Lucy nodded. "I understand how you feel," she said. Then she smiled. "But if I were you, I'd smoke a peace pipe with Curt Nolan. I think you have more in common than you think, and he's not somebody you want to have for an enemy."

Rumford shrugged in response and got in his van, giving her a nod as he drove off. As Lucy watched him go, she doubted he'd follow her advice, and maybe he was right. Curt Nolan didn't seem eager to make peace with anyone.

CHAPTER 6

Sometimes controversy was a good thing, thought Lucy, as she pulled her cleaning supplies out from beneath the kitchen sink. Thanks to the fact that the Metinnicuts' petition was so controversial, the selectmen's meeting had been scheduled for Tuesday evening, instead of the usual afternoon time, so more people could attend. That meant Lucy had all day to get the house in shape for Toby's homecoming.

Cleaning was never her favorite activity, but today she really didn't mind. She wanted everything to be perfect for Toby and his roommate Matt—or at least as perfect as it could be considering the house was over a hundred years old and occupied by an active family.

Oh, she loved the old farmhouse that she and Bill had worked so hard to restore, but she had to admit the years had taken their toll. As she went from room to room with her dustrag and vacuum, she noticed the woodwork was smudged with fingerprints, the paint on the back stairway was scuffed and the wallpaper in the downstairs powder room was peeling. In the family room, the sectional sofa was looking awfully worn and the rug was past cleaning—it needed to be replaced. She sighed. There wasn't any hope of getting new carpet anytime soon; Toby's college bills made that out of the question. She went into the dining room to cheer herself up. There, the ceiling was freshly plastered and new wallpaper had been hung last spring.

As she polished the sideboard with lemon oil, she wondered about Matt, Toby's roommate. What kind of home did he come from? Coburn University had a smattering of scholarship students like Toby, but most of the students came from families that had plenty of money and didn't even qualify for financial aid. Did Matt come from a home like that? Would he expect a guest room with a private bath when all she could offer him was the trundle bed in Toby's room. And that was if she could convince Elizabeth to move back to her old bed in the room she used to share with the other girls—a big if.

All of a sudden the room she had been so proud of didn't look that great after all. The furniture didn't match; she'd found the big mahogany table at an estate sale but the chairs came from an unfinished furniture warehouse and she'd stained and varnished them herself. The rug was a cheap copy of an Oriental and the sideboard's only value was sentimental because it had come from her grandmother's house.

She flicked the dustcloth over a framed photo montage that hung above the sideboard and paused, studying the kids' faces. The montage had been hanging there for quite a while. Zoe was still a baby, Sara still a chubby preschooler, and Elizabeth was actually smiling. Perhaps that was her last recorded smile, thought Lucy, her eyes wandering to the photograph of Toby.

It was one she particularly liked, snapped just after Toby had scored a goal playing soccer in his freshman year of high school. He looked so young and boyish, with his chipmunk cheeks and enormous adult teeth, and so thoroughly pleased with himself.

Her hand lingered over the photo. She would never admit it to anyone, not even Bill, but she had missed Toby terribly since he'd left for college. Maybe it was because he was her firstborn, maybe because their personalities were so similar, but she had felt as if a part of herself had suddenly gone missing. She smiled. But now he was coming home again and the family would be whole again. She would be whole again.

Hearing the school bus she glanced at her watch. Goodness, where had the day gone? She'd been so busy she hadn't noticed the time, and no wonder. She'd cleaned both bathrooms and the kitchen and had tidied and dusted the entire house. Only one job remained: evicting Elizabeth. She went to greet the girls.

"Where's Toby?" demanded Zoe, breathless from running all the way up the driveway.

"He's not here yet," said Lucy.

"Why not?" demanded Sara, dropping her bookbag on the floor with a thud.

"It's at least a five-hour drive, and he probably had classes this morning. I bet he'll get here around dinnertime."

"Oh, goody," said Elizabeth, her voice dripping with sarcasm. "I can't wait."

Lucy bristled. "You still haven't moved your things out of Toby's room like I asked you to," she said.

"I'll take care of it," replied Elizabeth, draping herself languidly on one of the kitchen chairs.

"It's still his room, even if you have been using it. I don't want Toby to feel that this isn't his home anymore."

"Well, it isn't, is it?" demanded Elizabeth. "He's not here

anymore. Why does he get a whole room that he's not even using when I have to share with these cretins."

"What's a—" began Zoe.

"Am not!" screeched Sara, spraying everyone, and the table, with milk and chocolate chip cookie crumbs.

"That's disgusting!" exclaimed Elizabeth, reaching for a napkin to wipe her face as Sara beat a hasty retreat.

"Sara! Get right back here and clean up the mess you made, including your backpack!" yelled Lucy, shouting up the stairs.

"And you . . ." Lucy had turned to glare at Elizabeth. "I want you to clear your stuff out of Toby's room right now."

Lucy narrowed her eyes and Elizabeth shrugged. "Okay."

"And as for you . . ." Lucy turned her baleful stare on little Zoe, who was struggling with a gallon jug of milk. "Let me pour that for you."

By 6 P.M. everything was ready for Toby's homecoming. Elizabeth had taken her things out of his room and Lucy had made the beds with fresh sheets.

The table was set for seven and Toby's favorite meal, lasagna, was cooking in the oven.

Lucy inhaled the aroma of herbs and cheese as she went from room to room, closing the blinds and turning on the lights. In the lamplight, she decided, the house looked attractive and welcoming.

"Hey," called Bill, as he pushed open the door and dropped his lunch box on the kitchen counter. "Where's Toby?"

"He's not here yet," said Lucy, taking Bill's jacket and hanging it on a hook.

"Not here? What's keeping him?"

"I don't know," said Lucy in a tight voice. "I haven't heard a word from him."

"Now don't worry," said Bill. "I'm sure everything's fine. They probably left later than they planned. You know how kids are."

"I'm sure that's it," said Lucy, pushing thoughts of squealing brakes and ambulances to the back of her mind. "Besides, we'd have heard if . . ."

"Right," said Bill. "The roads are clear. It's not like there's a storm or anything. I'm sure they're fine."

"Fine," repeated Lucy, peeking in the oven. "I know. Let's have a glass of wine and I'll hold dinner for a while. Say fifteen minutes? After all, it's Toby's favorite."

Bill opened a bottle of chianti and they sat at the kitchen table, fingering their glasses.

"How was work?"

"Fine." Bill took a sip of wine. "How was your day?"

"Okay. I have a meeting tonight."

"What time?"

"Seven."

Bill looked at the clock.

"Don't you think we'd better eat?" he asked.

"I guess so," said Lucy with a big sigh.

CHAPTER 7

Zipping down Red Top Road on her way to the town hall, Lucy had only one thought on her mind: She didn't want to go. She wanted to stay home to wait for Toby. Instead, she would have to sit in an overcrowded meeting room, facing the members of the board she'd so self-rightously blasted in last week's paper. What would their reaction be? Would Howard White publicly admonish her from his lofty perch as chairman? Would Bud Collier give her hurt, reproachful glances?

Worst of all was the knowledge that Ted had offered to cover the meeting for her and she'd turned him down. She had been sure Toby would arrive earlier in the day and there would be plenty of time to catch up at dinner. What had she been thinking? she wondered. How could she have forgotten that college students operated on a different clock from the civilized world, staying up until all hours of the night and sleeping late in the morning?

She braked to turn into the town hall parking lot and groaned aloud. Every spot was filled. That meant she was going to have to park across the street at the library. Not a good sign. The meeting room was obviously packed with people eager to express their opinions; it was going to be a very a long meeting, indeed.

She wouldn't be home until eleven, at the earliest, and that was assuming she survived the roasting the board was sure to give her.

Getting out of the car, she spotted Ellie Martin and gave her a big wave. This was better; she'd feel a lot more comfortable going into the meeting with a friend.

"Looks like a full house tonight," said Lucy, as they waited for a car to pass so they could cross the street.

"I hope there's room for everybody," said Ellie. "I don't want to be shut out."

"Oh, you won't be," Lucy reassured her as they stepped off the curb. "Open meeting law. If the room's too small they have to relocate the meeting."

"Really?"

"Really. Trust me on this. If they could get away with it, the board would meet in a coat closet!"

Ellie was quiet as they walked along the sidewalk; then she stopped abruptly as they were about to enter the building.

"How do you think it will go tonight?" she asked in a serious voice. "Do you have any idea how they'll vote?"

"Not a clue," said Lucy with a little laugh. "They're a pretty unpredictable bunch."

She pulled open the door and paused, wondering what was bothering Ellie. "Does it matter to you, how the vote goes?" she asked.

"I didn't think it did, but now I'm not so sure," said Ellie, who was twisting the handles of her purse. When she spoke, she sounded tired. "I guess it's six of one and half a dozen of the other. You've heard of a win-win situation? Well, I'm afraid this is a lose-lose situation. No matter how the vote goes, everybody's going to lose."

Lucy wondered what she meant, as they entered the hearing room. She had feared they would have to stand, but discovered there were a few unoccupied seats in the last rows. They sat down together and Lucy rummaged in her bag for her notebook and pen. Flipping the notebook open, Lucy found the agenda she'd picked up last week and unfolded it, holding it so Ellie could also read it.

"Where's the Metinnicut proposal?" asked Ellie, scanning the long list of items that included new parking regulations for Main Street, budgets for the cemetery, shellfish and waterways commissions, and an executive session to discuss upcoming contract negotiations with the police and fire unions.

"It's last," said Lucy, realizing with dismay that the meeting could run well past midnight. "We'll never get out of here."

"Maybe they're hoping everybody will run out of patience and go home," said Ellie, hitting the nail on the head.

"Not much of a chance of that," said Lucy, scanning the jam-packed room. "These folks aren't leaving until they've had their say."

Even from her seat in the back of the room, Lucy could see that all the players were in place, almost as if in a courtroom.

In the front row, on one side, sat Jonathan Franke, executive director of the Association for the Preservation of Tinker's Cove and Bob Goodman, Rachel's husband and the lawyer representing the association.

Franke's once long hair and casual workclothes had gradually been giving way to a more professional look; tonight he was wearing a denim shirt and knitted tie, topped with a tweed sport coat.

Bob, Lucy noticed, looked as if he'd come to the meeting straight from a long day in court. His suit was rumpled and he definitely needed a haircut. He was bent over a thick sheaf of papers and occasionally consulted with Franke.

On the other side of the room, the Metinnicut faction seemed more relaxed. Bear Sykes, the tribe's leader, was sitting with his arms folded across his chest. His thick black hair was combed straight back, and when he turned to confer with Chuck Canaday, the tribe's lawyer, Lucy saw he was wearing a wampum bolo tie with his plaid flannel shirt.

Canaday, as always, was impeccably dressed in a neat gray suit. Tall and fair, he was a dramatic contrast to Syke's stocky, barrel-chested figure. Next to him was Andy Brown, wearing his trademark farmer's overalls and a smug expression, as if he had counted his chickens and was certain they would hatch a casino. The three looked up when a fourth man approached them—a man Lucy didn't recognize.

From his city-tailored suit, with no vents in the jacket, Lucy guessed he probably represented a bank or a real estate development company. This guess was confirmed when he bent down and whispered to Sykes, who immediately left the room and returned a few minutes later carrying a cardboard box, which he carefully set on a table in the front of the room. Lucy figured they were going to be treated to an architect's model—plans for the casino had indeed progressed further than anyone suspected.

"Look at that," snorted Ellie, glancing at Bear. "They treat him like an errand boy."

"If the casino gets approved, he won't be an errand boy anymore," said Lucy. "As tribal leader he'll be a very influential man."

"That's what I'm afraid of," said Ellie. "When's this meeting going to start?"

Lucy glanced at the empty bench in the front of the room and checked her watch; it was already ten minutes past seven.

"It's a power thing," she said, leaning toward Ellie. "The board keeps everybody waiting so they know who's in charge."

"I'll let them know who's in charge come the next election," said Ellie. "I'm missing my favorite TV show."

"Hiya, Ellie! What's happening?"

It was Curt Nolan, sliding into the seat beside Ellie.

"Did I miss anything?"

"Nothing. They haven't started," said Ellie. Lucy couldn't help noticing her voice suddenly sounded a lot brighter than it had before Curt Nolan arrived.

"Good." Curt settled himself in the chair, planting his feet firmly on the floor and letting his knees splay apart. His hands rested easily on his denim-covered legs.

Lucy checked her watch again—it was a quarter past. Time for the selectmen to appear. A side door opened and Lucy slid down in her chair, hoping none of the board members would notice her as they marched in and took their places behind the raised bench. Last to enter was Howard White, the chairman, who walked briskly across the room to his seat at the center of the bench and picked up his gavel.

"This meeting is called to order. First on the agenda: parking regulations."

Lucy sighed with relief and sat up a little straighter. If Howard were going to scold her, he would have done it first thing.

"Point of order." Joe Marzetti's voice boomed out, unnaturally loud. "I'd like to move that we table all other business and take up the Metinnicut proposal first."

Lucy raised an eyebrow and scribbled furiously in her notebook.

"I second the motion," announced Bud Collier before White even had a chance to ask for seconds.

"Any discussion?" From White's tone, it was a challenge rather than a question. Howard White was clearly unhappy at this evidence of rebellion in the ranks.

Lucy was surprised. In her experience with the board, she had never seen individual members take any initiative whatsoever. Someone must have put a bee in Marzetti's and Collier's bonnets, and she suspected it was Chuck Canaday, who had gotten his ducks in a row before the meeting.

"Considering the very great interest in the Metinnicut proposal, I think we should act as expeditiously as possible," said Sandy Dunlap.

Lucy doubted that Sandy had come up with such big words on her own; she was probably quoting Chuck. What a busy bee. Lucy wondered if he was working on a retainer or if he stood to get a share of the casino.

"Any objections?" White looked hopefully to Pete Crowley, who was usually a stickler for proper procedure.

Receiving no encouragement in that quarter, White called for a vote, and the motion passed with only one no vote.

"All right, then" said White, with a disapproving humph. "We'll take up the matter of the Metinnicut proposal."

There was a buzz in the room as Bear Sykes stepped forward to address the board, reading nervously from a prepared statement.

"The Metinnicut Tribal Council has asked me to request your support, as the board of selectmen, for the tribe's petition for federal recognition.

"We all know that the history of the Metinnicut people is interwoven with the history of this town—Tinker's Cove. When I was a little boy growing up here, I shared many of the same experiences as most American boys. I was a Cub Scout. I played Little League baseball. I went to the public schools and served in the army.

"I was also aware, however, that because of my Indian ancestry I was descended from people whose culture and values were different from those of most Americans. I felt a desire to acknowledge this separate identity, but I was unable to do so. My tribe, the Metinnicuts, were not recognized.

"In recent years, I spoke about this with family members and others and learned I was not alone in my desire to reclaim my Metinnicut heritage. As time went on, we formed a tribal council and conducted genealogical research. Now we are now ready to request federal recognition as a tribe. As citizens of this town, we ask your support for this petition. Thank you."

There was scattered applause, which White quickly silenced.

"Do I have a motion?" he asked, casting an evil eye toward Marzetti.

Marzetti swallowed hard and raised his hand. "I move that the board support the Metinnicut tribe's petition."

"Second?"

Collier nodded.

"Discussion?" asked White, looking extremely annoyed as hands shot up throughout the room.

"Do I have a motion to limit discussion?" Lucy, for once, found herself agreeing with White. Unless discussion was limited, the meeting could go on all night.

This was met with silence by the board.

Defeated, White recognized Jonathan Franke.

"With all due respect to Mr. Sykes and his Indian heritage, I want to point out that the main reason the tribe is seeking federal recognition is so that they can negotiate a casino deal with the state government. It's important to recognize that fact and consider the possible impact such a project would have on our town."

There was a loud buzz from the audience and Chuck Canaday stood up.

"If I may . . ." he began, catching Howard White's eye but continuing without waiting for his permission. "Mr. Franke has brought up an important point, which we are prepared to fully address tonight. With us is Jack O'Hara of Mulligan Construction in Boston. Mr. O'Hara has plans and a model of the proposed casino project."

"Ah, Mr. O'Hara," said White, shooting his cuffs. "Didn't I see your name in the business pages of the *Boston Globe?* They say you're the top contender for my old golfing buddy Joe Mulligan's job when he retires next year."

As Lucy wrote the quote in her notebook she felt a rare surge of sympathy for Howard White. It must be quite a comedown for a man like him—the former CEO of a paper company—to find himself reduced to managing an unruly group of local yokels.

O'Hara shrugged off the comment. "You know, sir, you can't

believe everything you read in the papers. But I'll be sure to give your regards to Mr. Mulligan."

White was charmed. "Heh, heh," he chuckled. "That's right. Well, let's see what you've got there."

O'Hara stepped forward and stood next to the table with the box, but didn't lift the cover.

"By way of preamble," he began, "I want to tell you that we at Mulligan Construction believe we were presented with a tall order: a request for a modern, innovative design that would also honor the unique tradition of our clients, the Metinnicut Indian tribe."

A hush of expectation fell over the room. Feeling a slight vibration, Lucy's attention was drawn to Curt Nolan, who was sitting a few seats from her. He was so tense that his knee was twitching; his hands were clenched anxiously. Ellie was watching him nervously.

"With all due modesty," O'Hara continued, "I think you will agree that we have risen to the challenge and exceeded it."

With a flourish he lifted the cardboard cover and revealed the architect's model.

Involuntarily, Lucy blinked. There was a stunned silence, then a collective gasp, as audience members absorbed the two gleaming hotel towers, each at least fifteen stories tall, and the accompanying casino, a monstrous version of a traditional Iroquois long house rendered in glass and steel.

Lucy wondered what Nolan's reaction was and looked curiously at him. His knee, she saw, was jumping and his knuckles were white.

"What may not be obvious," said O'Hara, flicking a laser point over the model, "is that the complex will provide parking for two thousand cars, accommodations for five hundred overnight guests, numerous gift shops, and a wide variety of restaurants catering to all tastes from fast food right on up to a five-star dining experience."

As soon as he'd finished speaking, hands shot up around the room and Curt Nolan was on his feet.

"This is a travesty, an outrage," exclaimed Nolan.

From his perch behind the selectmen's bench, Howard White was nodding in agreement. He made no attempt to silence Nolan but let him continue.

"This prop-proposal has nothing to do with Metinnicut heritage," said Nolan, so angry he was stumbling over his words. "Metinnicuts never lived in long houses—and they certainly didn't have skyscrapers. And what about that museum we were promised? If you ask me, the only thing this looks like is the Emerald City of Oz!"

He sat down with a thump, and Ellie gave him a little pat on the knee.

White, for perhaps the one and only time, was nodding in agreement with Nolan. Looking around the room, he next recognized Bob Goodman, certain that he, as the lawyer for the Association for the Preservation of Tinker's Cove, would also be against the proposal.

"Putting all aesthetic considerations aside," began Bob, pausing to remove his glasses and wipe them with a handkerchief, "I feel compelled to point out that, as presented here tonight, this design does not comply with the existing zoning and site plan regulations of this town."

Canaday was immediately on his feet. "Point of order," he said, managing to get everyone's attention without raising his voice. "We believe there is some precedent here. If built on land that is owned by the tribe, and that can be shown to have been traditionally occupied by the tribe, local zoning ordinances do not apply."

At this pronouncement, the room exploded in an uproar as citizens loudly debated with their neighbors whether this could possibly be true.

Howard White pounded his gavel, and gradually the roar subsided and order was restored.

"I want to remind everyone that the merits," he spat the word out, "of the proposed casino are not the issue tonight. The question is whether the board will support the Metinnicut petition for federal recognition. I'm going to close the public debate now and bring that issue back to the board."

Pete Crowley took his cue.

"I'm sympathetic, of course," he began, "to the desire of the citizens of our town who are of Native American heritage to reclaim that, uh, heritage. But let's face it: Most of these so-called Metinnicuts are just about as much Indian as I'm Swedish, and for your information, my maternal grandmother was half Swedish which, as far as I can tell, makes me one hundred percent American!"

This was met with murmers of approval.

"The tribe's real interest, as we've seen tonight, is getting this casino built and as far as I'm concerned a casino is just going to bring organized crime and a lot of other problems to our town."

Crowley paused and shook his head sadly. "I'm sorry. I've lived with these people my whole life and I don't see how they're an Indian tribe. They're just like the rest of us."

"Well, I'm Italian and proud of it," proclaimed Joe Marzetti.

"It doesn't make me any less American, but in my family we enjoy Italian food. We keep in touch with relatives in the old country. And I understand what Mr. Sykes is talking about. He has a right to his heritage. And if recognizing that right brings certain advantages to our town, like legalized gambling, so much the better."

He turned to Bud Collier and, noticing he had dozed off, poked him in the side.

Lucy couldn't help rolling her eyes. Mrs. Collier might not have liked her story, but it apparently hadn't affected Bud Collier in the least.

He roused himself, blinked a few times, and spoke. "There aren't enough jobs in this town. The kids are all moving away. We're going to become a town of old people if we don't watch it. These Metinnicuts—they're fine people. I've lived with them my whole life. Give them what they want."

He paused and cast a baleful eye on the model. "There'll be plenty of time to talk about *that* later." His chin sank on his chest and he resumed his slumber.

"Oh, dear," fretted Sandy Dunlap as Howard White looked in her direction. "I just don't know what to say. I mean, I'm sympathetic to the Metinnicuts . . . but after what we've seen tonight . . . I can't say I'm in favor."

Concluding that he had three no votes, White seized the moment.

"Are we ready to vote?" he asked.

"I vote yes. We should endorse the Metinnicut petition," said Marzetti.

"Yes," said Collier, expending as little energy as possible.

"I vote no," said Crowley, narrowing his eyes at the others.

"I, of course, vote no," said White. "That makes it a tie. Mrs. Dunlap?"

"Oh, dear, I just don't know."

Lucy leaned forward, pen in hand, to get every word.

"Of course, I value the Metinnicut heritage, but this is such an important decision, it could change our town forever. Of course, we can't stand in the way of progress, but we do want to preserve our treasured way of life. . . ."

Suddenly, Sandy's eyes brightened and her curls bounced.

"I know! Frankly, this is much too important a decision for people like us to make. This is one time I think we should rely on the experts in the federal government."

Lucy glanced at White; she thought he would explode with rage.

"The folks at the Bureau of Indian Affairs have developed expert criteria for determining whether a tribe is really a tribe," continued Sandy. "We should let them do their job. I vote yes."

Again, the room exploded. There was celebration on the Metinnicut side, anguish and head shaking among the preservationists. Lucy only felt relief. She had the quotes; she had the votes—she could go home. She grabbed her bag and fled, never looking back.

CHAPTER 8

"You're cutting it kind of close, aren't you?" growled Ted when Lucy arrived for work on Wednesday.

It was ten o'clock, just two hours before deadline.

"Not to worry," said Lucy, glancing at Phyllis, the receptionist, with a questioning raised eyebrow.

Phyllis responded with a nervous grimace. Lucy knew she was in some sort of trouble.

"I worked at home this morning," she continued, "while my pies were baking. I've got the whole story on this disk."

"I can't wait to read it," said Ted. "I heard there was quite a little dustup."

"Just what you'd expect. Howard White almost had apoplexy a few times, but he managed to control himself."

"What about Curt Nolan and the Mulligan guy? What's his name?"

"O'Hara," said Lucy, wondering what Ted was getting at. "Nolan had a few words with him."

"From what I heard, it was more than words."

"I don't know what you're talking about," said Lucy, feeling her stomach drop a few inches. "I stayed for the whole meeting."

"This was after the meeting. Nolan took a swing at this

O'Hara fellow and he's pressing charges. Nolan's going to be arraigned this morning—I was hoping to have you cover it."

"Oh, shit," said Lucy, sliding into her chair and pounding her fist on the desk. "This is big. I can't believe I missed it."

"Me, either," said Ted, looking rather put out. "I thought I could count on you. What happened?"

"I stayed until they took the vote," said Lucy, sounding defensive. "Toby was supposed to come home yesterday but he hadn't arrived when I left for the meeting. I was in a hurry to get home and see him."

Ted nodded.

"The stupid thing is, he wasn't there when I got home either. He didn't actually roll in until one-thirty, and then he showed up with three friends instead of the one we'd been expecting." Lucy rubbed her eyes. "It was absolutely crazy. I mean, I was so worried I had Bill calling hospitals and the state police. When Toby finally did show up I didn't know whether to hug him or smack him." Lucy paused for breath. "And I didn't have a clue where all those extra people were going to sleep."

"Where'd you put them?" asked Phyllis, who had been keeping a low profile.

" 'No problem, Mom,' " said Lucy, imitating her son's laid-back attitude. " 'We'll just crash in the family room.' This, mind you, comes after weeks of delicate negotiations to convince Elizabeth to move out of his room and back in with her sisters. I mean, I could've used Madeline Albright!"

Phyllis laughed, and even Ted gave a weak chuckle.

"How are you going to feed them all?" asked Phyllis.

"Don't ask me. That was my next stop. After dropping this

story off, I was going to get some groceries—with my Visa card."
She looked at Ted. "What am I going to do about the story?"

He shrugged. "Go the official route. We don't have time for
anything else. Get the police to give you the arrest report. Court's
still in session, so you can't get the DA—I'll call the clerk's office
and see if Mabel remembers those chocolates I gave her for her
birthday."

While Lucy waited for the computer to boot up, she tried
to get control of her emotions. It was tempting to blame the
whole mess on Toby. After all, if he'd come home when he was
supposed to, she wouldn't have been worried about him and
wouldn't have hurried out of the meeting and wouldn't have
missed the fight. Now, thanks to his inconsiderate behavior, she'd
missed the biggest story that had come her way in a long time.

No, she thought. Shifting blame was the sort of thing kids
like Toby did. She had every reason to be angry and disappointed
with Toby, but she'd chosen to leave the meeting and she would
have to live with her decision. Maybe she could still save the
story. She reached for the phone and dialed Ellie Martin's number.

"Ellie," she began, "this is Lucy Stone. I guess I missed all
the excitement last night. Can you tell me what happened?"

Ellie was cautious. "Is this for the paper?"

Lucy sighed. "You can talk off the record. I won't quote you.
I'm just trying to find out what happened after I left. I heard that
Curt took a swing at O'Hara. Did you see it?"

"I wish I hadn't," said Ellie. "I mean, if he has to lose his
temper, why does he have to do it in front of a roomful of

witnesses? I think he really hurt O'Hara—they called the ambulance. Curt's in big trouble."

"Do you know why he was so mad?" asked Lucy, making a note to check with the hospital on O'Hara's condition.

"He felt O'Hara had tricked the tribe. They'd been promised a museum and the casino was supposed to have a traditional design." She paused. "I think Curt really thought the casino was a way to recapture the Metinnicut legacy."

"Does he have a lawyer?"

"I don't know." Ellie sighed. "This morning I was all set to go down to the courthouse to bail him out. Then I thought, if he's so good at getting himself in these messes, maybe it's time he figured how to get himself out."

Lucy understood completely.

An hour later, Lucy had finished the story. Thanks to Mabel, Ted had learned that Nolan had remained in police custody overnight and had been arraigned on assault-and-battery charges. He'd been assigned a court-appointed lawyer and released on his own recognizance. The hospital hadn't been willing to release any information about O'Hara but Phyllis checked with her sister, who was a nurse in the emergency room, and learned he had been treated and released.

Lucy didn't linger in the office after finishing the story. She told Ted to call her at home if he had any questions and headed straight for the Quick Stop. There she picked up extra gallons of milk and orange juice, a dozen eggs, and a pound of bacon so she could give Toby and his friends a decent breakfast. Well, brunch, since they were probably still asleep after their late night.

As she expected, the house was quiet when she got home. Lucy peeked in the family room and saw the kids were dead to the world in a tangle of couch cushions, sleeping bags, and blankets. She closed the door and stood staring at it, wondering what to do.

It was almost one. Surely they didn't want to sleep the entire day away.

In the kitchen, Lucy brewed a pot of coffee and whipped up some blueberry muffins. While they were baking, she got some bacon started in her big cast-iron skillet.

" 'Morning, Mom."

She smiled at hearing Toby's voice and turned to greet him. Her jaw dropped. He was standing there in nothing but a pair of boxer shorts.

"Toby! Put some clothes on!"

"What's the big deal?" he asked, pouring himself a cup of coffee and sitting down at the table.

Lucy stared at him. Who was this person with the shaggy hair and wispy little beard and mustache?

"You can't sit there like that. I won't have it. Go and put some clothes on."

"Okay, okay," muttered Toby, heading upstairs.

Lucy poked the bacon with a spatula and wished she didn't feel quite so miserable. She'd looked forward to Toby's homecoming for such a long time and now nothing seemed to be going right.

Hearing the rattle of hot water pipes that announced the shower was being used, she opened the door to the stairs.

"Don't use all the hot water," she yelled. "The others might want showers, too."

She was turning back to the stove when Toby's roommate Matt appeared. He, she was relieved to see, was wearing jeans and a shirt. The same ones he'd been wearing last night. Lucy suspected he'd slept in them.

"Toby's taking a shower," she told him. "There's coffee."

"Coffee," he repeated, making it sound like some sort of rare and exotic drink. "That's great."

She poured a mug for him and set it on the table with the cream and sugar.

Matt sat down and stared at his coffee.

"So how was your trip? Was there a lot of traffic?"

"No," said Matt, obviously a man of few words.

Lucy turned over a piece of bacon. "We expected you much earlier."

Matt noisily slurped his coffee.

"Was there a reason why you were so late?" persisted Lucy.

"Late?"

Lucy gave up. "Would you like some bacon and eggs?"

That got a more positive response.

"Sure."

Toby and Matt were just finishing their meal when the two girls appeared in the kitchen.

"Mom, this is Amy and Jessica," said Toby, tilting his head in their direction.

Lucy looked from one to the other.

"I'm Amy," said the plump, dark-haired one. "That's Jessica."

Jessica had light brown hair and was tall and extremely thin.

"Would you like some breakfast?" "

"Maybe just some juice," said Amy.

"How about a blueberry muffin?" offered Lucy.

"No, thanks. I'm a vegan. I don't eat animal products."

"You can't eat a muffin?" Lucy was incredulous.

"Made with eggs, right? Listen, I don't mean to be any trouble. A glass of juice is all I want, really."

"And what about you?" Lucy turned to Jessica, who was watching with a horrified expression as Toby mopped his plate with a piece of muffin, lifted it dripping with egg yolk, and popped it in his mouth.

"Just some water," she said.

"Okay," said Lucy brightly. "That's easy."

What wasn't going to be easy, she thought, was coming up with something for supper that the entire group would eat. She'd been planning to serve beef stew, but that obviously would not do.

"So what are your plans for the day?" asked Lucy, joining the group at the table to eat a bacon, lettuce, and tomato sandwich.

"I don't know," answered Matt. "Say, Toby. What's doing in this burg?"

"Not much."

"There's the pep rally," said Lucy. "Or you could help out at the pie sale."

"Pie sale?" Amy was intrigued.

"They have it every year. To raise money for the Boot and Mitten Fund."

"Don't ask," said Toby. "It's so poor kids can have winter clothing."

"You don't want to miss the pep rally, Toby," said Lucy. "All your friends from high school will be there. Besides, don't you want to support the team? The Thanksgiving game is the biggest game of the year."

Toby rolled his eyes. "Oh, yeah. The Tinker's Cove Warriors against the Gilead Giants. I wouldn't want to miss *that*."

"Toby, I'm surprised," said Lucy. "You always used to enjoy it."

No sooner had she spoken than she realized she'd said the wrong thing. Toby didn't want to be reminded of his youthful enthusiasms in front of his college friends.

"Well, it's up to you," she said, picking up her plate and carrying it to the sink, "but this is the country. There isn't a heck of a lot to do."

"How about a movie?" asked Amy.

"Only on the weekends," admitted Toby.

"I bet there's an arcade," said Matt.

Toby shook his head.

"A mall?" asked Jessica in a hopeful voice.

"Nope."

"Well," said Amy, "we might as well go to the pep rally."

"Rah, rah," said Jessica in a slow drawl.

Lucy had been listening to them as she loaded the dishwasher. She had to hustle, she realized. It was past two and she was late for the pie sale. She was just turning the machine on when the phone rang.

"For you, Mom. It's Dad."

"Sweetheart," he began.

Lucy new he wanted something. "What is it? I'm running late."

"This'll only take a minute. You know my clients, the Barths?"

"Um-hmm," said Lucy. "The old Tupper place?"

"Right. Well, they're having a little trouble with their car. It's a Range Rover and the garage says they can't get the part before Friday at the soonest."

"Bill, we have a full house," she protested. "We can't put them up."

"No, I know that. Matter of fact, they're staying at the Queen Vic," he said, referring to a very posh bed-and-breakfast on Main Street. "I was wondering if we could invite them for Thanksgiving dinner. It seems a shame for them to have Thanksgiving in a restaurant, especially since any decent place has been booked for weeks."

"I guess two more won't matter," said Lucy, glancing anxiously at the clock.

"Great! Thanks, honey."

By the time Lucy got to the pie sale, which was held in the fellowship hall of the community church, it was in full swing. Several long tables at the front of the room were covered with an impressive array of homemade pies, which customers could buy whole or by the slice. More tables were set up in the rest of the room, where people could eat their pie along with a cup of coffee or tea. As always, business was brisk and the room was crowded and noisy. Lucy finally found Pam in the kitchen, filling a coffeepot from a huge urn.

"Looks like you got a crowd," said Lucy by way of greeting. "Sorry I'm late."

"No problem," said Pam, giving her a big smile. "Did you bring your pies?"

"Sure did," affirmed Lucy, pleased to have gotten something right. "Six pumpkin."

"Bless you. I've been worried about running short. Patty Wilson came down with the flu and you know she always makes a dozen."

"What can I do to help?" asked Lucy.

"Here, take this coffee around and see if people want refills," said Pam.

"Aye, aye, Captain. Will you save an apple for me and a mince one, too, if you have it?"

"Sure thing."

As she made her way among the tables, Lucy saw many people she recognized. Oswald Crowley, the chief of police, gave her a wave and she went over to his table. As she went, she heard snippets of conversation. Everybody seemed to be talking about the same thing: the casino.

"Here you go," she said as Oswald held out his cup to be filled. "Who else wants some more coffee?"

She looked at the faces gathered at the table and fought the impulse to flee. It seemed the entire board of selectmen, minus Sandy, was sitting there.

"If it isn't our own little newshound," said Joe Marzetti.

"I just write it the way I see it," said Lucy, keeping her voice light. "More coffee?"

"I'll have some," said Bud Collier, looking at her somewhat curiously. It suddenly dawned on Lucy that he didn't know who she was; he hadn't connected her face with her byline, which was the way she wanted to keep it.

"I've got no complaints about Lucy," said Howard, surprising her so much that she almost dropped his cup. "She's a good reporter. And I'm sure we can count on her to cover all sides of this casino issue fairly." He put great emphasis on the word *fairly*.

"Absolutely," said Lucy, passing his cup back to him. She gave Bud a big smile, just in case he was following the conversation. "And anything I hear today is off the record."

"So, Howard," she heard Fred Smithers ask as she filled his cup, "is it true that town zoning regulations don't apply to the Indians?"

"That's nonsense," said Howard, setting his fork down. "We have very strong zoning regulations in this town. I don't think the Metinnicuts are going to find they can just ignore our bylaws."

"That's right," said Jonathan Franke, who was sitting at the same table. "The zoning bylaws were revised just last year and passed with a large majority at a town meeting. It was a long, hard battle but I think we finally have an effective tool for controlling development."

"Any court is going to have to take that vote into account," agreed Bob Goodman, dropping a lump of sugar into his coffee and stirring it with a spoon. "I've noticed in quite a few recent decisions that the courts have given community character quite a bit of weight."

Someone snorted at the far end of the table. Lucy was surprised to see Curt Nolan digging into a big wedge of blueberry pie.

"It's amazing," he said, hoisting his fork and popping a piece in his mouth. "You see what you want to see."

"Out of jail so soon?" asked Jonathan Franke, glaring at him.

"On my own recognizance," said Nolan. "It's a nice place to visit but I wouldn't want to stay there."

"I wouldn't be so cocky," said Crowley, giving him a nod. "You might be going back . . . for a while."

"You'd like that, wouldn't you?" said Nolan, looking at Franke.

"I'd like nothing better," replied Franke, shoving away his empty plate.

"Now, now, don't get all excited," said Nolan, looking over the rim of his cup. "I'm just as against that Mulligan proposal as you guys are, but I don't see how you can stop it with the zoning bylaws. Not when you let Andy Brown put up electric signs and that mechanical talking pumpkin. And a train ride. How come the association didn't have any problems with Mrs. Lumpkin, the Talking Pumpkin?"

As Lucy watched, Howard White's face grew quite red. "I can assure you that Mr. Brown went through all the proper channels," said White. "He obtained variances for those improvements."

"If you say so."

"Just hold on," said Franke. "You saw that model, and there was no sign of any museum. It looks to me like Canaday and Mulligan Construction are taking the tribe for a ride."

Lucy held her breath, waiting for Nolan's reaction.

"I wouldn't be so sure if I were you," he said, clenching his fist.

"If I were *you*, I'd listen to him," said White. "What he's saying makes sense."

"We don't need *him* to explain things to us," said Nolan, pointing at Franke and rising to his feet. "We're not a bunch of dumb Indians who can't look out for own interests, you know."

"Now, now, I didn't say that—" began White.

"Well, I'll say this," said Franke, standing and facing Nolan. "The tribe used to be strong advocates for the environment. In fact, quite a few were APTC members. But now that you all stand to make a lot of money from the casino, well, I guess the environment takes a backseat to the almighty dollar. It's pretty hypocritical if you ask me."

"You have a lot of nerve, talking like that," said Nolan. "You haven't exactly been working for the environment for free, have you? What do you make as director? Fifty, sixty thousand? You know what the average Metinnicut income is? It's under the poverty line. Being environmentalists hasn't been quite as profitable for us as it has for you."

Franke glared at him, facing off. Lucy fully expected them to come to blows. Then, suddenly, Franke turned and stalked off.

Nolan laughed, then sat down. He looked at Lucy, who was standing speechless, coffeepot in hand.

"How about some more of that coffee?" he asked, giving her a big grin.

"Sure thing," she said, wasting no time in filling his cup.

Lucy stayed until the last cup had been washed and put away, the tables wiped, and the chairs neatly stacked in a corner. Then she bought her pies, said good-bye to Pam, and headed over to the football field to meet the girls. Remembering the trouble she'd had finding a parking spot last year, she put her pies in the car and left it at the church parking lot, walking the few blocks to the high school.

As she walked down the tree-lined street, where bare limbs reached up to the blank gray sky, she wondered what made Curt

Nolan tick. He'd only gotten out of jail that morning and he had been arraigned on assault-and-battery charges, yet only a few hours later, he almost got in a fight with Jonathan Franke. He seemed nice enough, she thought, admitting to herself that she actually found him rather likable. But he always seemed to be involved in some kind of confrontation. In fact, he seemed to make a habit of provoking and angering people. Why did he do it? What satisfaction could he possibly get out of it? It seemed a terrible waste of energy to her, an exhausting way to go through life.

Stopping at the corner to let a car go by before she crossed the street, she realized how tired she was. No wonder. She'd gotten only a few hours of sleep; then she'd spent the morning baking pies and working on her story. Then there'd been the stress-filled hour or two at the *Pennysaver* office, the rush home to cook for Toby and his friends, topped off by the pie sale, where she'd spent a couple of hours on her feet running around with the coffee pot.

Maybe Nolan had it right, she thought, trudging up the hill to the field and keeping an eye out for the girls. Maybe it was her way, trying to please everybody, that was exhausting. Maybe she ought to tell Ted to cover meetings himself if he wasn't happy with the way she did it, and maybe Toby needed to understand he couldn't be quite so inconsiderate and maybe Bill could cook Thanksgiving dinner for the Barths himself if he was so keen on inviting them. And what gave those girls, Toby's friends, the right to be vegans? The way she was brought up, you took what you were offered and said thank you.

"Mom! Mom!"

Lucy looked up and saw Sara standing by the gate, holding on to Zoe's hand.

"Are you okay, Mom?" asked Sara.

"Sure. Why?"

"You looked kind of worried."

"You looked mad," volunteered Zoe.

Lucy laughed. "I guess I am kind of tired."

"Toby was late." Zoe's little face was serious.

Lucy thought for a minute. "You haven't seen him yet, have you?"

"Nope."

"Me either," added Sara.

"Well, maybe we'll see him here. He said he was coming."

There were so many people on the field, however, that Lucy soon gave up looking for him. Instead, she led the girls to the top of the grandstand, where they could get a bird's-eye view of everything.

They had just sat down when the high school band could be heard approaching. Rapt with excitement, Zoe stood up and clapped enthusiastically when the band members finally appeared in their red uniforms with brass buttons.

As usual, they were playing out of key and several members were straggling behind, finding it difficult to keep in step while playing an instrument. Finally, they formed a loose rectangle on the field and waited while the drum major climbed onto an elevated platform. He raised his baton and the band responded with a blast of sound; he lowered the baton and they began rearranging themselves, finally resting in a ragged zigzag.

"What is it, Mom? What is it?" demanded Zoe.

Lucy frowned and furrowed her brow. After a moment, enlightenment came. "It's a W for Warriors."

"That's not a W," insisted Zoe.

"I think it's supposed to be a W."

"If you say so, Mom."

The drum major raised both arms dramatically, the final chord rang out, and everybody clapped like mad as the cheerleaders ran onto the field.

"Look, Zoe. It's the cheerleaders. Aren't their outfits cute?"

Zoe was enraptured. Lucy guessed she was picturing herself in a red-and-white cheerleader's skirt.

"What are they holding?"

"Pom-poms."

"Can I get one?"

"I don't know where you get them."

"You have to be a cheerleader," said Sara.

Zoe's face fell.

"Maybe we can make some," Lucy said, "out of crepe paper or something."

"I'll help," promised Zoe.

"We'll see," said Lucy.

"Give me a W," yelled the cheerleaders.

"W!" yelled back the crowd.

The cheer finally ended with everybody screaming, "Warriors! Warriors! Warriors!"

The band played a drumroll and all eyes went to the end of the field, where two girls dressed in fringed deerskin dresses were holding a large paper hoop. The band began playing the Warriors' fight song and the crowd roared as quarterback Zeke Kirwan broke through the paper circle, followed by the other members of the team. They ran down the field and formed a circle around a big pile of wood that had been stacked at the opposite end of the field.

The music finally stopped playing and everyone was silent, waiting for the big moment. They were rewarded with the sight of the two girls in Indian dress holding torches, escorting team captain Chris White, who was carrying the Metinnicut war club.

Everyone began chanting together: "Go! Go! Go!"

Chris raised the war club above his head, gave the traditional Warrior yell, and sped down the field followed by the torchbearers.

Still holding the club above his head, Chris joined the circle of his teammates. The girls threw the torches onto the pile of wood and the crowd roared as the flames grew steadily higher.

All of a sudden, everybody seemed to be moving, gathering around the huge bonfire. Holding Zoe carefully by the hand, Lucy made her way down from the grandstand. They joined the throng and stood watching the fire, roaring in approval as a dummy dressed in a Gilead Giants uniform was thrown into the flames.

"Mom, we'll win the game, right?" asked Zoe.

"Maybe," said Lucy, who subscribed to the glass-half-full theory.

"Not a chance," said Sara. "Gilead's already in the finals for the state superbowl."

"Winning's not the important thing," said Lucy mechanically. She was wondering what to have for supper. Something everybody would eat. "It's how you eat the rice."

"You mean play the game."

"That's what I said."

Zoe and Sara looked at each other and laughed.

CHAPTER 9

Lucy was just putting the finishing touches on a brown rice and carrot casserole when the phone rang. She picked up the receiver and was surprised to hear Fred Rumford's voice.

"What can I do for you?" she asked as she slid the dish into the oven.

"I have to get something in tomorrow's paper," he said.

"I'm sorry, Fred, but it's too late. The deadline was noon."

"Damn," he said.

Something in his tone made Lucy suspect that, whatever it was, it was something a lot more important than an announcement for a bake sale or a flintknapping workshop.

"Is something the matter?" she asked.

"You bet something's the matter! The Metinnicut war club is missing."

Lucy's hand tightened on the receiver. This could be a big story. "Are you sure?"

"Of course I'm sure. When I handed it over to Chris White I made him promise to bring it right back to me as soon as the pep rally was over. We agreed on a meeting place—by the ticket booth—and I was there right on time. In fact, I was early and I stayed for an hour, but there was no Chris. I went back to the museum, thinking he might have misunderstood and gone there instead, but there was no sign of him. I called his house and his mother told me he wasn't home yet and she didn't expect him until late because it was the night before the big game."

"Did you call the police?"

"Of course I did. And they picked up Chris, drunk as a skunk."

"On the night before a big game?"

"Not just him. Most of the team!"

"No wonder we never win."

"More to the point, there was no sign of the war club. Chris said he was approached after the pep rally by someone who offered to return the club for him and he handed it over."

"I can't believe he did that," said Lucy. "Did he know the person?"

"Apparently not. But he did say he looked like an Indian, with long black hair and a bear claw necklace."

Lucy sighed. "That sounds like Curt Nolan."

"Exactly," said Rumford.

"Are the police looking for him?"

"They are, but so far they haven't had any luck. He wasn't home and nobody seems to know where he is. For all we know, he could have left the country."

"I wouldn't jump to conclusions," said Lucy, who had learned as a reporter that there were always at least two sides to any story. "We don't really know much for sure. It's not even certain that it was Nolan who took the club."

"Oh, I'm certain," said Rumford.

Lucy didn't like his tone. He sounded as if he were ready to act as judge, jury, and executioner.

"What now?" she asked.

"Well, I'd hoped to get the news out. Ask for anyone who has any information about the club or Nolan to contact the police." He paused. "But you say it's too late."

As much as she hated it, Lucy knew she had to tell him, even though it meant the *Pennysaver* would lose a scoop.

"You could call the Portland paper," she said. "And the TV station. Why not try the *Boston Globe?*"

"You think they'd be interested?" Rumford sounded doubtful.

"I'm certain they will," said a resigned Lucy.

As she hung up, she thought of Ted. He'd be furious that he'd missed such a big story, but that was the problem with publishing only once a week. It meant you lost out on news that happened the other six days of the week.

There was really no point calling him with the bad news, she thought, as she started cleaning up the mess she'd made preparing the casserole. He'd find out soon enough.

CHAPTER 10

On Thanksgiving day, Lucy woke up a half hour before the alarm was set to go off. It was a luxury she was unaccustomed to: time to herself. Careful not to disturb Bill, who was sound asleep beside her, she rolled on her back and stretched. Then she tried to work up some enthusiasm for the long day that stretched ahead of her.

Truth be told, Thanksgiving had never been her favorite holiday, consisting as it did of football and food. Food that she had to cook and dishes—lots of dishes—that she had to wash. This year she'd been able to summon up more excitement than usual, but that was because Toby was coming home.

She sighed. Somehow Toby's homecoming hadn't gone at all as she'd expected. He and his friends seemed interested in using the house only as a place to sleep and leave their stuff. Yesterday, much to her irritation, after she'd gone to the trouble of making that vegan brown rice and carrot casserole for supper, they'd gone on to Portland after stopping only briefly at the pep rally and hadn't returned until around eleven. She hadn't seen much of Toby, and the girls hadn't seen him at all. They'd either been asleep or at school when he made his brief appearances. There was plenty of evidence of his and his friends' presence, however, in the huge pile of sleeping bags and backpacks that practically filled the family room, in the wet towels left on the bathroom floor, in the litter of dirty snack dishes that filled the kitchen sink.

Lucy didn't know exactly what she wanted. Certainly not cozy family games of Monopoly, such as he used to enjoy when he was younger. But she had thought he would join the family at dinner. She'd thought he'd be around for a while in the evenings, perhaps watching a video with the rest of the family. And she had hoped to have a little time with him by herself.

Now, she realized with a start, if she did get him to herself she'd like nothing better than to shake some sense into him. She would like to yell and scream and let him know he was behaving like a pig. She'd like to make him understand how much he was hurting her and how very angry it made her feel.

No, she thought. That wouldn't do. If he was the prodigal son, it was her job to set aside her petty little negative feelings and welcome him. To kill the fatted calf in celebration—or in her case, to cook the turkey and reheat the brown rice casserole.

Doing a quick count, Lucy realized there would be twelve for dinner, instead of the eight she'd been figuring on, presuming Toby and his friends deigned to eat Thanksgiving dinner with them. She counted again. Herself and Bill and the three girls— that was five. Toby and his friends made nine. Add the Barths and Miss Tilley, the total came to twelve.

That meant she would need some extra chairs. She'd have to round up all the strays from the bedrooms and Bill's attic office. There were plenty of dishes, but her silver service only had eight place settings, so she'd have to use the kitchen stainless, too. So much for the elegant table she'd hoped to set. Oh, well, she told herself as the alarm sounded, Thanksgiving was about being grateful for what you had, not wishing you had four more sterling place settings.

A few hours later, Lucy was savoring the sweet satisfaction of revenge. The college kids weren't sleeping late this morning thanks to Zoe, who wanted to watch the Macy's Thanksgiving Day Parade on TV. She had settled herself right in front of the TV, a bowl of cereal on the floor, a spoon in one hand, and the remote in the other. Any attempts to dislodge her—and there had been a few—had been repulsed with fits of noisy squealing. She had now solidified her position, calling on her sisters to act as reinforcements. The college kids had finally given up and had begun the hours-long ritual of morning showers.

Busy in the kitchen, peeling potatoes and mixing up stuffing and arranging plates of condiments, Lucy thought smugly to herself that things had a way of working out. They hadn't eaten the cassserole last night; they could jolly well eat it today. They didn't want to behave like proper guests; the family didn't have to act like gracious hosts.

Glancing at the clock, Lucy saw it was almost time to leave for the football game. She turned on the oven and opened the door, preparing to slide the turkey inside so it could cook while they were gone, when Sara ran into the kitchen.

"You'll never believe it, Mom."

"What won't I believe?" asked Lucy, straightening up.

"I saw Katie Brown on TV!"

Lucy looked at her doubtfully. "How can you be sure it was her?"

" 'Cause she was with her dad and her mom and her brothers. They were all there. At the parade, like she said they would be."

"Really? You saw them in New York?"

"Yeah, Mom. Isn't that cool? She told me in school yesterday, to look for her, and I did and I saw her! I can't wait to tell her."

"That is pretty cool," said Lucy. "Is the parade almost over?"

"Yeah."

"Good, because it's almost time for the game. Would you tell the others so they can get ready to go?"

"Sure thing, Mom."

A miracle. A small miracle. She'd asked one of her children to do something and she'd done it willingly. *Treasure the moment*, Lucy told herself as she checked the dining room table.

Everything was in place: the linen tablecloth and napkins, the cornucopia of fresh fruit and nuts, the twelve place settings with assorted flatware. Three pies—pumpkin, apple, and mince— were sitting on the sideboard along with dessert plates and coffee cups and saucers. It all looked very nice, she thought, pausing to admire the new wallpaper.

In the kitchen, the turkey was stuffed and roasting in the oven; it would be almost done when they got home. The brown rice casserole only needed a few minutes in the microwave; the potatoes were peeled and in the pot, covered with water and ready to cook. Cranberry sauce, pickles, and celery with olives were arranged on crystal dishes and covered with plastic wrap, cooling in the refrigerator. So was the wine, and the coffeepot was set up and ready to go.

And so was she. Ready to go and cheer for the home team at the football game.

Taking her place beside Bill in the Subaru, Lucy firmly

pushed all thoughts of Toby and his friends from her mind. They had transportation. They could come to the game if they wanted to. She wasn't going to worry about them. She and Bill and the two younger girls would have a lovely time on their own. Elizabeth, never a big football fan, had offered to stay home and keep an eye on the turkey. What a contrast to her thoughtless, irresponsible, selfish brother!

"It's a perfect day for football," said Bill, interrupting her thoughts.

Lucy considered. The sun was shining brightly in a cloudless blue sky, there was no wind to speak of, and there was just a slight nip in the air.

"It's perfect," Lucy agreed, hoping that Toby and his friends wouldn't miss the game. It would be a shame, on such a nice day, to stay cooped up in the house.

Instead of going straight into town, Bill took the long way round on the shore road. There, big, old-fashioned, gray-shingled "cottages" stood on the bluff overlooking the cove. The trees were bare, and brown leaves had drifted into the road, but tall, pointed fir trees provided a touch of green here and there. Beyond the houses they could see the sea, deep blue with a scattering of tiny whitecaps. Farther out, on the horizon, they could see the humped shape of Metinnicut Island.

"See the seals!" exclaimed Sara, pointing to a small cluster of rocks.

Bill pulled off the road and stopped the car. Lucy took a closer look and saw several seals lounging in the sun. As she watched, one slid into the water.

"It's not a bad place to live," said Bill as they turned back onto the road.

"Not bad at all," agreed Lucy, resolving to concentrate on her many blessings rather than dwelling on her problems with Toby. After all, he was in college. It wasn't as if he were in jail or unemployed or working at a dead-end job somewhere.

Traffic grew heavier as they approached the field, so Bill decided to park alongside the road rather than try to find a spot in the parking lot. They climbed out and joined the crowd of walkers on the sidewalk.

As they marched along, Lucy kicked the dry brown leaves that covered the sidewalk and sniffed their sharp, musky scent. She grinned at the girls and slipped her arm through Bill's. When they turned the corner, they could hear the band playing, and Lucy felt as if she were back in high school herself. She squeezed Bill's arm. A roar went up from the crowd already gathered in the stadium and Lucy guessed the teams were being introduced.

They took their places in the line at the ticket booth and soon were climbing up the stands to claim the few remaining seats near the top. Lucy held Zoe's hand, but Sara insisted on going ahead of them.

They sat down just in time for the kickoff. The Warriors had won the toss and elected to receive the ball; Bill approved of their decision.

"Brian Masiaszyk, the kid who was on the state all-star team last year—he's really fast. If he gets the ball they'll gain a lot of yardage."

Lucy thought she understood what he meant. Maybe. She held her breath as the ball soared throught the air and landed in Brian's arms.

"Yes!" said Bill, leaping to his feet.

Suddenly everyone was standing and cheering as the all-star

player ran down the field, dodging and even slipping through the arms of the Giants to make a touchdown. The Tinker's Cove fans roared their approval. On the other side of the field, the fans of the Gilead Giants sat silently, looking glum.

"What happened?" asked Zoe, tugging on Lucy's sleeve.

"A touchdown, stupid," said Sara.

Lucy's eyes widened in surprise. "That was unnecessary," she said.

"I'm sorry," mumbled Sara.

Lucy knew that Sara often squabbled with her older sister, but she was usually sweet-natured toward Zoe. Lucy wondered if the fact that Toby had ignored her since her got home was upsetting her, causing her to vent her frustration on her little sister.

"Is something bothering you?"

"Nah."

"Are you sure?" Lucy reached out and touched Sara's arm.

"I'm sure," said Sara, shaking herself loose.

"Okay."

The Giants now had the ball and were making slow, steady progress down the field. Despite their brave showing at the beginning of the game the Warriors seemed unable to put up much defense. By the half the Giants were leading thirteen to seven.

"Want something to eat?" asked Bill, standing up and stretching as the teams straggled off the field.

"And spoil our appetites?"

Lucy was starving but didn't want to admit it.

"I'm starving," said Bill. "It's been hours since breakfast. How about some hot dogs and hot chocolate?"

"Make it popcorn and black coffee for me."

"You got it. Come on girls—I'll need help carrying the food."

Left to her own devices, Lucy decided to head for the ladies' room. She was standing in line when Sue saw her and stopped to chat.

"How's it going?" she asked, flipping her tartan scarf over her shoulder and straightening her matching gloves.

To her surprise, Lucy felt tears pricking her eyes. She blinked furiously. "Great," she said.

Sue narrowed her eyes. "If things are so great, how come you look so miserable?"

"I'm just feeling sorry for myself, I guess. Toby looks great. He's doing fine at school. He has lots of friends."

"But he doesn't have any time for you?"

"No." Lucy shook her head and her bangs bounced.

Sue wrapped an arm around her shoulder.

"I told you. You never get back the same kid you sent away. When Sidra was in high school she was hard working and organized. She kept her room neat as a pin. She played field hockey every fall and stayed in shape the rest of the year by running. She'd bring me little things she found: a perfect acorn, a seashell, a pink pebble." Sue sighed. "She came back from her first semester a completely different person. She would only wear black. She spent the whole vacation lounging on the couch. When I suggested she get some exercise she actually growled at me. I didn't know what to do. I was frantic. Finally, I dragged her to the doctor."

"What did he say?"

"After he examined her, he took me into his office and wrote me a prescription for tranquilizers!"

"Did they help?"

"I didn't take them. I decided I just had to let her grow up. I couldn't wreck my life worrying about her. It was time to let go."

"Easy to say," said Lucy, tempted to growl herself.

"Not easy to do," agreed Sue. "See you later."

Back in the stands, Lucy propped her popcorn in her lap and wrapped her hands around the paper coffee cup. The warmth felt good. She slid a little closer to Bill and rested her head on his shoulder. He turned his head, brushing her forehead with his beard.

"They've gotta turn it around," he said, as the teams lined up for the kickoff. "Go, Warriors, go!" he roared.

The Warriors' cheerleaders were doing their best, leading the crowd through the familiar litany of cheers. It seemed to work; the Warriors played a lot better in the second half and got two more touchdowns, thanks largely to the heroic efforts of Brian Masiaszyk.

By the fourth quarter, the Warriors were obviously tired and getting sloppy. The Giants started putting pressure on the Warriors, quarterback, Zeke Kirwan. In a desperation move, he threw a long pass that missed and the Giants got possession of the ball. They didn't go for any flashy maneuvers. They just drove down the field like a machine to score a touchdown. When the Warriors got the ball back they couldn't make a first down and the Giants had the ball once again. The Warriors had lost their lead. The game was tied at nineteen to nineteen, and there were two minutes left to play when the hometeam finally got the ball back.

Nevertheless, hopes were high on the Tinker's Cove side of the field. Fans stood and cheered, hoping for a miracle as the teams lined up on the thirty yard line. Maybe Masiaszyk could score again? Maybe it was time for Kirwan to try another Hail Mary pass?

The stands fell silent as the players crouched down, waiting for the referee to signal the snap. All eyes were on the field, practically everyone was holding their breath in the tension of the moment. Raising his arm, the referee seemed to move in slow motion. He had the whistle in his hand and was bringing it to his lips when, suddenly, a woman's high-pitched scream ripped through the stadium.

It was one of the cheerleaders, Megan Williams. She was standing on the sidelines, shaking and sobbing. An EMT approached her and she pointed behind the concession stand; then she collapsed in his arms as he wrapped a blanket around her. He stood holding her as a couple of police officers ran up to them. There was an exchange of words and one of the officers signaled that the game should resume.

Once again the players took their positions, but Lucy knew Ted would expect her to find out what was going on.

"I'll meet you at the car," she told Bill and made her way down from the bleachers. Once she was on firm ground she ran over to the refreshment stand, oblivious to the struggle that was taking place on the field.

Several more officers had arrived when she joined the small group of curious onlookers. Spotting her friend, Officer Barney Culpepper, she elbowed her way through and went up to him.

"What's going on?" she asked.

Barney considered for a minute, glancing left and right as

he removed his cap. Then he brushed his hand through his crew cut and carefully replaced it.

"We've got a homicide."

Lucy gasped in shock. "Who?"

"Curt Nolan."

For an instant, Lucy didn't register the name. Then it hit her. Her hand flew to her mouth. "Oh, no."

"You know him?"

"A little."

Lucy tried to remember when she'd seen Curt last. Of course, it had been yesterday at the pie sale. She could practically see him raising a fork loaded with blueberry pie to his lips, a glint of mischief in his eyes.

"You're sure he's dead?" asked Lucy, unwilling to believe the bad news.

Barney nodded. "Brain's bashed in."

Lucy grimaced but Barney wasn't through. "Murder weapon was right there beside him. Some sort of Indian club."

The roar of the crowd rang in her ears and she was jostled aside as the police cleared the area. For a second, she got a glimpse of Nolan lying on his back, his face to the sky.

That's where he's gone, she thought. *Up above the clouds into the bright sunshine beyond.*

CHAPTER 11

"I can't believe it," moaned Bill as they were driving home.

"Neither can I," agreed Lucy, whose face was white with shock.

"Absolutely no defense," continued Bill.

"I wouldn't say he was defenseless," said Lucy. "I would've thought he could take care of himself."

Bill gave her a sideways glance.

"Are we talking about the same thing? I'm talking about the game."

"Me, too," lied Lucy.

Bill stared at her. "No, you weren't. You were talking about Curt Nolan."

"Well, I am going to have to report on it for the paper."

"Reporting is one thing. Getting involved and trying to figure out who did it is another. You'd better leave that part to the police."

Mindful of the two girls in the backseat, Lucy didn't want to argue.

"Absolutely," she said, thinking it was time to change the subject. "So how did the game end? Did we win?"

In the backseat, Sara and Elizabth laughed. In the front, Bill snorted.

"The Giants intercepted the ball. Some guy ran seventy yards for a touchdown. I tell you, there's no excuse for that. Where was the defense?"

"No excuse," echoed Lucy. "No defense."

An hour later, alone in the Subaru as she went to fetch Miss Tilley, Lucy's thoughts returned to Curt Nolan.

No two ways about it, she admitted to herself, he was confrontational. He loved an argument and was never one to go along just to get along. A man like that made enemies, no doubt about that. There were plenty of people in town who had their problems with him, but that didn't mean they would actually kill him. This was New England, after all. The more ornery and cantankerous a person was, the more likely his neighbors were to grant him a grudging respect.

Lucy felt tears sting her eyes and blinked. She was surprised at herself. She wouldn't have thought she cared that much about Curt Nolan.

She remembered the day at the turkey farm, when the kids had been so frightened and he'd come to their rescue by distracting TomTom Turkey. She thought of him at the dog hearing, where he'd defended his pet.

By now the tears were really flowing and she had to pull off the road. This was ridiculous, she told herself as she fumbled in her purse for a tissue. She hadn't even known the man, not really.

But, she realized with surprise as she blew her nose, she had liked him. And why not? There was something awfully attractive about a man who was so comfortable in his own beliefs that he wasn't afraid to stand up for them. Not to mention the fact that he was good with animals and children.

Then her heart felt heavy as she thought of Ellie. She was already a widow, and losing Curt would be another terrible loss for her. Even more difficult, in a way, because the death of a good friend didn't elicit the same sort of sympathy that the death of a husband did. It was an awkward situation and people wouldn't know what to say or even if they should say anything at all.

Making the situation worse, thought Lucy, was the fact that Curt Nolan had been murdered. Tinker's Cove was a small town where nearly everybody knew everybody else. There was no random crime here as you would expect to find in a big city. Whoever killed Curt Nolan had done it deliberately, for a reason.

Why? wondered Lucy. *Why kill him?* It hardly seemed that the murderer would have taken such a huge risk, assaulting him at a crowded football game, just because Curt was occasionally obnoxious. There had to be a reason, thought Lucy, flicking on her turn signal and pulling back into traffic. A reason worth committing murder.

Arriving at Miss Tilley's little antique Cape-style house, Lucy leaned hard on the doorbell. She knew Miss Tilley—whose age was a secret but who had been old for the twenty-odd years Lucy had known her—was hard of hearing. She also moved slowly these days, so Lucy waited patiently, giving her plenty of time to answer the door.

After it seemed at least five minutes had gone by, Lucy gave the doorbell a second try. When this ring also failed to bring

Miss Tilley to the door, Lucy began to worry. Perhaps her old friend had fallen or had taken sick. It happened to frail elders all the time and sometimes they weren't found for days.

Lucy swallowed hard and tried the door. It opened and she went in, preparing herself for the worst.

"Hello," she called out loudly. Then she paused a moment in the little entry hall, listening for a reply.

"No need to yell," said Miss Tilley. "I'm right here."

She spoke slowly, without her usual snappish tone. Lucy thought she sounded tired.

"Is everything okay?" Lucy asked, entering the front parlor.

Miss Tilley was seated in her usual rocking chair by the fireplace but there was no fire in the hearth. The electric lights hadn't been turned on either, making the room dim.

"No. It's not all right. It's dreadful."

"Are you ill?"

"Oh, no. I'm fine. A horrid, decayed old wreck like me is perfectly fine and a big, strong young fellow like Curt Nolan is dead. Is that all right?"

"No, it's not all right." Lucy sat on the footstool and put her hand on Miss Tilley's knee. She sat quietly for a moment, then spoke. "How did you hear about it? It only happened a few hours ago."

"The radio. I was listening to the game."

This was a new side to Miss Tilley that Lucy hadn't suspected.

"I didn't know you followed football."

"Just the high school team. I like to keep track of the youngsters." Miss Tilley had been the town librarian for many years and knew everyone. "Curt played, you know. He was a very good player."

"I'm not surprised," said Lucy, spying something in Miss Tilley's hand. "What have you got there?"

"A little change purse." Extending her wrinkled claw of a hand she held it out for Lucy to see. "Curt made it for me many years ago."

Lucy took the little deerskin purse and examined the fine beaded design and the fringe decoration.

"It's lovely."

"I've always treasured it." Even in the poor light Lucy could see her eyes brighten at the memory. "He was such a sweet child, so interested in Indians. He read everything in the library, then asked me to get him more books from the interlibrary loan. By the time he graduated from high school, he must have been quite an expert. I hoped he'd go on to college to study anthropology or archaeology, but he didn't." She sighed. "He gave this to me just before he left for the army. It was the Vietnam war and he was drafted. Imagine. He survived all that and came back to Tinker's Cove, only to die at the Thanksgiving football game."

It was later, when they were in the car, that Miss Tilley finally asked how Curt died.

"Didn't they say on the radio?" asked Lucy.

"No. Just that his body had been discovered."

Lucy didn't want to tell her. It would only upset her, but there didn't seem any way around it. She drove carefully, watching the road, trying to think of the best way to say it. Finally, she came to the conclusion there was no good way.

"He was assaulted with the Metinnicut war club."

Miss Tilley drew in her breath sharply. "You mean he was murdered?"

"I don't see how it could have been an accident," said Lucy.

"That's awful!"

"I know."

For a few minutes, they drove on in silence. It was when they were turning into Lucy's driveway that Miss Tilley challenged her.

"You have to find out who did this, you know."

"It's not that easy," said Lucy, braking. "Bill's already made it very clear he doesn't want me getting involved. And I'm sure the police won't want me poking my nose into their investigation. I can just imagine what Lieutenant Horowitz would say."

"You're a reporter, aren't you? Asking questions is your job and they can't stop you. Freedom of the press is a constitutional right."

Lucy was sympathetic, but she wasn't going to be bullied.

"You know perfectly well that means newspapers can print what they want within reason. It doesn't mean reporters have carte blanche to interfere in a police investigation."

"As a favor for me?"

Lucy found herself looking at Miss Tilley: her faded blue eyes, her wrinkled cheeks, her wispy white hair.

"Please."

The word hit Lucy like a bucketful of cold water. Over the years Miss Tilley had threatened and argued and cajoled her into doing many things she'd rather not have done, but she'd never before said that word, never said *please*.

Lucy blinked hard and smiled.

"Well, if you put it that way, how can I refuse?"

Besides, she told herself, she already had a suspect in mind.

* * *

Entering the hall, where she paused to hang up Miss Tilley's coat, Lucy heard voices in the living room, where Bill was entertaining the Barths.

"Lucy," said Bill, rising to greet them. "I'd like you to meet Clarice and St. John Barth."

"I'm so glad you could come," said Lucy.

The Barths were seated together on the couch, and they nodded amiably at her. Clarice was just as she had expected: tiny, trim, and toned, dressed entirely in black. Just looking at her made Lucy feel huge, out of shape, and hopelessly out of style.

In contrast, St. John was shorter and pudgier than she expected. He seemed ready to burst out of his stiffly starched shirt and tightly knotted tie. Seeing Miss Tilley appear behind Lucy, he jumped to his feet.

"I'd like you to meet a dear family friend, Julia Tilley," said Lucy.

"Nice to meet you, Julia. St. John Barth, here, and this is my wife Clarice."

Lucy's eyes widened in shock. No one, except a sadly diminished group of contemporaries, ever called Miss Tilley by her first name. Today, especially, Lucy didn't think she'd tolerate such disrespect.

"I'm afraid I'm hopelessly out of date," Miss Tilley purred. "I prefer to be called Miss Tilley."

That seemed pretty mild, thought Lucy, relaxing.

"No problem, Miss Tilley," said St. John with a smile. "Thank you."

A gleam appeared in Miss Tilley's eye and she screwed up her mouth.

Oh, no, thought Lucy. *Here it comes.*

"Since we're speaking of names, why do you pronounce yours *Saint John?* Don't you know it's properly pronounced *Sinjin?*"

Clarice bristled and came to the defense of her husband. "It's a family name and that's the way the Barths have been saying it for generations."

Miss Tilley's back stiffened and Lucy jumped in, hoping to avoid bloodshed.

"The Barths are clients of Bill's," she said. "They've bought the old Tupper place and are restoring it. It's going to make a lovely home."

From her place on the couch, Clarice gave a small, smug smile.

"Would anyone like a glass of wine?" asked Lucy.

Receiving nods all around, Bill disappeared into the kitchen.

Lucy helped Miss Tilley get settled in an armchair, then perched on a hassock. She tried desperately to think of something to say.

"Tinker's Cove must be quite a contrast to New York," she finally ventured to say.

"Oh, it is," agreed St. John.

Clarice was examining her fingernails, which were polished bright red.

This was going to be tough, thought Lucy.

"I suppose you'll be using the house for vacations and weekends?"

"Actually, we're thinking of moving here year-round."

"Really?" Lucy was surprised. "Don't you have jobs in the city?"

"Clarice works in fashion—she designs displays for outfits like Guess and Banana Republic," said St. John, a note of pride in his voice. When he continued, his voice had dropped and he was practically mumbling. "I used to work for a big construction outfit, Mulligan, but I'm between jobs at the moment."

Lucy recognized the name immediately; she knew Mulligan Construction had designed the plans for the casino. Before she could ask about it, Clarice jumped in.

"St. John wants to write a book."

"A writer!" exclaimed Miss Tilley. "What's it going to be about?"

"He's not sure yet," said Clarice. "But it's sure to be a bestseller, whatever he writes."

Just then Bill appeared with a tray of wineglasses and passed them around. Lucy waited until he had pronounced a toast and then she fled.

"I have a few things to do in the kitchen," she said.

When she got there, she discovered that Bill had started cooking the potatoes, and they were ready to mash. That was good, she thought, guessing he wouldn't be able to keep the combatants in the living room apart for long. But when she started to whip the potatoes, she discovered the centers weren't quite cooked. No matter how high she turned the electric beater, stubborn lumps remained. She finally gave up and spooned the mess into a dish, plopping a big lump of butter on top. She tucked the potatoes in the oven, then went to peek in the family room, where the younger set, college kids included, were watching a video.

"Dinner in fifteen minutes," she said, noting with surprise that the news was well received.

"I'm starving," confessed Matt.

"Mom makes great stuffing," said Toby. "And wait till you taste her gravy."

Lucy beamed at him and smiled at the girls. She was pleased to notice that Amy and Jessica had changed out of their usual jeans and had dressed up for the occasion in attractive dresses complete with panty hose and heels.

Back at the stove she pulled the turkey pan out of the oven and set it on the counter, perched on a trivet so as not to burn the countertop. With one oven-mitted hand, she held the pan, and with her other hand she began loosening the turkey with a spatula. Plenty of greasy juice had cooked out of the turkey, which was great for the gravy but made the tricky task of getting the twenty-five-pound turkey onto the platter awfully difficult. Making matters worse was the fact that the bird had become firmly adhered to the pan. No sooner would she get one part loosened than she discover another stuck to the pan.

Finally, after poking away at the bird for what seemed an eternity, she thought she could risk lifting it onto the platter. She jabbed a fork into the breast and slid her biggest spatula under the bird and attempted to lift it. Halfway between pan and platter it slipped and crashed back into the roaster, showering her with greasy juice before the whole thing, pan and bird, slid off the tipsy trivet onto the floor.

Lucy slapped her hand over her mouth to keep from screaming. Lord knows she wanted to scream and wave her arms and
stamp her feet, but that would only attract attention, which was
the last thing she wanted to do. She was alone in the kitchen.
She was the only one who knew what had happened. She was
going to keep it that way.

"Mom?"

It was Sara, staring openmouthed at the turkey on the floor.

"Don't say a word to anyone, or I'll kill you."

Lucy wrapped a dishtowel around the bird and wrestled it
onto the platter.

"You can't serve that. It was on the floor." Sara was shaking
her head.

"Oh, yes, I can," growled Lucy. "Now go back to the TV
room and act as if nothing is the matter."

"But, Mom," protested Sara.

"Go! Now! And remember: One word and you die!"

After Sara disappeared into the family room, Lucy began
mopping up the grease that had spilled from the pan and covered
the floor. As she wrung out the mop she wanted to cry, watching
her beautiful golden turkey juice swirling into the soapy water.
Finally, the floor was clean and she turned her attention back to
the dinner.

So far she had mashed potatoes (lumpy) and turkey (dusty).
No matter, there would be plenty of other food. She slipped the
brown rice casserole into the microwave. Then she popped a pan
of sweet potatoes into the oven to warm beside the mashed
potatoes. She dumped a couple of packages of frozen baby peas

into the steamer and set it on a back burner behind the double boiler filled with creamed onions.

There was no question of making gravy; the juice was gone. She found a couple of cans of pork gravy in the cupboard and emptied them into a saucepan, adding a little soy sauce to darken the pale glop. She gave the spoon a lick, grimaced, and splashed in some cooking sherry. Maybe it would help.

"How much longer?" It was Bill. There was a note of desperation in his voice.

"It was your idea to invite them," she said, glaring at him. "You can't imagine what I've been going through in here."

Bill wasn't moved. "You think it's been a picnic out there?"

Lucy laughed. "Just a few more minutes."

Finally, everyone was seated at the table. Zoe recited a simple grace and Bill began carving the turkey.

As she surveyed the table, Lucy crossed her fingers and took a deep breath. The turkey didn't seem any the worse for its fall to the floor. She didn't think anyone would notice (and she had wiped it off with paper towels). As for the rest of the meal, well, she couldn't guarantee it would taste good but it sure looked good.

Bill stood and raised a glass. "To the cook!"

"Hear, hear!" chorused St. John.

Lucy tossed back her glass of wine and held it out for a refill.

"What did I tell you?" Toby asked Matt. "Doesn't my mom make great gravy?"

"I've never had anything like it," said Matt. His mother would have been proud of his tact.

"It's certainly unusual," said Clarice, furrowing her perfectly plucked brows.

"More stuffing, anyone?" asked Lucy.

"Yes," said Miss Tilley, taking the bowl of potatoes. "How about you?" She had turned her beady eyes on Jessica. "No wonder you're so thin. You're only eating celery. Here, have some mashed potatoes. Put some meat on your bones!"

Jessica's eyes widened in horror as Miss Tilley waved the bowl of potatoes in front of her. Looking somewhat green, she rose and fled from the table.

"I'll see if there's anything I can do," said Matt, following her.

"And you?" Miss Tilley had turned her basilisk gaze on Amy. "At least you're not all skin and bones, but what is that muddy stuff you're eating?"

"It's delicious. It's brown rice and carrots."

"You can't live on that! You need protein." Miss Tilley plunked a drumstick on Amy's plate. "Try this."

Amy studied the burnt offering for a moment, then shook her head. "Excuse me," she said, leaving the table.

"What's the matter with her?"

"She's a vegan, for Pete's sake." Toby pushed his chair away from the table and left the room.

"They don't eat turkey in Las Vegas?" Miss Tilley didn't understand.

"No. It's vee-gan. They don't eat animal products," explained Clarice.

Miss Tilley stared at the drumstick. "Oh, dear."

"You certainly have a knack for clearing a room," said Lucy. "At the rate you were going, I was beginning to wonder if anybody would be left for dessert."

"Wouldn't miss it for the world," said St. John. "Pumpkin pie is my favorite."

"Mine, too," said Miss Tilley, eyeing him with new appreciation. "I had my doubts about you, Sinjin, but you're all right!"

CHAPTER 12

All in all, Lucy thought Thanksgiving dinner had gone pretty well.

"There were a few tense moments, but it never actually came to blows," she told Bill the next morning as they sat at the kitchen table, taking advantage of the fact that the kids were all sleeping in to enjoy a second cup of coffee by themselves.

"Not even one fatality," said Bill, grinning.

His joke reminded her of Curt Nolan's death and she guiltily remembered her promise to Miss Tilley.

"I have to go in to work," she said, staring out the window at the fog-filled yard.

"What about the kids?"

"Zoe's going to spend the day with Sadie, and Elizabeth and Sara are going to the food pantry to sort out the stuff from the canned goods drive." She paused. "As for the others, I don't know and I don't care."

Bill put his hand over hers. It felt warm and good. "I know you're upset about Toby."

"Don't I have the right to be upset?" demanded Lucy. "King Lear was right—an ungrateful child is sharper than a serpent's tooth. I can't believe he's acting like this."

"I can," said Bill. "Don't you remember what it was like when you first went away to school and didn't have to ask your parents for permission anymore? You could come and go, and there was nobody to ask you what the hell you thought you were doing. Nobody to tell you what you could and couldn't do. You just started getting used to all that freedom when, all of a sudden, it was Thanksgiving and you had to go back home."

"I remember," said Lucy, thinking of how she used to dread the holidays when she was in college. For the first time, she wondered how her parents had felt. Had she hurt them as much as Toby was hurting her?

"Just a few more days," said Bill, standing up and putting on his jacket. "They'll be gone Sunday."

"You're right," said Lucy, stroking his beard when he bent down to kiss her good-bye.

"Lucy, thank goodness you're here," said Ted, when Lucy finally arrived at the *Pennysaver* a half hour late. "I was afraid you weren't coming, what with the holiday and all your company."

"I had to drop the girls off," she said, giving her damp jacket a shake and hanging it up. "Any progress on Nolan's murder?"

"Nope. The state police are holding a press conference later this morning. Maybe they'll have something to announce then."

"I'll go," offered Lucy eagerly. She could think of a million questions she'd like to ask the police.

"That's okay," said Ted. "I can handle it. I want you to start working on Nolan's obit."

"Not the obit," groaned Lucy. She hated writing obituaries. It was the worst part of working for a newspaper.

"I've already got some information from the funeral home," said Phyllis, trying to be helpful.

Lucy gave Ted an evil look. "I don't suppose you'll be happy with that, will you? You'll want quotes."

"Just a few," said Ted in an apologetic tone. He knew how hard it was to call up grieving survivors and ask them to talk about a lost loved one.

"A lot of people didn't like him," began Lucy.

"You can say that again," cracked Phyllis.

Lucy clucked her tongue and continued. "Do you want me to get negative quotes, too?"

"Sure," said Ted, turning back to his computer. "But I think you'll find people don't like to speak ill of the dead. Curt's probably a lot more popular dead than he was alive."

"Maybe I'll use that for a lead," said Lucy in a sarcastic tone. She turned on her computer and waited for it to boot up. "You know Fred Rumford called me Wednesday night? He was all upset that Chris White hadn't returned the war club. I was worried we were missing a big story." She sighed. "It's funny how things turn out, isn't it?"

"I can't believe that Chris was so irresponsible," said Phyllis. "That war club is priceless."

Lucy and Ted, both parents, laughed together.

"Doesn't surprise me," said Lucy, remembering Nolan's reaction that day at the library when he'd seen Zoe carrying the club. "Maybe Nolan saw Chris fooling around with it or something. He always said the club belonged with the tribe instead of in the museum. Didn't the cops follow up? Why didn't they question him on Wednesday and get the club back?"

"They tried to," said Ted, "but he wasn't home. There was

even an APB out on him but there was no sign of him until he turned up dead."

"You mean they think Nolan absconded with the club?" Lucy was puzzled. "But that makes no sense because he brought it back with him to the game."

"Maybe he didn't take the club," said Phyllis. "Maybe the murderer took it."

A thought occurred to Lucy. "Maybe nobody took the club at all. Maybe Rumford had it all the time."

"But that would make him the murderer," said Ted.

"Maybe he is," said Lucy, remembering how angry he was that day outside the library.

"*Professor* Rumford?" Phyllis was incredulous.

"Why not?"

"I don't think you're on the right track, Lucy," said Ted, checking the clock. "But you've given me some good questions for the press conference." He got up and reached for his jacket. "You'll have that obit done when I get back?"

"No problem."

After he'd gone, Lucy stared at the blank computer screen wondering who to call. Ted was right: Nobody would want to be quoted saying what they really thought of Curt Nolan. Certainly not Howard White or any of the other members of the board of selectmen. All she'd get from them would be a lot of hypocritical double-speak and she didn't have the stomach for it. Andy Brown? He was Nolan's boss, after all. But he was out of town.

Reluctantly, she decided there was nothing for it but to call Ellie Martin. She dialed Ellie's number quickly before she could change her mind.

"Hi, Ellie," she began, speaking in a soft voice. "This is Lucy Stone. I just wanted to tell you how sorry I am about Curt."

"Thank you, Lucy." Ellie's voice sounded distant, as if she were very far away instead of just a few miles down the road.

"I'm working on Curt's obituary for the *Pennysaver*. I wonder if you could tell me a little about him."

"I don't know. . . ."

"You knew him better than most people," coaxed Lucy. "Don't you want people to know what he was really like and to remember him that way?"

"I do." Ellie paused. "People didn't understand him, even people in the tribe. You know, I think that, if he'd lived in the old days, when the tribe was still strong, he would have been a shaman or something. He would have been a great leader. There would be legends about him. He saw things differently from other people. He saw behind appearances to the way things really are."

As she wrote Ellie's words down Lucy wondered if Ellie had given her the motive for Nolan's murder. Had he seen something that made him dangerous to someone? Had he known something that the murderer wanted to keep secret?

"Can you think of a particular example?"

"Well, he was very committed to his Indian heritage. It was more important to him than anything else. And it had to be the truth—what he understood to be the truth. He didn't like it when people tried to pretty up the facts, like saying Native Americans lived in harmony before the white men came. He'd say that was nonsense, that the tribes used to make war on each other." Ellie paused. "I don't think you should put that in the paper."

"Well, we could say he was committed to the cause of restoring and preserving Metinnicut heritage and culture," suggested Lucy.

"That's good."

"I guess we could say he valued the traditional ways, but not everyone approved of his unconventional and sometimes controversial tactics."

"I'm going to miss him," said Ellie, her voice breaking.

"Are you taking care of his dog?"

"Kadjo? Yeah. He really misses Curt. He won't eat. He keeps looking down the driveway, waiting for him."

"Are you going to keep him?"

"Oh, Lucy, I wish I could but I don't see how. Not if I want to raise chickens again next spring. You can't change dogs once they've got the taste. Sooner or later I'm going to have to give him up, and I guess it might as well be sooner before I get too attached to him. I called the dog officer but she wasn't too hopeful about finding a home for him. She says he's got a bad reputation."

"What happens if she doesn't find a home for him?"

"They'll destroy him."

"That's horrible!"

"I know." Ellie was sniffling on the other end of the line. "Would you be interested in taking him? You've got a big place and you don't have any neighbors to speak of. How about it? He's an awfully nice dog."

Lucy remembered Kadjo. She'd often seen him sitting in the cab of Curt's truck, usually grinning, with his ears pricked up, waiting for his master's return.

"Okay," she said, then thought better of it. What would Bill say? "Well, maybe. I guess I'd better take another look at him."

"Come on over. Anytime."

"In an hour?"

"Sure."

Lucy pounded out the obit and headed over to Ellie's. By the time she got there, she had made up her mind. As much as she would like to save Kadjo, she didn't really think she could take him. So far the family's only experience with pets had been a few assorted cats through the years, and after Elizabeth was diagnosed with asthma, they hadn't had any pets at all. Lucy had suggested getting a dog a few times but Bill had always nixed the idea. "Too expensive," he'd say. "Too dirty." If she pressed the point, she thought she could probably convince him to accept a small dog, like a Jack Russell terrier or a poodle, but Kadjo was enormous. Eighty or ninety pounds at least. Furthermore, he did have a reputation as a problem dog. She knew perfectly well what Bill's reaction would be if she brought him home and she didn't want to have to deal with it. So when she knocked on Ellie's kitchen door, she had resolved to say she was very sorry, but she would not be able to take the dog after all.

"Hi, Lucy. Come on in." Ellie waved her arm at Bear Sykes, who was seated at her kitchen table. "You know my uncle Bear. He was at the meeting the other night."

Lucy hesitated for a minute. She didn't want to intrude on a family meeting.

"Sit down," said Bear. "Take a load off your feet. I see you running all over town, chasing the news. I bet you could use a break."

Lucy laughed. "I sure could."

Bear's black hair was combed back from his face, and he was wearing a beaded choker under his plaid flannel shirt. His skin was ruddy, and with his high cheekbones and curved beak of a nose, Lucy thought he looked very much like the stereotypical Native American.

"Coffee?" asked Ellie. "How about a cup of tea?"

"Tea would be great," said Lucy.

Ellie put the kettle on and joined them at the table. She smiled but didn't say anything. Neither did Bear. The silence stretched on and Lucy felt she had to speak.

"I'm awfully sorry about Curt," she said. "I didn't know him well, but I know you'll miss him."

Bear glanced at Ellie. "Ellie was a lot fonder of him than I was," said Bear, picking up a spoon and stirring his coffee. "He had a big mouth."

"He did a lot for the tribe." said Ellie, defending him. "He made people proud of their heritage."

"I'll give him that," said Bear. "But the trouble with Curt was he didn't know when to stop. Wouldn't compromise. I could've killed him at the meeting the other night when he started talking against the casino." Bear slapped his fist on the table. "I mean, here we've worked so long and come so far, and he has to start throwing a monkey wrench in things. When we all stand together, folks are a lot more likely to take us seriously. But if it seems like we aren't agreed on what we want, well, then they're not going to stick their necks out for us. That vote could have gone either way, you know. We got lucky with that Dunlap woman."

The kettle shrieked and Ellie got up to make the tea.

"What do you think your chances are for federal approval?" asked Lucy.

"A lot better now that Curt isn't spouting off—that's for sure."

Ellie passed Lucy a cup of tea, then sat down. She pulled a handkerchief out of her pocket and dabbed at her eyes.

"I'm sorry, Ellie," said Bear, patting her shoulder. "I know you're upset about what happened."

Ellie nodded, sniffling. "I'm going to miss him no much," she said.

"Well, I've got to get going," Bear said, rising to his feet. "I've got a meeting."

"You always have meetings," said Ellie, blinking back her tears.

"Ain't that the truth," he said.

For a moment he stood behind her chair. Then he bent down and enfolded her in a big hug. After a moment he straightened up and headed for the door, giving Lucy a little salute.

After he'd gone, Lucy sat staring at the door, a thoughtful expression on her face.

"He talks tough, but he's upset about Curt, too," said Ellie, reading her mind and answering Lucy's unspoken thoughts. "It's funny about the tribe. It's like a big family. We get mad at each other, but if one of us gets hurt in some way, it's like all of us got hurt. He's a lot more upset than he's letting on, believe me. Especially since Curt was killed. Maybe whoever did it had it in for Curt, or maybe they hate all Indians. It wouldn't be the first time."

"Curt made a lot of enemies," said Lucy.

"Yeah," agreed Ellie. "So you want to see the dog? I put him outside."

Lucy followed Ellie outside through the fog and drizzle to

the empty chicken coop Ellie was using as a temporary kennel. Inside the wire fence, Kadjo was lying down with his chin on his front paws. He didn't get up as they approached. He just cocked an eye at them and sighed. It was a huge sigh—a sigh that seemed to express immense sadness.

"If I didn't know better, I'd say he's mourning for his master," said Lucy.

"He is mourning for him." Ellie pulled the hood of her jacket over her head.

"How could he know?"

"Dogs know. Always. Bees, too."

"Bees?"

"When a beekeeper dies . . ."

"I don't believe it," said Lucy, sticking her hands in her pocket for warmth.

Ellie shrugged and opened the gate. When they entered the pen, Kadjo got to his feet, but he didn't make any gesture. He didn't wag his tail in welcome; he didn't growl in warning. Ellie reached down and scratched him behind the ears. He looked up at her with sad yellow-brown eyes.

Lucy stroked his neck, feeling the muscles beneath his thick, coarse coat, which was beaded with moisture. "Poor old boy," she said.

He expelled another huge sigh and leaned his shoulder against her leg.

"I'll take him," she said.

"Great," said Ellie. "You won't regret it."

Lucy was regretting it already.

"But not until Sunday when my company has left and the house is quiet."

"That's good." Ellie patted Kadjo's massive head. "That way you'll be able to get acquainted in peace."

"Not likely," said Lucy. "This will probably cause a divorce."

"Look on the bright side—at least you'll have a dog."

"Might not be such a bad deal after all," said Lucy with a small smile. She started to go, then remembered something she'd meant to ask Ellie about. "Fred Rumford called me Wednesday night. He accused Curt of taking the war club from Chris White. Do you know anything about that?"

"Kids! Curt saw Chris and some other members of the team loading a keg of beer into a car. They also had the war club. They'd left it lying on the roof of the car, in fact, so he told them to give it to him for safekeeping. He was going to take it back to the college."

"Even though he thought it should belong to the tribe?"

"Of course. The tribe doesn't have a safe place for it now. He wanted it for the museum—the one that's supposed to be part of the casino deal."

"You're sure about this?"

"Absolutely."

"But the police couldn't find him Wednesday night. Do you know where he was?"

A look of peace settled on Ellie's face and she smiled. "He was with the ancestors, showing them the war club and promising to keep it safe."

Lucy nodded, as if she understood; then she realized she didn't. "And where did he find the ancestors?" she asked, hoping she wasn't being rude.

"On the island, of course. Metinnicut Island in the bay."

"Did he go alone?"

Ellie nodded. Then her face crumpled and Lucy wrapped her arms around the sobbing woman. They stood there together—two women and a dog in the cold November drizzle—for a long time.

CHAPTER 13

What had Lucy done? Was she out of her mind? How on earth was she going to convince Bill to accept Kadjo when she didn't even know herself why she had agreed to take the dog?

This was insane, she thought as she drove down Ellie Martin's driveway and turned onto Main Street Extension. It must be some sort of empty-nest syndrome, she theorized. Maternal instincts gone awry. Toby had flown off to college. He preferred his friends over his family, and she was reeling from the snub. What other explanation could there be?

All that was perfectly understandable, she could hear Bill saying as the Subaru wagon whizzed past the brown fields and bare trees, but why should the whole family have to suffer because of her motherly neurosis? Why should they have to put up with a huge, unruly, smelly beast of a dog that nobody wanted but her? A dog like that must eat an awful lot. How much did dog food cost? Did she have any idea? Not to mention vet bills. What if he got sick or was hit by a car? How would they afford that?

She didn't have any answers, she admitted to herself as she passed a deep stand of dark pine woods. All she knew was that she wanted to adopt Kadjo and she was determined to do it. Besides, she rationalized, she didn't ask much for herself. She never bought anything—clothing or shoes—that wasn't on sale, and when the kids asked what she wanted for Christmas or her birthday, she always told them to make her a nice card because that would mean more to her than anything they could buy. And it was true.

Now, for the first time in a very long time, she wanted something. She wanted Kadjo, and she decided as she pulled up at a stop sign that she was going to have him no matter what.

That settled, she found herself feeling remarkably cheerful and lighthearted. She could hardly wait until Monday when she could bring the dog home.

She had just pulled out onto Route 1 and was speeding along, eager to tell the kids about her decision, when an avalanche of guilt overwhelmed her. Here she was rejoicing in the fact that she was going to have Kadjo and entirely forgetting the reason why he needed a good home. Her good fortune had come at Curt Nolan's expense. If he hadn't been killed, she certainly wouldn't be getting the dog. And what about her promise to Miss Tilley? She'd been so busy feeling sorry for herself that she hadn't given much thought at all to finding Curt's killer.

The blare of a horn and the zoom of an accelerating car as it passed startled her. She was halfway home and she had no recollection of the drive. Shaken, she pulled off the road and tried to collect herself.

She took a deep, cleansing breath and closed her eyes, only to see Rumford's image pop up. Okay, she admitted, so he hadn't faked the war club's disappearance as she had suspected. But what if he had encountered Nolan at the game with the club? It was extremely unlikely Rumford would have accepted Nolan's explanation. They would have argued and Rumford might well have lost his temper and bashed Nolan with the club. It was a scenario that seemed all too probable, considering the argument she'd witnessed outside the library.

In fact, she thought, considering the number of times she'd seen Nolan embroiled in some conflict or other, there was no shortage of people who could have argued with Nolan at the game. After all, even Bear Sykes had admitted he wanted to kill Nolan at times.

Not that she thought for a minute that Bear had killed Nolan. It was just an expression. People said it all the time but they didn't really mean it. For instance, at this very moment she would like to kill Toby. She'd like to wrap her hands around his neck and shake some sense into him. Of course, she would never do it. But the urge was there. He certainly knew how to push her buttons. Was that what had happened to Nolan? Had he made someone, probably Rumford, so angry that Nolan had gotten himself killed?

Or had somebody seen some benefit in killing Nolan and cold-bloodedly taken advantage of the moment? That theory expanded the list of suspects even more. Nolan had managed to make enemies on both sides of the casino issue. By insisting on the rights of the tribe, he'd alienated the anticasino forces, and by criticizing the proposed plan, he'd made enemies of the procasino faction. There was no love lost between Howard White and Nolan, and she suspected Pete Crowley didn't think much of him either. Come to think of it, she'd even seen him arguing with his own boss, Andy Brown.

Andy Brown! He had more to gain from the casino than anybody, considering it was going to be built on his land. He'd be sitting pretty—no more pumpkins and turkeys for him!

Of course, Brown had an unshakable alibi. He'd been in New York at the Macy's Thanksgiving Day Parade on the day Nolan was killed. Sara had seen Katie and the rest of the Brown family on TV.

Suddenly, she had an unsettling thought. The Browns were in New York and Nolan was dead. That meant nobody had been taking care of poor TomTom Turkey. He must certainly need some food and water, and as it happened, she wasn't far from the farm. She couldn't just let the poor old thing starve, she decided, flipping on the directional signal and pulling back onto the road. Besides, it wouldn't hurt to check Andy Brown's alibi.

When she pulled into the driveway at the farm, Lucy was struck by the silence. When she'd been there before, it had always been crowded with people. In summer, Brown did a big business with his fruit and vegetable stand. September brought apples, and hordes of weekenders visiting the old-fashioned cider press. October was pumpkins and the haunted house, and in November, of course, it was the fresh turkeys.

That explained the silence, she realized. The turkeys were gone. All the noisy gobblers had either been sold or frozen for Christmas. All except TomTom.

Lucy pulled up beside the barn and got out of the car. She felt a little bit like a trespasser, but she did have a good excuse for being there. She was on a mission of mercy. Entering the cavernous barn she went straight to the corner where the giant turkey was penned.

"Hi, there, TomTom," she said, studying the situation. "Are you hungry?"

The huge bird cocked his head and blinked at her. As she watched he began to fan his tail.

"Now calm down," she told him. "I'm not going to hurt you. I just came to see if you've got any food."

Moving with stately slowness, the bird approached her, lifting first one enormous clawed foot and then the other.

Good Lord, thought Lucy, watching in fascination. Suddenly the relationship between birds and dinosaurs, which she'd read about in numerous books when Toby was in his dinosaur phase, didn't seem so preposterous.

Her instinct was to make a hasty exit, but TomTom's feed tray was indeed empty. Also, it was close to the side of the pen and she could probably fill it with feed without entering the cage. The water, however, posed a problem. The galvanized metal can hung from a chain attached to one of the rafters and was in the exact middle of the pen.

"This is a pretty kettle of fish," said Lucy, keeping a wary eye on the big bird as she explored the barn looking for the feed bin.

She found it under a window and next to it stood a sillcock with a hose.

Lucy first filled the feeder tray, hoping the bird would be too busy eating to bother her while she filled the water can. But as soon as she opened the gate he turned to look at her, once again spreading out his tail.

"Okay. Be thirsty. See if I care."

Realizing the hose was quite long Lucy decided to try to toss it into the container, which fortunately had no lid. After a few tries she succeeded, then turned on the faucet. From the sound of the water pouring in, Lucy guessed it had been empty. TomTom immediately marched over and took a long drink, lifting his beak to let the water slide down his long neck.

"You are indeed a strange creature," said Lucy, watching the performance. As she turned the water off, she wondered if it really was true that turkeys could drown in the rain because they wouldn't shut their beaks.

"Not even turkeys are that stupid," she told TomTom.

He blinked in agreement.

Returning to her car, Lucy congratulated herself. Between Kadjo and TomTom, she had really become quite a friend to animals. Furthermore, she'd made some progress on her investigation. She could now eliminate Andy Brown from her list of suspects. All indications were that he and the rest of the family were away from the farm. His alibi appeared to be ironclad.

CHAPTER 14

"Sara, will you get that?" Lucy was stripping the meat off the turkey carcass so she could make soup and her hands were too greasy to answer the phone.

"It's for you," said Sara, covering the mouthpiece with her hand. "It's Miss Tilley."

Lucy felt exactly as if the teacher had called on her in class and she hadn't done her homework. She washed her hands and took the phone.

"You caught me up to my elbows in soup fixings," said Lucy to explain the delay.

"Is that what you've been doing, making soup instead of finding out who killed Curt?"

"I've made some progress," said Lucy. "I've eliminated Andy Brown from my list of suspects."

"I wouldn't call that progress," said Miss Tilley, adding a little snort. "Everybody knows the Browns are in New York—they were even on TV."

"Well, I went out to the farm to make sure," said Lucy, wishing she didn't feel quite so incompetent. "That's one thing I've learned, you know. When it comes to an investigation like this, you can't take things for granted. You have to check and double-check everything."

"Maybe you'd like to double-check this," snapped Miss Tilley. "Rachel's here, you know, and she told me the police have some solid evidence. It's supposed to be very hush-hush but the police chief told Bob, Rachel's husband. Those two are thick as thieves, you know, Bob being a lawyer and all."

"What kind of evidence?"

"Rachel didn't know but she said it's something important."

"I wonder what it is," said Lucy.

"I thought you'd be interested," said Miss Tilley, sounding smug. "Rachel also said that Bob had a meeting with Howard White and Jonathan Franke and some other people who are opposed to the casino. Bob told her they were shedding no tears over Curt."

"I can see why," said Lucy, remembering the pie sale. "Curt could have been quite an embarrassment to them. He was claiming the town couldn't use the zoning regulations to keep the casino out because they'd ignored them and given Andy Brown preferential treatment."

"Of course they did," said Miss Tilley. "Electric signs, a talking pumpkin—it's scandalous. I never could abide Howard White, you know. He's the sort who puts overdue library books in the book return slot so he won't have to pay the fine. Sneaky— that's what I'd call him."

Lucy couldn't help smiling at this proof of Miss Tilley's willingness to think the worst of everyone.

"Oh, Howard seems okay to me," said Lucy. "And he's right. It was all by the book. Brown applied for variances, just the way he was supposed to."

"Well, maybe you'd better do some of your double-checking," said Miss Tilley, adding a humph. "If you ask me, I don't doubt for one minute that Howard White is capable of murder. He routinely returned books with broken backs."

"I'll look into it," said Lucy.

As she turned to put the heavy stock pot on the stove, Lucy's eye was caught by Elizabeth, who was making herself a cup of coffee. This was not the usual mussed-up version of herself that Elizabeth typically presented in the morning; today she had dressed and combed her hair before coming downstairs. She had even, Lucy noticed on closer inspection, applied mascara and eyeliner.

Lucy was dying to know what the occasion was, but she knew better than to ask. All would be revealed, she told herself, if she were patient. Biting her tongue, she wrapped the extra turkey meat into a neat package and tucked it in the refrigerator.

She was wiping off the counter when Toby and Matt staggered in, barefoot and unshaven, in the same rumpled T-shirts and jeans they'd apparently slept in.

"Do we have any eggs?" asked Toby. "Matt and I want to fry some up."

"Sure. Help yourselves."

Lucy poured herself a second cup of coffee and joined the girls at the table. Elizabeth, she noticed, was watching Matt as he and Toby jostled to open the refrigerator door.

"Would you make one for me?" asked Elizabeth.

Lucy's eyes met Sara's across the table.

"You never eat eggs!" exclaimed Sara.

"Is that true?" asked Matt, lifting up his shirt and scratching his stomach.

"Of course not," said Elizabeth, furiously batting her eye-lashes. "I love a well-cooked egg and I bet you know how to make them just right."

"I am pretty good with eggs," admitted Matt.

"Yeah, right," said Toby, handing him the box. "Just try not to break all the yolks this time."

"Sure thing. Elizabeth, how do you want yours?"

"Oh, over easy," said Elizabeth, seductively drawling the words.

Lucy almost choked on her coffee. "So what are you guys going to do today?" she asked. "Are you going to the parade?"

"There's a parade?" Matt paused, holding an egg in his hand.

"Every year. Santa Claus comes."

"The elves, too," added Sara.

"Well, that is tempting," said Matt, cracking the egg on the side of the pan. "But I think I'll pass."

"Well, if you're looking for something to do, Pam Stillings told me they could use some help at the food pantry. It's open today and they're expecting quite a crowd."

Toby and Matt nodded. "Sure. We can help."

"I'll come, too," said Elizabeth. "After all, I was the chairman of the canned goods collection at the high school."

"You were?" Matt carefully lifted an egg with the spatula and flipped it over. "I bet it was very successful."

"This year was the biggest ever," said Elizabeth, coyly running her finger around her coffee mug. "Of course, it wasn't just me. I had a lot of help."

Lucy couldn't take it anymore. She finished her coffee and went upstairs to make the bed.

* * *

"I think Elizabeth likes Matt," said Lucy as she and Bill and the younger girls were driving into town to see the parade."

"No way," Sara said. "She told me he was a dork. Almost as much of a dork as Toby, but not quite because Toby is the king of the dorks."

Sara had a way with words, thought Lucy.

"That's right," chimed in Zoe. "She said Matt is Dork Number Two and Amy is Dork Number Three and Jessica is a bitch."

"Zoe!" Lucy and Bill spoke in one voice.

"Well, that's what Elizabeth said."

"She shouldn't have said it and you shouldn't have repeated it," said Lucy. "Besides, I think she may have revised her opinion—at least concerning Dork Number Two."

Bill parked the car on a side street, hoping to avoid the inevitable traffic jam that took place after the parade every year, and they walked along the sidewalk past neat white clapboard houses to Main Street. At the corner, they encountered Officer Barney Culpepper, who was standing behind a sawhorse and making sure no cars tried to sneak onto the parade route. The assignment wasn't very taxing and he had time to talk.

"Hi, Barney. It's a fine day for a parade, isn't it?" Lucy asked.

"Unseasonably mild," he agreed. "They say it's that El Niño."

"We'll get plenty of cold before winter's over," said Bill.

"Mom, can we go ahead?" Sara was clearly bored with this adult conversation. "We'll wait for you right in front of the news store."

"Okay. Catch you later."

Barney gave his whistle a short blast and waved a Ford Explorer onto the detour.

"Never fails." He shook his head. "There's always some that think they can drive right onto Main Street."

Lucy shook her head at this example of human folly. She wanted to ask Barney about the new evidence Miss Tilley had told her about but didn't want him, or Bill, to suspect she was more than casually interested.

"Wasn't that awful about Curt Nolan?" she asked. "Killed in broad daylight, right here in town."

Barney looked down at her from his considerable height. "I hope you're not planning on playing detective, Lucy. You'll just get yourself in a mess of trouble. Remember the last time at the lobster pound?"

Lucy shuddered at the memory and reached for Bill's arm, giving him a little squeeze. "No. I've given up investigating," she said, telling herself it really wasn't a lie if she judged by the progress she'd made in the case so far. "I was just wondering if there was any new information I could pass along to Ted at the paper."

"There was a press conference this morning at the station and Ted was there. Lieutenant Horowitz gave his usual spiel. 'The case is under investigation by the state police and we'll keep you informed.' Never gave us any credit at all, and it was our department that turned up the only piece of evidence that looks like it's worth anything."

Lucy knew the local cops resented the way the state police took over investigations of serious crimes and rarely acknowledged the ability and expertise of local officers who often had firsthand knowledge of both the victims and perpetrators.

"Sounds like the same old story," said Lucy, adding a sympathetic cluck. "You guys do all the work, but the state guys get the glory. It's really not fair. If you found something important, you should get the credit." She paused, letting him think it over. "Whatever it was, it probably wasn't that important, huh?"

"It might be, might not. It all depends. It could link the killer to the crime—that's why Horowitz didn't want it to get in the papers. They're holding it back."

Lucy knew this was standard procedure, but she couldn't help being curious.

"I won't put it in the paper, Barney. Promise. Scout's honor."

He laughed. "We had some fun times when the kids were Cub Scouts together, didn't we? Hey, Bill, remember that chuck wagon you and I built for the Chuck Wagon Derby? It's still going strong."

"That's great," said Bill. "Of course, we built it to last."

Lucy didn't like the turn the conversation was taking, "You really ought to tell me about the evidence, off the record, of course. That way I can make sure the department gets credit when the case is solved."

Barney considered.

"You know you can trust me," said Lucy.

He sighed. "Like I said, it might not be anything, but they did find a button in Nolan's hand."

"A button? What kind of button?"

"Leather, I think. Kinda woven. You know the type. 'Course it might've been dropped there by anybody and he just happened to pick it up. It didn't have to come from the murderer."

"That's probably what happened," said Lucy, determined

not to show her excitement at getting the information. "But you never know."

"We'd better get a move on," said Bill. "We don't want to miss the parade."

"Have a nice time now," said Barney, raising his hand to halt a pickup truck.

When Lucy and Bill found the girls, standing just where they had said they'd be, Sara was holding a big pink cone of cotton candy.

"You're going to ruin your teeth," scolded Lucy. "It's nothing but sugar, you know. Empty calories."

"Want some, Lucy?" asked Bill.

"Sure."

Soon she was happily enjoying the way the cotton candy melted on her tongue and watching the other people in the crowd waiting for the parade to start. That was one thing about living in a small town like Tinker's Cove: Even if you didn't know everybody by name, almost everyone looked familiar.

"When's it gonna start, Mom?" Zoe asked.

"Pretty soon. I think I hear the drums."

Just then a siren blared, causing the girls to cover their ears and scream with delight. The parade was approaching, led as always by the fire department's gleaming white pumper truck. The town's pride and joy—a brand-new hook-and-ladder truck— would be at the end of the parade, carrying Santa in a crow's nest atop the ladder.

The high school band was marching past, and everybody was smiling and clapping in time to the music. The band was followed by a band of clowns driving funny little cars, actually Shriners in costume. Everybody laughed at their antics and the children scrambled to catch the candy they tossed.

Lucy was enjoying the spectacle when, suddenly, someone fell against her almost knocking her off her feet. As she staggered to keep from falling, Bill took in the situation and leaped to her aid.

"Here you go, fella," he said, grabbing the man by the upper arms. "Steady now."

"I'm so sorry," the man said.

Lucy was surprised to recognize Howard White.

Pale and drawn, he hardly seemed the imperious chairman of the board of selectmen.

"Are you all right?" asked Lucy. "Should we call the rescue squad?"

"Oh, no." White spoke with some effort, he was out of breath and his chest was heaving.

"The fire station's just down the street—I'll get an EMT," said Lucy.

"I'm all right." The words came out in a rush. White continued to breathe heavily. "I just need to catch my . . . my breath. It's the cold you see."

Lucy hesitated. Her instincts told her he needed help, but she knew White would hate the embarrassment of causing a fuss at the parade. Indeed, he did seem to be getting back some of his color and to be breathing more easily.

"How foolish of me," he said. "I was fooled by this mild weather and was rushing to meet my wife. I should have taken my time. It's this darned asthma."

"Shall I go and get her?"

"No, no. I'll be fine. I'll just go on slowly, as I should have in the first place. I apologize for being so much trouble."

"Not at all," said Lucy, watching as he made his way cautiously down the street.

"Poor old fellow," said Bill.

"Yup," agreed Lucy, mentally scratching another suspect off her list. Miss Tilley was undoubtedly correct that Howard White wasn't mourning Curt Nolan's death, but Lucy doubted very much that he would have been physically capable of committing the evil deed. That war club was heavy; Lucy herself had held it when Rumford had brought it to the flintknapping workshop at the library. There was simply no way Howard White could have lifted the club and delivered a fatal blow, especially since it had been at least twenty degrees colder on the day of the football game. If temperature triggered his asthma and he was having trouble on a mild day, he would have been in serious trouble on a really cold day.

The parade continued but Lucy wasn't watching; she was lost in her thoughts. She was thinking of the button Barney had described. It sounded like the sort of button that was often used on tweed sportcoats—the sort of sportcoat that Fred Rumford almost always wore. Once again she remembered that day at the library.

"Mom! Mom!" Zoe was screeching, waving madly at Santa atop his fire truck. "I want to tell Santa what I want for Christmas!"

"Okay. What do you want to do, Sara? Do you want to visit Santa Claus?"

Sara rolled her eyes in disgust. Her mother should surely

know better than to ask a question like that of such a mature individual as herself.

"You take Zoe to see Santa," said Bill. "Sara and I will go on over to the football field and see who wins the prize for the best float. You can meet us there."

Taking Zoe's hand, Lucy headed for the fire station, where Santa traditionally held court. By the time they arrived, however, the line of children eager to tell him their Christmas wishes was halfway down the street.

"I hate standing in line," said Lucy.

Disappointment clouded Zoe's little face and she stuck out her bottom lip in a pout.

Lucy pulled a schedule from her pocket and checked the time.

"Look. Santa's going to be here for another hour. Why don't we do something else for a while and come back in forty-five minutes or so? The line will be much shorter then."

"What could we do?"

"How about this," said Lucy excitedly, spying an opportunity to continue her investigation. "There's an open house at the college museum. You know you love the mummy."

Zoe nodded. She was fascinated by the exhibit of a drab and dusty mummy case that contained the well-wrapped remains of an ancient Egyptian workman.

"Okay," she said.

As they walked the three blocks to the museum, Lucy told herself she wasn't really involving her child in a murder investigation. Of course not. She was taking Zoe to see the mummy, which was just one of the many strange artifacts William Winchester had collected on his grand tour and later donated to the college he had created back in 1898. No, her main interest was amusing Zoe, but if the opportunity rose to question Fred Rumford, she would certainly take advantage of it.

As she had expected, few people were attending the open house at the college museum. Lucy and Zoe helped themselves to lemonade and cookies from the table set up in the lobby. Then they wandered through the largely empty rooms studying the old-fashioned glass exhibit cases.

One case contained artifacts collected in Polynesia, including spears, drums, and a plaster model of a woman wearing a grass skirt. Lucy looked at the faded photograph of William Winchester surrounded by several half-naked native women and noticed he seemed remarkably dour for a man in that situation.

"Come on, Mom. The mummy's in the next room."

Lucy followed as Zoe ran up to the glass case, then stopped short.

"Is it really a dead person?" Zoe asked.

"Yes, it is. But the person has been dead for a very long time. Thousands of years."

"Why did they wrap it up like that?"

"It was their religion."

"I wouldn't like to be tied up like that."

"Neither would I. Not if I was alive. But once you're dead, it doesn't matter. You don't know what's happening to you."

Zoe had crouched down, trying to get a better view of poor old Asherati the stonecarver, and Lucy wondered what the poor fellow would think of his new situation if he were able to. He had died secure in the knowledge that his remains would be properly prepared for the afterlife; he would probably be horrified to find himself a subject of curiousity in a New England museum.

Leaving, they passed the empty display case that usually contained the war club. Lucy paused for a minute, thinking sadly of Curt Nolan. When she was leaving, she spotted Fred Rumford coming out of his office. To her disappointment he was wearing a blue blazer with brass buttons.

"I see the police still have the war club," she said, approaching him. "Do you know when you'll get it back?"

He shook his head. "They say it's evidence. We may not get it back until after the trial—if there is a trial, that is." Rumford grimaced. "Considering they have to figure out who killed Nolan and catch him before they can even have a trial, it could be years before we get the club back."

"What if they don't make an arrest? What if the case is never solved? Do you get the club back?"

"That," he said with a grim nod, "is the sixty-four-thousand dollar question. The answer I got was, 'maybe.'"

"I guess you could sue them," said Lucy, ignoring Zoe's tugs on her arm. She'd gotten the chance to question Rumford and she wasn't going to let it pass.

"I guess I'd have to if it came to that," said Fred. "The problem is, of course, that the war club is centuries old. It's extremely fragile and needs special care. Controlled humidity and temperature. Which I'm pretty sure it's not getting in some evidence locker at state police headquarters."

Rumford's voice had gotten louder as he spoke; he was clearly very upset. "It's bad enough that they take it out of the museum and wave it around at the pep rally every year, but there's nothing I can do about that. Believe me, I've tried. It's outrageous, but people didn't understand how to properly care for primitive artifacts when William Winchester wrote his will specifying the annual display at the football game." He seemed to run out of steam. "I've learned to live with it. I mean, it's been going on for nearly a hundred years. And it was never a problem until now."

Lucy nodded, hugging Zoe to her side. The little girl was getting restless and Lucy didn't want her to wander off.

"I know how upset you were when Chris White didn't return it after the rally."

"You bet. I called the cops and they were great. They tracked the kid down, but no club. Chris couldn't be bothered getting it back here—he gave it to Nolan. Of all people!"

"You know," said Lucy, looking at Rumford closely and watching his reaction, "I think Nolan might have been just as concerned as you about the club. I heard he took it for safekeeping and intended to return it to the museum."

"That's ridiculous!" exclaimed Rumford. "You know as well as I do that Nolan's always said the war club belongs with the tribe."

"Ellie told me he wanted it for the tribal museum—the one that's part of the casino deal." Lucy held tight to Zoe's hand; the little girl was squirming, trying to run away. "She's certain he was going to return it to you. What I wonder is whether he tried to do that at the game? Maybe you were the last person to see him alive."

Rumford looked at her suspiciously. "You know, the police asked me that same question."

"The police questioned you?"

"Oh, sure." His face reddened with the admission. "I guess I'm a suspect." He looked around the museum, as if to reassure himself it was still there and he was still its director. Then he gave a short, abrupt laugh. "Oh, well. I'm probably in good company. Half the town would have liked to kill him!"

That was exactly the problem, thought Lucy as she and Zoe left the museum: too many suspects and none at all. Reluctantly, she crossed Rumford from her list of suspects. Not because he couldn't have killed Nolan; Lucy thought that Rumford would have liked nothing better. It wasn't that he couldn't have committed murder, but he wouldn't have, not using the war club. He would never have risked damaging such a precious artifact.

"I'm going to ask Santa for a Barbie Bakes Cakes oven," said Zoe, her mouth full of cookie. "You're too big to sit on Santa's lap, aren't you?"

"Yes, I am."

"Then how does he know what you want for Christmas?"

"He just knows."

"He does? How?"

"Magic, I guess. Santa magic."

That was what it would take, she thought, to get what she really wanted for Christmas. Even Santa would be hard-pressed to come up with a lead in this case.

CHAPTER 15

Looking out the laundry room window, Lucy saw it had started to snow. Not heavily, but scattered tiny flakes were drifting down and a light frosting had collected on the cars in the driveway.

It was almost noon on Sunday and Lucy had spent most of the morning doing laundry. The girls had been up for hours. Elizabeth had gone ice-skating with some friends, Sara was working on a school project at a classmate's house, and Zoe was at the Orensteins', playing with her best friend, Sadie.

Lucy pulled one of Toby's shirts out of the laundry basket and began to fold it. Snow had been forecast, and if the kids had been smart, she thought, they would have gotten up early for the drive back to Coburn. If they had, they would almost be there by now. But as it was, it was nearly noon and they were still asleep in the family room, and it would probably be snowing heavily by the time they got going.

Lucy didn't like to think of them driving on the interstate in heavy snow; she doubted Matt was an experienced winter driver. He probably would try to go 65 miles an hour in spite of bad visibility and slippery roads.

Pulling another shirt out of the basket—an expensive

designer shirt Toby had received as a graduation present—Lucy groaned. The pocked was ripped, a cuff was dangling loosely, and several buttons were missing. Whatever could have happened to it?

It was hard to understand how his clothes could become quite so stained and torn in the library, where he ought to be spending most of his time. Summer camp, basic training, survival courses—she could see how such programs would be tough on clothing. But French 101, freshman composition, calculus, and theories of government? It hardly seemed they could account for the sorry condition of Toby's wardrobe.

The pipes began to hum; the college kids were starting the series of showers with which they began every day. Lucy sent up a quick prayer to the plumbing gods, begging that the hot water heater would hold out.

It was at times like these that she missed her father. He had served in North Africa in World War II and had been a master of the one-minute shower. She smiled, remembering him acting out the process for her, fully clothed, of course, in the living room. He could teach these kids a thing or two about conserving water, she thought, as she headed for kitchen.

"I've got some clean clothes for you—don't forget to pack them," she told Toby, who was pulling a carton of eggs out of the refrigerator.

Matt was standing at the stove, cooking bacon, and Jessica was sitting on the floor, reorganizing her duffel bag. That was the only explanation Lucy could come up with for the mess of clothing and personal articles that was strewn all around her.

"Toby, a lot of your clothes are ripped. What have you been doing?"

Matt laughed. "I told you your mother would be ticked," he said.

"I was on the rugby team," said Toby.

"Don't they have uniforms?"

"It's a club sport."

"Oh. Well, from now on, if you're going to play, wear sweats, okay?"

"Okay," said Toby. Then, surprising her, he wrapped his arms around her and enveloped her in a bear hug. Lucy responded with a squeeze and ruffled his hair.

"Tough guy, huh?" Matt said, smacking him with the spatula. Toby grinned and put up his fists.

Watching them scuffle, Lucy hoped Toby's T-shirt, already ripped at the shoulder, would last a little longer. She tiptoed through Jessica's assorted piles and went into the family room, intending to put Toby's clean clothes by his backpack. The sight that greeted her, however, made her gasp.

The normally neat, pleasant room looked like a disaster area. The couch had been stripped of its cushions. Clothing, shoes, blankets, sleeping bags, and pillows covered the floor. And for some inexplicable reason, the shade had been removed from one of the lamps. The window blinds, of course, were tightly closed. What did she expect? she thought, snapping the cord. You couldn't sleep until noon if the light came in, could you?

She was sitting on the uncushioned sofa, staring glumly at the mess, when Bill came in.

"I wish they'd gotten an early start," he said, looking out the window. "The snow's starting to come down pretty heavily."

"It'll take them hours to pack all this stuff," she said with a weak little wave of her arm. "Maybe the storm will be over by the time they leave."

"Buck up, Bucky," said Bill, pulling a couch cushion out from under a tangle of bedding. "We can have them packed and on the road in no time."

"Aye, aye, Captain," said Lucy, jumping to her feet and rolling up a sleeping bag.

An hour later the snow had petered out, leaving a scant inch on the roads. Lucy and Bill stood on the porch, waving as Matt floored the gas pedal and sent his battered Saab lurching down the driveway.

"So how does your empty nest look now?" he asked, slipping his arms around her waist.

She stroked his beard and looked up at him. "There's something I have to tell you," she said.

Bill's back stiffened. "You're not pregnant, are you?"

"Oh, no," she said quickly. "It's not that. But we are getting a dog."

"That's okay, then," he said, nibbling on her ear.

Lucy wasn't sure he'd heard right, but she wasn't going to press the issue. "You know what?" she said, slipping her arms around his neck. "We've got the whole house all to ourselves."

"Darn," he said, pulling her closer. "Another boring Sunday afternoon. Nobody home. Nothing to do."

"Oh, I can think of something to do."

"You can?"

He was kissing her.

"Oh, yes," she said, taking his hand and leading him back into the house.

* * *

Lucy had promised to pick up Zoe at the Orensteins' at three o'clock. Since she was already out, she decided to swing by Ellie's house to get Kadjo, too. Zoe wasn't sure this was a good idea.

"Mom, what if he bites?"

"He won't bite. He's a nice dog."

"Are you sure?"

"Of course I'm sure. I wouldn't adopt a mean dog."

"We've never had a dog before. Why do we have to get one now?"

"Kadjo needs a home."

"But why does he have to come to our house? Why can't he go somewhere else?"

"You'll like him."

"I don't think so."

Lucy pulled into Ellie's driveway and braked, then turned to face Zoe. "We're taking Kadjo on a trial basis. If it doesn't work out, we won't keep him."

"Promise?"

"Promise."

Together they walked up to the house and knocked on the door. Ellie greeted them warmly and invited them in to the kitchen, where Bear was seated at the table.

"Tea for you, Lucy? How about some hot cocoa for Zoe?"

"Sure," said Lucy, sitting down. "You know, I bet Zoe would like to see your dolls."

"Would you like that?" Ellie asked Zoe.

"Yes," answered Zoe.

Ellie led her down the hall to her workroom, leaving Lucy and Bear alone.

"You're a reporter, right?" he demanded, scowling at her over his coffee cup. "You heard anything about Curt's murder? Have they got any suspects?"

"I heard they've been questioning a lot of people," said Lucy, unwilling to admit she didn't really know how the police investigation was going. "And they've got some physical evidence."

"What's that mean?"

"Something they think belonged to the killer." She paused. "They're not saying exactly what it is."

He narrowed his eyes. "You've been talking to people, asking questions?"

Lucy wondered what he was getting at. "It's my job."

He shrugged. "Nothing wrong with that. If you ask me, it's the cops that aren't doing their job."

The kettle whistled and Lucy got up and turned the stove off. Ellie had left the cups ready to add water. Lucy poured and brought the hot drinks back to the table.

"You surprise me," said Lucy, lifting the tea bag out and squeezing it with a spoon. "Last time I talked to you, you said you would have liked to kill Curt yourself."

His black eyes seemed to bore into her for a long time. Then he grinned at her, reminding her of a fox. "People say funny things when they're upset. Shock takes people differently."

Studying Bear's broad, impassive face, Lucy didn't think he would shock easily. She listened as he continued.

"No two ways about it: I had my differences with Curt. That

doesn't change the fact that one of my people was killed in cold blood and nobody seems to be doing anything about it."

"These things take time," said Lucy, turning around to smile at Zoe and Ellie, who were returning to the table. "Your cocoa's ready." She patted the chair. "What did you think of the dolls?"

"Nice," said Zoe, taking a big slurp of cocoa.

Lucy laughed. "Is that all you have to say?"

Zoe pursed her lips and thought for a moment. "Thank you for the cocoa," she finally said.

Lucy's eyes met Ellie's and she gave an apologetic smile. "How are you doing?"

"Okay." Ellie glanced at Bear. "It's hard."

Lucy patted her hand. "I know."

"I really appreciate your taking the dog. It's a load off my mind knowing he's going to a good home."

"I'm happy to take him."

When they finished their drinks, Ellie led Zoe and Lucy out to Kadjo's pen.

The dog was on his feet, not barking, but watching them approach. As they drew closer, his tail began to wave.

"Hi, boy," said Ellie. "Are you ready to meet your new family?"

She opened the gate and snapped on a leash and Kadjo bounded forward. When Ellie handed the leash to Lucy, however, he suddenly halted.

"Good boy," said Lucy, holding her hand out for him to sniff. "We're going to call him Kudo."

"That's a good idea," said Ellie. "Give him a fresh start."

When Kadjo, now Kudo, was satisfied with her scent, Lucy gave him a little scratch behind his ears. When she led him toward the car, he didn't resist but trotted along beside her. She opened the rear hatch for him and he jumped in willingly. She slammed the door down and looked at him through the window; he gazed back at her.

Zoe didn't want to sit in the backseat, where she would be close to the dog, so Lucy let her sit in the front passenger seat. She made sure Zoe's seat belt was tightly fastened, then started the car.

Ellie came up and stood by the car door; Lucy opened the window.

"Remember to be firm with him and you won't have any trouble," said Ellie.

"I'll remember," said Lucy. "Thanks."

"I'm the one who should be thanking you," said Ellie. "By the way, I don't know if you want to come, but the funeral is tomorrow. Ten o'clock at the meeting house in Hopkinton."

"Thanks for telling me. I'll be there."

"Better come early if you want to get a seat." Ellie bit her lip. "I just wanted a private graveside service but Bear said that wouldn't do. He said Curt was a tribal leader and deserved a traditional ceremony. Personally, I think it's a big waste. It isn't as if Curt is going to know."

Lucy recited the usual platitude. "It's not for him. It's for the people left behind."

Ellie shrugged, holding her hands out in a helpless gesture.

Lucy gave a little wave and shifted into drive, checking that the driveway was clear before accelerating. Seeing Bear climbing into his truck, she waited, watching with disapproval as he carelessly careened down the icy drive holding a cell phone to his ear.

As she followed, driving slowly, Lucy checked the rearview mirror to make sure Kudo was behaving himself in the cargo area. He seemed to be doing fine, not minding the motion of the car. She braked carefully when she got to the road so he wouldn't be knocked off his feet; then she proceeded to turn. She had no sooner got onto the highway, however, than he jumped into the backseat, causing Zoe to shriek. Signaling, Lucy immediately pulled off onto the shoulder and stopped the car.

She climbed out of her seat and opened the rear door. Kudo sat on the backseat, grinning at her, his tongue lolling. He seemed to be saying he much preferred riding in the backseat, sitting like a person, to sliding around in the cargo area.

"We're not getting off to a good start," Lucy warned him, looking him straight in the eye.

She took hold of his leash and pulled, but Kudo resisted. Lucy snapped the leash and yanked him out of the car. To her surprise, once he was on the ground he followed her easily around to the rear of the car. She opened the hatch and he leaped in. She got back in the driver's seat and started the engine, checking the rearview mirror before pulling onto the road. In the mirror her eyes met Kudo's.

"You'd better behave," she said.

Kudo grinned.

Still not trusting the dog to behave in the car, Lucy chose to drive home over back roads rather than to risk being distracted on busy Route 1. She liked taking the less traveled route through the woods anyway, especially since today the trees and bushes were still frosted with snow from the morning storm.

"Aren't the woods pretty today?" she asked Zoe.

"Like a fairyland," agreed Zoe.

"Fairyland," repeated Lucy. "But only for a little while. It's already starting to melt."

Suddenly spotting a fast-approaching dirt bike that was apparently headed straight for her car, Lucy slammed on the brakes. Zoe lurched forward, but was restrained by her seat belt, and Kudo slammed into the seat back.

"Are you all right?" Lucy's arm had instinctively shot out across Zoe's chest.

"I'm fine, Mom."

Looking over her shoulder, Lucy saw that Kudo had recovered without any damage. He was standing with his chin resting on the top of the seat back, staring at her reproachfully.

"It wasn't my fault," she told him before proceeding down the road.

She had no sooner got started again, however, than the dirt bike reappeared in her rearview mirror. This time Lucy continued driving slowly, trying to get a good look at the biker. Although she could see he was dressed in black motocross leathers, she couldn't make out his face. It was hidden behind a black visor.

Once again, she heard the motorcycle engine roar and once again he zoomed past her with an ear-deafening vroom. She tensed, ready to brake if he stopped again, but this time he continued on his way, disappearing down a side trail.

When Lucy finally reached Red Top Road, coming out just a few hundred feet from her driveway, she was much relieved. She hadn't thought the dirt biker intended her any harm, but his antics had been dangerous. What if she had hit him? He seemed to be playing a very dangerous game. If he was going to seek thrills, she wished he wouldn't do it at her expense.

She flipped the lever, signaling the turn into her driveway and tapped her brakes. When she checked the mirror, she flinched at the unexpected reappearance of the dirt biker. He had pulled up on the side of the road, oppoosite the driveway, and he remained there, watching, as she hurried Zoe and Kudo out of the car and into the house. Once they were safely inside, she looked to see if he was still there, but he was gone. Standing on the porch, Lucy could only hear the faint sound of the motorcycle engine as it grew more and more distant and finally ceased altogether.

Satisfied that he was gone, she went into the house herself. She wondered if she should call the police and report the incident. Looking at the phone, trying to decide, she rememberd Bear Sykes and his cell phone. Had he called the biker? she wondered briefly before dismissing the thought.

She was reminded of more pressing duties by Kudo, who was rubbing his wet nose against her hand.

"Come on and meet the family," she said, pushing open the door to the family room.

CHAPTER 16

That evening, having reclaimed the family room, Bill switched off the TV at ten and he and Lucy headed for bed. Kudo had been sleeping at Lucy's feet, but as soon as she stood up, he also got up and stretched. Then he looked at her expectantly. She went through the kitchen and he followed, nails clicking on the bare floor. She opened the back door for him and he trotted out, obviously with a mission in mind.

Lucy decided she might as well use the bathroom herself; then she opened the door and called the dog. He appeared out of the darkness almost immediately and she let him in, pointing to the bed she had put down for him in a corner of the kitchen. Kudo approached it cautiously, suspiciously sniffing the expensive, flea-repellent bedding.

"Go on," said Lucy in a reassuring voice. "It won't bite."

Then she turned out the light and opened the door to the back stairs. As she started up, Kudo was right at her heels.

"Oh, no," she said, turning around and pointing him to the dog bed. "You sleep in the kitchen."

Kudo dropped his head and made a little whining sound.

"That's enough," said Lucy sternly. "Down you go."

The dog turned and went down a few steps, then paused, shivering pathetically.

"It's not cold in the kitchen. It's a lot warmer than my room—that's for sure," she told him.

He raised his head and looked at her, somehow turning his yellow dog eyes into pools of melting chocolate.

"Okay. You win," said Lucy, resuming her climb up the stairs. "Just for tonight. I know it's hard getting used to a new home."

"What's he doing up here?" asked Bill, who was in bed reading a homebuilder's magazine.

"He followed me up the stairs."

"You know, Lucy, I'm not at all sure why we have this dog, but he's sure as hell not sleeping with us."

Lucy looked wounded. "You said it would be okay."

"I don't remember that," said Bill. He got out of bed and snapped his fingers. "C'mon, boy."

Kudo stepped closer to Lucy and made a noise that began as a whine but ended with a throaty rumble.

Bill looked at the dog, narrowing his eyes.

"I think he wants to stay with me," said Lucy.

"That's obvious," said Bill as he climbed back in bed. "But do we want him to stay with us?"

"I don't mind," said Lucy. "Do you?"

Bill sighed. He'd lost this battle before, when the kids were little and wanted to sleep in their parents' bed. He'd believed the books that said children must learn to sleep by themselves, but Lucy could never stand to send them back to their cold, solitary beds, where frightening monsters lurked in the dark.

"I guess not," he finally said. "But not on the bed."

Lucy settled herself on the pillows, propping a book on her chest. Kudo stood beside the bed, resting his chin on the mattress.

Lucy gave her head a little shake and the dog expelled a huge breath and curled up on the carpet next to the bed. Lucy let her arm drop and gave his head a scratch.

The next morning, after Bill and the kids had left the house, Lucy pulled on a warm jacket and took the dog out for some exercise along the old logging roads that ran behind their house. Lucy walked at a good pace, enjoying the fresh air and sunshine. Kudo ran ahead of her, sniffing the ground and chasing rabbits, but returning frequently as if to check that she was still there.

Lucy picked up a stick and threw it. Kudo ran after it and brought it back to her, grinning proudly. She threw the stick a few more times, then realized it must be getting late. She checked her watch and discovered it was time to go home if she planned to go to Curt Nolan's funeral service.

Back at the house she gave Kudo a fresh bowl of water and a dog biscuit, then hurried upstairs to change her clothes.

As she tugged on her black panty hose, Lucy considered the best route to the Indian Meeting House in Hopkinton. The most direct way was along the back roads she had taken the day before, but remembering the dirt biker she decided to take the long way round on the highway. Chances were that the biker, whoever he was, was just some kid who'd been having fun at her expense. Sure, the leathers and helmet had looked menacing, but that was just the style. They all wore them. No doubt the biker was back in school today or maybe even back on the job.

Lucy slipped on one black leather pump and sat holding the

other. Maybe the biker wasn't a kid at all. Come to think of it, dirt biking was an expensive sport when you added up the cost of all the equipment, and there weren't too many kids in Tinker's Cove who had that sort of money.

But if he were a grown man, she wondered, what was he doing harrassing her like that? It was the kind of stunt a kid would find funny, but it wasn't the sort of thing an adult would even think of doing.

She put the shoe down and slipped it on. Rocking back on her heels, she lifted her toes, then slowly lowered them and put her hands on her knees. Why had that biker been so interested in her and why had he followed her home? Had it been an intentional move to find out where she lived?

Even more disquieting was the thought that Bear Sykes might have summoned the biker, using his cell phone. What possible reason would he have for doing that? she wondered as she stood up and fastened her faux pearls around her neck.

Come to think of it, Sykes had seemed awfully interested in what she knew about the murder. That didn't mean he was involved in any way, she told herself. As the tribe's leader he would naturally want to know how the investigation was proceeding.

After one last check in the mirror to make sure her slip wasn't showing, she decided she was ready. She was probably being paranoid, but she wasn't about to risk another encounter. Today, she'd stick to the highway.

It was funny, she thought as she carefully closed the door behind so Kudo couldn't get out. She hadn't felt a bit nervous this morning when she was walking with Kudo; she had felt sure that the dog would protect her. But even in a car she didn't want to risk the same deserted roads by herself.

As she started the car, she thought it might be a good idea to pay attention at the funeral and see who was there and who wasn't and to keep an eye out for strange behavior.

Arriving at the plain little country church with only minutes to spare before the service was scheduled to start, Lucy felt a surge of sympathy for Ellie. Judging from the number of cars and the crowd of people, not to mention the large white trucks topped with satellite dishes bearing the logos of the Portland TV station and Northeast Cable News parked along the road opposite the church, it was going to be a three-ring circus. It was bad enough to lose someone you loved, but to have your private grief turned into a public spectacle made it all that much worse.

Lucy had to park at least a quarter of a mile farther down the road and had to hike back to the church in her uncomfortable high heels. She arrived, out of breath, just as the bell was tolling. As she drew closer she realized she hadn't needed to worry about getting a seat—this crowd wasn't interested in attending the service. The people gathered on the church lawn were demonstrators, content to stand outside in view of the TV cameras. A few were holding placards with a photograph of Nolan demanding *Justice for our Brother*.

Lucy looked for a familiar face, but the only person she recognized was Bear Sykes. Dressed in a denim shirt with a beaded chestpiece worn over it, he was being interviewed by a TV reporter. As she mounted the steps, she heard him deliver a ringing declaration and stopped to listen.

"If Curt Nolan were white, you can be sure the police would not be dragging their feet in investigating his murder. We demand equal treatment—justice in life and in death!"

He raised a fist and the crowd of protesters erupted in cheers and applause. Placards were held aloft and someone began beating a drum.

The crowd began chanting, "Justice! We want justice!"

Watching the spectacle unfold before her, Lucy found herself reaching for her reporter's notebook and camera. She didn't have them, of course. She'd left her big everyday bag at home and had brought her small, dressy purse. Maybe Ted was here, she thought, hopefully scanning the crowd of reporters gathered outside the churchyard for his face.

There was no sign of him. Lucy wondered what to do. She had come to attend the funeral service, but maybe she should stay outside and cover the demonstration. A few police cars had arrived without sirens, but the barking of their radios could be heard and their roof lights were flashing. A certain tension seemed to be building among the demonstrators and their chanting was getting louder. Lucy remained on the steps, hesitating.

A few organ chords made up her mind and she pulled open the heavy door. Inside, the church was quiet and dim and smelled like old wood and chrysanthemums. She waved away the usher, declining to sit and instead remained standing in the rear of the church. From that vantage point she could see the whole church and the fifty or so people who had come to the service.

In the front row she spotted Ellie and two attractive young women she took to be Ellie's daughters sitting on her left. On Ellie's right, Lucy was surprised to see a man. She couldn't tell who he was from his back, but he was very solicitious of Ellie, who was leaning against his shoulder.

When the hymn began and everyone stood, the man turned around as if to check and see how many people had come. Lucy was astonished to recognize Jonathan Franke.

As the hymn droned on, Lucy struggled to make sense of this new development. Perhaps he was simply an old friend who had put aside his dislike of the deceased to offer support to Ellie. Or perhaps, thought Lucy, he was taking advantage of the death of a hated rival to advance his own case as a suitor. The final amen sounded and Lucy wrestled with a vague sense of guilt. Here she was in church and all she could think of was sex and murder.

"Let us pray," began the minister, a stocky, white-haired man with a ruddy complexion, and Lucy took the opportunity to check out her fellow mourners.

Just a few rows behind Ellie she saw Chuck Canaday and Andy Brown, along with Joe Marzetti. *Ah,* she thought rather cynically, *the business community.* Never ones to alienate customers, they showed up at almost every funeral.

On the other side of the narrow aisle she spotted a few more members of the board of selectmen: Sandy Dunlap and Bud Collier. There was no sign of Pete Crowley or Howard White; even this prime opportunity to win some votes had not been attractive enough to overcome their dislike of Nolan. She didn't see Fred Rumford either, even though he could have used the funeral as an occasion to bridge the widening gap between the museum and the tribe. Perhaps knowing he was a suspect, he hadn't wanted to draw attention to himself.

Listening with half an ear to the minister, Lucy followed her own thoughts. Maybe the absentees had been afraid of appearing hypocritical, since they had all had their differences with Nolan. Personally, Lucy thought they were mistaken. By attending the funeral they could have shown respect for Nolan and for the Metinnicut people.

A sudden increase in the noise level from the crowd outside drew Lucy's attention and she decided she'd better see what was going on. She tiptoed to the door and, opening it as little as possible, slipped through. Once outside on the stoop she paused, horrified.

Dozens of police officers in full riot gear were advancing on the demonstrators with raised shields and batons. At first the demonstrators stood fast, huddling together in passive resistance behind their leader, Bear Sykes. Then a sound like a shot was heard.

Lucy was never convinced it actually was a gunshot; she thought it was probably a backfire from a passing car. Whatever it was, it had the effect of terrifying the crowd of demonstrators, who suddenly broke ranks and began running for safety, pursued by police officers through the churchyard and adjacent cemetery. Sykes remained in place, vainly calling for order, until he was collared himself and led to a cruiser.

Lucy watched in dismay as the officers wrestled people to the ground and handcuffed them. She winced at the thwack the batons made when they connected with human flesh. She heard the screams of fear and pain. Nevertheless, she was able to remain a detached observer until she saw a young child in a familiar threadbare lavender jacket. Tiffani had apparently become lost and separated from her family and was wandering about, dazed, with tears streaming down her face.

Jumping down the stairs Lucy ran to the little girl and scooped her up in her arms.

"Hold it right there," said a gruff voice.

Lucy froze, hugging Tiffani to her chest and patting her back. Next thing she knew she was seized roughly by the shoulders, the screaming Tiffani was torn from her arms and her wrists were restrained.

"I'm not—" she began in protest, attempting to make eye contact with her captor.

All she saw was her own face, very small, reflected in his aviator sunglasses.

"Tell it to the judge," he said as he thrust her inside the crowded paddy wagon.

CHAPTER 17

Judge Joyce Ryerson wasn't interested in what Lucy had to say. She tapped her long polished nails on the bench impatiently.

"How do you plead?"

"There's been a misunderstanding."

Receiving a warning glance from the judge, Lucy decided this was not the time to argue. "Not guilty."

"Thank you," said the judge, with exaggerated politeness. "You're due back in court on December fifteenth."

"That's so close to Christmas," protested Lucy.

The judge ignored her and studied a sheet of paper.

"I see no reason not to release you on your own recognizance. See the bailiff."

She banged down her gavel and Lucy got in line behind the other accused lawbreakers at the bailiff's desk. When it was her turn she waited while he scribbled on an official-looking form.

"That'll be fifty dollars," he finally said without even raising his head.

"Fifty dollars?" Lucy knew she didn't have that much money in her wallet. She guessed she had something in the neighborhood of five dollars. "Can I write a check?"

He raised his head and lifted an eyebrow.

"Do you take Visa?"

He shook his head.

"I understand I get a phone call?"

He nodded and she was led back to the holding cell.

When she finally got her turn at the phone, Lucy didn't know whom to call. Bill was on the job and nobody was home. She could leave a message on the answering machine, but the odds of one of the kids actually listening to the message and taking action weren't good. She could call the paper, but suspected Ted was most likely out on assignment. Phyllis usually only worked mornings, which meant she'd have to leave a message and trust he'd check the machine before quitting for the day. Besides, it was getting late and the banks would be closing soon. She knew he refused to carry an ATM card and the chances he would have fifty dollars in cash were slim.

Her best bet, she finally decided, was to call Bob Goodman, Rachel's husband. He was a lawyer, after all. He would know what to do.

"The law office of Robert Goodman. May I help you?"

Martha Bennett's voice was music to Lucy's ears. "Martha, this is Lucy Stone. Could I speak to Bob?"

"Lucy, I'm afraid he's not in right now. Can I take a message?"

Lucy didn't want to tell this very proper, silver-haired lady that she needed bail, but she didn't really have a choice.

"I'm in a bit of a jam and need Bob to bail me out."

Martha Bennett didn't seem at all surprised. Lucy supposed she'd gotten calls like this before.

"Don't worry, Lucy. I'll page Bob immediately. How much do they want?"

"Fifty dollars."

"He's on his way."

This time, as Lucy was led back to the holding cell once again, she felt encouraged. Bob was on the way; Bob would rescue her.

She sat down on the steel bench, squeezing in between a rather heavy woman in flowing handwoven garments, who was obviously one of the protesters, and a tiny, shrunken woman, who was shaking uncontrollably.

"DTs," said the heavy woman with a knowing nod. "Better give her plenty of room."

She had no sooner spoken than the tiny woman doubled over and vomited on the floor. Some of the other women in the crowded cell made sounds of disgust; the gray-haired woman called for the guard.

Nobody came to clean up the mess. There was no place to go; no other seat was available in the crowded cell. Lucy concentrated on a brown water stain on the opposite wall. She tried to ignore the smell; she tried not to notice the woman's trembling. Instead, she tried to frame the story she would write for the *Pennysaver* about the morning's events.

The thing that most struck her, she decided, was the contrast between the quiet mourners inside the church and the pandemonium outside. To her, it seemed the protesters and the police were equally guilty of disturbing the funeral service.

Her thoughts turned to Ellie and the figure beside her: Jonathan Franke. There had been something in the way he'd angled his body toward Ellie, something in the way his hand lingered on her back, that made Lucy doubtful he was acting simply as a friend. She would have bet her bail money that Jonathan Franke was hoping to take Curt Nolan's place as Ellie's boyfriend.

If that was true, she thought, it gave Franke a real motive for killing Nolan. She remembered the pie sale, where the two had argued. Now that she thought about it, the two men had exhibited more animosity than could be accounted for by their differing views about zoning regulations. In fact, she remembered, Franke had been so angry he had stalked off without finishing his pie—a definite first for the pie sale.

The more she thought about it, the more convinced she became that Franke was a prime suspect for Nolan's murder. It was obvious the murder hadn't been premeditated; the murderer had acted on impulse. And everybody knew Franke had trouble controlling his temper. Years ago, when the Association for the Preservation of Tinker's Cove had been in its early stages, he'd been involved in a few scuffles and had even been charged with assaulting a contractor in an effort to halt a construction project in a watershed area.

Lately, however, he'd made a real effort to be more reasonable and professional in his role as the association's executive director. He'd given up the wild, curly hair that had been his trademark and had taken to wearing casual business clothes instead of the jeans and plaid flannel shirts he'd once favored. Now he was usually seen in khaki pants and tweed jackets—the sort of jackets that had leather patches on the elbows and woven leather buttons.

The thought brought Lucy up sharply: woven leather buttons, just like the one that was found in Curt Nolan's hand.

Feeling pressure on her upper arm, Lucy glanced at the alcoholic woman next to her. She wasn't a pretty sight and Lucy struggled not to gag. The woman had passed out and was leaning against Lucy. A stream of saliva was dribbling down her chin and she reeked of booze and vomit.

"Lucy Stone," called the officer.

"Here," yelled Lucy, gently easing herself away from the unconscious woman and lowering her to the bench before presenting herself to the guard.

She watched impatiently as he fumbled with the keys. Enough, already. She'd been here for an eternity and couldn't wait to get out.

"What took you so long?" she demanded as Bob led her to his car. "Do you know what it's like in there? People were throwing up! It was disgusting! I don't know how they get away with treating people like that, keeping them in such appalling conditions! It's outrageous!"

"I knew you'd be glad to see me," said Bob, unlocking the car door for her.

"I must've been in there for hours," said Lucy, fuming as she fastened her seat belt.

"Well, you're out now—until December fifteenth. Want to tell me how you got in this mess so I can convince Judge Joyce not to lock you up and throw away the key?"

"She could do that?" Lucy was horrified.

"I'm exaggerating," admitted Bob. "But you've got to face the fact that this isn't over. You've been charged with assaulting a police officer, disorderly conduct, unlawful assembly, and kidnapping."

"That's absurd! I was there for the funeral. I wasn't involved in the protest at all. Then I saw one of the kids from the day care center wandering around and tried to get her to safety. I wasn't kidnapping her." Lucy stared out the window at the bare gray trees they were passing. "They grabbed her out of my arms. What's going to happen to her?"

"Probably social services is taking care of her until her parents can claim her. Were they arrested, too?"

"I don't know. All I know is her name is Tiffani. I don't even know her last name." She bit her lip. "I hope she's okay."

"She's in good hands."

"I wish I could be sure of that."

"All right," said Bob. "I'll check on her and let you know."

"Thanks," said Lucy.

"About time," said Bob. "Most of my clients are a lot more appreciative. This will definitely be reflected in your bill."

"I'll tell Rachel," said Lucy with a little smile.

"Touché," said Bob. "This will be pro bono."

"Thank you. That's really nice of you."

"Don't mention it," said Bob, turning into her driveway. "I'm just being realistic. If you couldn't come up with bail, what are the chances you could pay me?"

"My funds were temporarily unavailable," protested Lucy.

"Never mind," said Bob. "Just do me a favor and stay out of trouble between now and December fifteenth. Promise?"

"I promise," said Lucy.

CHAPTER 18

"Mom, you're on TV."

Lucy tossed the sponge she'd been using to wipe off the kitchen table into the sink and hurried into the family room. There she watched herself being unceremoniously tossed into the paddy wagon.

"Is my butt really that big?" she asked Bill.

He didn't answer but walked right past her to answer the phone that was ringing in the kitchen.

She stood there in the doorway, watching the rest of the report. Bear Sykes got a lot of play; he was shown in action leading the protest and was also interviewed afterward, when he had been released from jail.

"Why do you want to get mixed up with a guy like that?" said Bill, returning to his recliner and picking up the remote.

"I'm not mixed up with anything," protested Lucy. "I explained to you. All I did was go to the funeral. I didn't even know there was going to be a protest. I got arrested because I saw one of the day care kids had gotten lost and tried to get her out of the scuffle."

"Don't give me that," said Bill. "The cops obviously don't believe that story and I don't either. You told me you weren't going to get involved in this murder, and here you are, charged with ten counts of sticking your nose where it doesn't belong."

Lucy shifted uneasily and looked over at the couch, where Zoe and Sara had gotten very still and quiet. Bill, however, was too angry to notice and continued his tirade.

"You had no business going to that funeral. It isn't as if there isn't plenty for you to do around here. The house could do with a good cleaning and Zoe got stranded at her scout meeting without a ride home. Anybody with two working brain cells could have figured out there'd be some kind of demonstration at that funeral but you never gave it a second thought and went off to get yourself arrested and forgot all about your responsibilities."

"That's not fair," Lucy began, ready to argue in her own defense but Bill was having none of it.

"And if all this wasn't bad enough," he said, cutting her off, "you know who just called? The Barths. They don't want to move here anymore. They just want me to finish up the house as quick and cheaply as I can so they can sell it—and I don't blame them either. Who would want to live in a place with murders and a gambling casino and demonstrations? Nobody in their right mind—that's for sure!" He glared at Lucy as if it were somehow all her fault.

"Bill," she began, then realized she might as well talk to a wall. He had retreated behind the newspaper and she knew from past experience there was no point trying to talk to him when he was in this kind of mood.

Besides, she thought guiltily, returning to the kitchen, he did have a point. She had had no business promising Miss Tilley she would try to find out who murdered Curt Nolan and she should never have attempted to conduct her own investigation.

She could have saved herself a lot of trouble if she'd stayed home vacuuming or dusting instead of going to the funeral.

Angry and depressed, she yanked open the freezer and pulled out the emergency chocolate bar she kept behind the ice cube trays. She smacked it on the table, smiling with grim satisfaction as she felt it shatter into small pieces. Then she sat down and unwrapped it, popping a piece of chocolate into her mouth.

Sitting there with the sweet, delicious chocolate melting on her tongue, safe in the house she didn't seem to appreciate and surrounded by the family she had neglected, Lucy felt tears stinging her eyes.

She pictured once again Tiffani's frightened, tearstained face as she wandered in the midst of the disordered crowd, looking for a familiar face among the struggling police and protesters outside the church. She remembered the fear and outrage she'd felt when the police had grabbed her and how frustrated she'd been to find herself completely powerless, being carted off to jail. Worst of all was the way everybody had refused to listen to her explanation. To the cops and the judge, she was just another docket number, another case for the system.

And what a system. She hadn't had any idea how people were treated when they were arrested. All jumbled together in that appalling paddy wagon and then confined in that filthy cell. As soon as she'd gotten home she'd taken a shower and changed her clothes, but the stench of the jail seemed to linger stubbornly about her. She could still smell the disgusting reek of vomit, booze, and body odor.

She reached for a tissue and gave her nose a good blow, then took another and wiped her eyes. If she was this upset, she thought, popping another piece of chocolate in her mouth, what

must poor little Tiffani be going through? Was she spending the
night with strangers in some foster home? Had some unfamiliar
woman bathed her and dressed her in borrowed pajamas, then
tucked her into a bed that wasn't her own? Was she terrified that
she'd never see her family again?

Lucy sniffled again and Kudo raised his head from the dog
bed, where he had been snoozing. He looked at her curiously.
He got up slowly and stretched, then clicked across the floor to
her and rested his head on her lap.

At least someone understands, thought Lucy, stroking the thick
fur on the dog's neck. She hoped Tiffani had found some similar
comfort, maybe a teddy bear, to get her through the night.

Bob had promised to check on the little girl for her, but
Lucy wasn't entirely confident he'd remember. Tomorrow she'd
check with Sue at the day care center and make sure Tiffani was
back where she belonged. Then, she promised herself, she would
drop the whole thing.

But what about Jonathan Franke? she asked herself as she
sucked the chocolate off a piece of almond. She couldn't just
forget about him, especially since he seemed to have such a strong
motive for killing Nolan. No, she thought, picking up another
piece of chocolate, she had to alert the police to her suspicions.
Once she'd done that, then she could retire from the investigation
and turn her attention where it belonged: to her home and family.

CHAPTER 19

When Lucy stopped at the day care center the next morning her heart almost stopped when she didn't see Tiffani playing with the other children.

"You look like you've seen a ghost," said Sue.

"It's what I'm not seeing," said Lucy, frantic with worry. "Where's Tiffani?"

"Her mom called. She's keeping her home today." Sue paused, giving her an odd look. "What's it to you?"

"She's home and everything's okay?"

"Yeah. Why?"

"It's a long story," said Lucy.

"I'm not going anywhere," said Sue, casting an eye at the roomful of children. "I've got plenty of time."

"Well," began Lucy, taking a child-size seat next to Sue's desk. "I saw her at the funeral yesterday. She'd gotten separated from her mother or whomever she was with and was wandering around lost in the crowd. I tried to help her, but ended up getting arrested myself."

"No!"

"Yes. It was horrible. Jail isn't all it's cracked up to be."

"I can imagine," said Sue, expertly surveying the play area, where the little girls were chattering in the dress-up corner and the boys were divided between the blocks and the sand table. "How come you went to the funeral? I didn't know you knew Curt Nolan."

"I didn't. I went to support Ellie Martin. I got to know her when I interviewed her for the story I wrote about the dolls. She and Curt were in a relationship, so this has all been pretty tough on her. I've been trying to help—I even took the dog."

Sue stared at her. "You've got a dog?"

"Curt Nolan's dog."

"Kadjo?" exclaimed Sue in disbelief. "The one that killed the chickens?"

"We call him Kudo now. He's not a bad dog at all really. I've gotten kind of attached to him."

Sue gave her a knowing look. "Ah, an empty-nest puppy."

Lucy shook her head. "Don't be silly. He just needed a home."

"Right," said Sue, furrowing her brow. "Harry, please don't throw the sand."

"I never heard anything so silly," continued Lucy. "It would be crazy to try to replace Toby with a dog."

"If you say so," said Sue. "Harry, this is a warning. If you do that again you'll have to go to time-out."

Harry threw down his shovel and went over to the shelves, where he took down a big dump truck and started pushing it around on the floor.

"You know," said Lucy, "I never did get Tiffani's last name. What is it?"

"Sykes." Sue was on her feet, keeping an eye on Harry while she poured glasses of juice.

"Sykes! Is she related to Bear Sykes?"

"You bet," said Sue, carrying the tray of juice cups over to a low table and setting it down. "She's his granddaughter."

Lucy brought over the graham crackers and unwrapped them. "I guess that explains what she was doing at the demonstration."

Sue nodded, passing out the crackers to the children. "You won't believe this," she said, whispering. "He wanted me to bring all the day care kids, but I told him it wasn't appropriate."

"He wanted you to bring the kids to the demonstration?" Lucy was appalled. "Where'd he get such an idea?"

Sue took a bite of cracker. "About half the kids here are Metinnicut, you know. He's been after me for quite a while to add Metinnicut songs and stories to the curriculum."

Sue lowered her head, studying her carefully manicured nails. Her face was hidden by a fall of glossy black hair, which Lucy happened to know was testament to her colorist's skill. "I know I should. I mean, I really try to be multicultural. We sing songs from all over the world, so why not Indian songs? I'm really not opposed to it," she said, lifting her head, "but I don't quite see what business he has coming into my day care center with a couple of young toughs and telling me what to do. I told him to get lost."

Sue's attention shifted to the snack table. "Don't grab, Justin. There's plenty for everyone."

She turned back to Lucy. "And then he told me I'd better start looking for a new job because when the tribe makes money from the casino they're going to open their own day care center and I'll be out of work."

Lucy could hardly believe her ears. "That's ridiculous," she said, sputtering.

"No it's not. Like I said before, about half the kids are Metinnicut. If they go somewhere else, there won't be enough children left to justify funding the center. In fact, I wouldn't feel right asking the voters for the money for so few children."

"You could fight back," said Lucy. "I'll put it in the paper, how he's using strong-arm tactics."

"It's not such a big deal really," said Sue. "I don't have to do this. I'm not sure I want to anymore. It filled a need when Sidra went away to college. I admit it. It was a way to fill my empty nest." She smiled down at the children, who were seated around the snack table. "But I've worked that out. I'm ready for something new."

"I had no idea," said Lucy, giving her friend a hug. "I didn't realize you were that upset when Sidra went away."

"It was terrible—I almost got a dog," said Sue, struggling to keep a straight face.

"Ouch!" exclaimed Lucy. "I'm not taking any more of this abuse. If I want abuse, I can go to work. At least Ted pays for the privilege."

But when Lucy got to the *Pennysaver* office, there was no sign of Ted.

"He's interviewing Bear Sykes," said Phyllis, "for a story about the demonstration yesterday."

"Oh," said Lucy, digesting this information while she hung up her coat. All of a sudden it seemed as if Bear was popping up everywhere. He was the man of the hour, and as yesterday's protest seemed to indicate, the tribe was falling in step behind him.

"Lucy," said Phyllis, breaking into her thoughts, "since you're here, would you mind keeping an eye on things? I've got to go to the post office."

"No problem."

Lucy sat down at Phyllis's desk, where she could answer the phone and keep an eye on the door. Since she was alone, it seemed a good time to call Lieutenant Horowitz and tie up that last loose thread. Then she could retire from the investigation in good conscience.

Lucy reached for the receiver, then hesitated. This wasn't going to be pleasant, she told herself, recalling previous encounters with the lieutenant, but it had to be done. Bracing herself, she dialed the number of the state police barracks in Livermore.

"Ah, Mrs. Stone," he said when her call finally got through to him. "I was wondering why I hadn't heard from you."

"I didn't know you cared," said Lucy, picturing his long rabbit face and his tired gray eyes.

"I care very much," said the lieutenant, adding a long sigh. "It's the new buzzword in the department: community policing. We're supposed to get the public involved, maintain good relations with the media. So what can I do for you?"

"Well, since you asked, I was wondering if Jonathan Franke is a suspect in the Curt Nolan investigation?"

There was a long pause. "Well, in an investigation like this, the umbrella of suspicion covers a lot of people. Why are you asking about Franke in particular?"

"I happened to see him at the funeral yesterday and he was being very attentive to Ellie Martin, who used to be Nolan's girlfriend."

"Hmm. Jealousy. Could be a motive."

Encouraged, Lucy continued. "Plus, he happens to wear a lot of tweed jackets with the kind of button that was found in Nolan's hand."

"Who told you about the button?"

From the lieutenant's icy tone, Lucy guessed he was no longer interested in cultivating good media relations. "I can't tell you that," said Lucy. "My sources are confidential."

"I could take you into court for witholding evidence," said Horowitz. "I don't think Judge Ryerson would look very kindly on you, especially considering the list of charges pending against you."

"You know perfectly well that's all a big misunderstanding. Now, to get back to Jonathan Franke, I think you have to consider him a suspect. First there's the motive: jealousy. Then there's the question of whether he'd be capable of committing murder. I can tell you he has a very hot temper and I've seen him almost come to blows with Nolan."

"Mrs. Stone, just hold on a minute. Curt Nolan almost came to blows, hell he did come to blows—with lots of people."

"What about the button?"

"Every man in America has an article of clothing with that kind of button: a jacket, a sweater, a raincoat. Trust me on this."

"It isn't who's got buttons like that—it's who's missing a button," said Lucy, feeling rather pleased with her cleverness. "Have you checked his clothes?"

"Mrs. Stone, as a professional journalist—and I use the term loosely—you know perfectly well that I can't reveal the details of an investigation. But off the record, I will tell you that Jonathan Franke has been eliminated as a suspect in the murder of Curt Nolan."

"Eliminated? Why?"

"Again, off the record, he was having dinner with his mother at the time. Thanksgiving dinner."

"You believe that?" Lucy was incredulous. "You're taking the word of his mother?"

"Actually, no. He had proof. Turkey leftovers, wrapped in foil."

"You're teasing me. You know you are."

Horowitz chuckled. Lucy could hardly believe her ears. "You know, I understand your interest in the case. It's a big story. And I appreciate the coverage we've gotten from the *Pennysaver* in the past. The *Pennysaver*'s always been supportive and cooperative. But I've got to tell you that an investigation like this is best left to the professionals. We're not talking about someone who steals Girl Scout cookies here—this is a real bad guy and he won't hesitate to kill again. Do you understand me?"

"Yes," said Lucy, in a small voice.

"Good. Now I want to tell you about the department's unclaimed property auction next month. Got a pencil?"

"Sure," said Lucy.

She'd just finished jotting down the details when the bell on the door jangled and Ted came in. His jaw was set and he stomped across the office to his desk, tossing his notebook down. Then he pulled off his jacket and threw it across the room, missing the coat rack.

"What's the matter?" asked Lucy, ready to duck for cover.

"Bear Sykes—that's what's the matter."

"The interview didn't go well?"

Ted snorted.

"It wasn't an interview, it was a lecture. Sykes told me the kind of coverage he wants in the future, and he pretty much let me know that the *Pennysaver*'s continuing survival depends on it. And he had a bunch of young fellows from the tribe to back him up, too. Guys with nothing better to do than look tough."

"Wow. I guess power's really gone to his head. Sue said he's been throwing his weight around at the day care center, too." She paused, remembering the selectmen's meeting when Sykes had presented the Metinnicuts' petition. Ellie had called him an errand boy when he'd run out to fetch the architect's model of the casino. "It looks like he's really consolidated his position as tribal leader," she said. "You should've seen him at that demonstration yesterday. And the cops just played into his hands— those arrests will unify the tribe even more."

"I dunno," said Ted, perching restlessly on the edge of his chair. "Somehow I have a feeling that Curt Nolan must be turning over in his grave. He took pride in his Indian heritage. I don't think he'd like what's going on. Sykes and his boys looked more like the Mafia than anything else."

Lucy's and Ted's eyes met; they were both thinking the same thought. Before either could express it, however, the door opened with a jangle. They both looked up. Lucy recognized Jack O'Hara.

"Hi," she said, stepping behind the counter. "Can I help you?"

"Yes," he said. "I'd like to speak to the editor. You can say Jack O'Hara from Mulligan Construction is here."

"I know who you are," said Lucy with a big smile. "I covered the meeting."

"I'm sorry. I should have recognized you." He grinned apologetically. "I'm afraid I have a terrible memory for faces."

Yeah, right, thought Lucy. She was pretty sure he'd gone into that meeting knowing exactly who would be covering it; Chuck Canaday would have primed him.

"We're pretty informal here," she said, tilting her head at Ted. "That's Ted Stillings. He's the editor and publisher."

O'Hara pushed open the gate next to the counter and walked over to Ted's desk.

"Nice to meet you, Ted. Like I said, I'm Jack O'Hara from Mulligan Construction." He stuck out his hand and Ted shook it. "Mind if I sit down?"

"Not at all. What can I do for you?"

O'Hara spread his feet apart and leaned forward, resting his arms on his thighs and shifting his gloves from hand to hand. Lucy had the feeling she'd become invisible; O'Hara was talking to Ted man to man.

"As you probably know, Mulligan Construction has been selected by the Metinnicut Nation to build their casino. It's a big project, and we know it's bound to be controversial. This is a small town, and people in small towns don't usually like change very much. They like things to stay the way they are and I guess that's understandable."

Ted glanced at his watch, signaling it was time to skip the preamble and get down to business.

O'Hara cleared his throat and continued. "I understand just how influential a local newspaper like the *Pennysaver* can be in a situation like this, and I want to be sure we're all on the same page here. If you have any questions, anything at all you'd like to ask me about the project, I'd be more than happy to answer."

"Well, that's real nice of you," said Ted, reciting his stock answer. "I'll keep it in mind and give you a call if I have any questions."

O'Hara didn't take the hint. "A project like the casino can mean a lot to a town like this. It will give the local economy a big boost, believe me. And more business means more advertising, right?"

"Hadn't really thought about it," said Ted. Lucy could tell he was getting a bit hot under his collar.

"We happen to be fairly big advertisers ourselves at Mulligan," continued O'Hara. "I'm not sure of the total budget, but I can assure you it's substantial. And we're very selective. We place ads where they'll get the most results. And of course, we tend to favor publications that support our general goals. We play ball with people who are on the team, if you know what I mean."

Lucy watched, waiting for Ted's reaction. This was the second time someone had tried to pressure him in one day and she knew he must be pretty fed up.

"We'll be happy to run your ads," Ted said, spitting the words out. "As for supporting your goals or playing ball, I don't work that way. The paper's a public forum and we try to give equal coverage to all sides."

O'Hara looked down at his shoes, then turned his gaze on Ted. "I understand your reluctance," he said, practically winking at Ted. "I can assure you we would definitely make it worth your while to write a positive editorial. I understand that your opinion is valuable—more valuable than you might think."

Ted sat there, his eyes bulging and his mouth gaping like a goldfish. "Are you saying you would pay me to write an editorial in favor of the casino?"

"Oh, no. You misunderstand me," O'Hara said smoothly. "We would work something out. I hear you have a son in college—

perhaps he could win a Mulligan scholarship? How would that be?"

"Get out!" roared Ted, rising to his feet and pointing to the door. "This discussion is over! Get out of my office!"

O'Hara maintained his casual manner as he stood up and crossed the floor to the gate. He pushed it open, then paused.

"You're making a mistake," he said, slapping his gloves against his hand. "We can make things pleasant, or we can make them very unpleasant. It's up to you."

"Are you threatening me?" Ted took a few steps toward O'Hara.

"I think I've made myself clear," O'Hara replied, opening the door.

A moment later he was gone, with nothing to remind them of his visit except the jangling bell.

CHAPTER 20

"That was weird," said Lucy after O'Hara had gone. Ted didn't answer. He grunted and started flipping through the stack of papers on his desk. Then he shoved them aside, pushed his chair back and stood up.

"I'm going out for some fresh air," he said, dropping the stack of papers in front of her. "Would you mind typing in these listings for me?"

Lucy figured Ted had had enough for one day and needed to get away from the office for awhile.

"No problem," she said.

Once he'd gone, however, she realized it would take hours to go through the stack of press releases annoucing club meetings and used-book sales and holiday bazaars. She was struggling to decipher a particularly confusing notice about an amateur production of *Amahl and the Night Visitors* when the phone rang. It was Miss Tilley.

"I wondered if you'd like to join Rachel and me for lunch," the old woman purred.

Rachel worked as a part-time caregiver for the old woman, driving and cooking for her.

"I'd love to, but I can't. I've got too much work to do."

"That's too bad. Rachel and I were hoping you could give us an update on your investigation."

Lucy squirmed in her seat, remembering her conversation with Lieutenant Horowitz.

"I don't have much to tell you," she said. "In fact, I've been so busy—"

"You can't fool me, Lucy Stone," snapped the old woman. "I know you must have some idea by now of who killed Curt."

"Oh, I have some ideas," said Lucy. "But I think I'd better keep them to myself for the time being."

"I wouldn't tell a soul," coaxed Miss Tilley.

Lucy glanced around the empty office. She was dying to discuss her thoughts with someone, and Miss Tilley was a gold mine of local knowledge.

"My lips will remain sealed," continued Miss Tilley.

"I know you'll tell Rachel," said Lucy.

"Well, Rachel won't tell anyone either. She's married to a lawyer and she's used to keeping secrets. She's nodding in agreement as we speak, and making a sign of zipping her lips."

Lucy chuckled. "This is just an idea, now. I don't have any real evidence. But it does seem that one person has benefitted from Nolan's death more than anyone else. It's the *cui bono* thing."

"Bear Sykes!" exclaimed Miss Tilley, confirming Lucy's suspicions. "I just knew it!" Then she added, "Rachel thinks so, too."

"This is just a hunch."

"I'm sure you're right. It's obvious when you think about it. He's always had a power complex, and Curt Nolan was the one person who stood in his way as tribal leader."

"He's definitely in charge now," said Lucy. "He's really been throwing his weight around, you know."

"I'm not at all surprised. Why, I remember when he was a little boy. He wasn't much of a reader, you know, but he was looking for a topic for a research paper. It had to be about a famous person who changed history. I suggested Eisenhower—the supreme allied commander and such a dear man, too—but Bear wasn't interested. He said he'd rather write about John Wayne and wanted books about him."

"John Wayne? Isn't that an odd choice, considering Bear is a Native American?"

"Now that you mention it, I guess it is. Of course, I had to tell him that John Wayne was only an actor, that he hadn't really changed history." She paused. "I finally suggested Napoleon and Bear really got interested. For a while there he was constantly asking for books about Napoleon. Such a horrid little man, I've always thought, but Bear absolutely adored him."

"I wonder why," said Lucy.

Miss Tilley spoke slowly. "I suspect it was the fact that Napoleon was ultimately defeated but was still considered a great general."

"Like Geronimo and Sitting Bull?" Lucy said.

"I think so."

"Well, he's certainly acting like Napoleon now. He's turning the tribe into something like the Mafia."

"I can't say I'm surprised," said Miss Tilley. "Do you think the police suspect him?"

"I don't know," admitted Lucy.

"Maybe you could help them. Isn't there some way you could get evidence?"

"I can't think how."

"Search his house or something."

"You want me to break and enter?" Lucy was astonished. "That's illegal. What if I got caught?"

Miss Tilley clucked her tongue. "What's happened to you, Lucy Stone? You used to much bolder, you know."

"Let's say I'm older and wiser, unlike some people I know."

Miss Tilley wasn't about to give up. "If you applied yourself, I'm sure you could trick him into confessing."

"And how would I do that without risking my neck? You know, I have a family and they depend on me."

Miss Tilley didn't answer immediately, but Lucy could have sworn she heard her wheels turning through the telephone line.

"Use the telephone! Like that Linda Tripp person. Record him and take the tape to the police."

"That's illegal—they've filed charges against her, you know."

Miss Tilley sighed. "It was just an idea. You're probably not clever enough to trick him into confessing anyway."

"Thanks for the vote of confidence," said Lucy.

"I have to go. Rachel says lunch is ready—it's shrimp wiggle today," said Miss Tilley, naming a favorite dish of Lucy's.

"You have absolutely no mercy," said Lucy.

She hung up and picked up the next press release. It was for a square dance, and although it gave more information than she needed about callers and cuers, it didn't state the time of the dance. Fortunately, there was a phone number so Lucy called it.

While she listened to the rings, Lucy noticed there was a record button on her phone. She pushed it just as the other party answered.

She got the information she needed, hung up, and dialed

the code for the message system. Sure enough, she'd recorded the entire conversation. That was interesting, she thought, wondering if she dared call Bear Sykes, when the phone rang. She recognized Jack O'Hara's voice.

"I'm sorry," she said, "but Ted's not here. You can leave a message if you want."

"Actually, it's you I want to talk to," he said.

Lucy rolled her eyes; didn't this guy ever give up?

"You couldn't convince Ted, so now you're going to try me? You're wasting your time. I'm just the hired help. I have no influence whatever."

O'Hara laughed and Lucy found herself warming to the man despite herself.

"You can't blame me, can you? After all, this is a project I believe in. Not just because it will make a profit for Mulligan, but because it will improve the town's economy. You've got to admit there's an awful lot of poverty in your unspoiled rural paradise. I mean, people can't afford to buy mittens for their kids?"

Lucy thought of Tiffani and her ragged jacket. "I can't argue with you there."

"Andy Brown and I would like to go over the plans with you. I think you'll see that gambling is really just a small part. There will be shops, theaters, even a museum. In fact, it's been suggested we name it after Curt Nolan as a memorial. It's a lot more than just a casino. It's going to employ a lot of people— and they'll be able to make a lot more money than they're getting from jewelry piecework—that's for sure. This could mean opportunity for a lot of people."

Lucy's first impulse was to refuse, but she hesitated. The man had a point. She hadn't really considered the benefits the casino could bring; she'd made up her mind against it based on her own prejudices. Thanks to her Protestant upbringing, she had an unshakable conviction that gambling was sinful and the only proper place for money was in a savings bank.

"Okay," she finally said. "When and where?"

"There's no time like the present."

"No can do," said Lucy. "I have some work I have to finish up before deadline."

"Say in a couple of hours? At Andy Brown's place?"

Lucy checked the clock. It was almost one and she had to be at the selectmen's weekly meeting at four.

"How about three o'clock? But I won't be able to stay long."

"Great. See you then. I'll have Andy warm up some of his famous cider."

"Sounds good," said Lucy, suddenly hungry as she hung up the phone. She hadn't eaten lunch and she was ravenous. She knew she ought to eat something, but she still had pages and pages of listings.

Her stomach growled and she came to a decision. She'd go home and eat something and finish working on the listings there. That way she could check on the dog and she'd be closer to Andy Brown's farm. She could easily swing by there on her way to the meeting.

Satisfied with her decision, she stood up and stuffed the papers into her bag. She turned the sign in the window to read *closed* and pulled the door shut behind. As she hurried to the car she debated what to eat: leftover stew or a peanut butter and jelly sandwich?

CHAPTER 21

Lucy was sitting at the computer in the family room, working on the press releases, when the girls got home from school at a quarter of three.

"Home already? Gee, I didn't realize it was so late," said Lucy, ejecting the disk from the machine. "How was school?"

"School sucks," said Elizabeth. "I can't wait to go to college."

Lucy gave her a sharp look. "Don't swear."

"My group only got a B on our South America project because Lizzie Snider left Argentina off the map—it's not fair!" wailed Sara, who wasn't much of a team player.

"Mrs. Wilson put my picture up on the wall," said Zoe, beaming proudly.

"Great," said Lucy, bending down and giving her a peck on her forehead. "Listen, guys, I've got to go to a meeting, so I want you to hold the fort. I won't be home in time for supper so, Elizabeth, you'll have to cook the franks and beans. Sara, you can make a salad and, Zoe, you set the table. Got it?"

"Got it." Elizabeth was reaching for the phone, which had begun ringing right on schedule minutes after the girls got home.

Lucy shrugged off the guilt that invariably accompanied her

when she left the kids in charge of dinner and headed for the door. Kudo was right at her heels.

"Sorry," she told him. "I don't have time for a walk today-and believe me, you wouldn't like the selectmen's meeting."

Kudo didn't seem convinced. He wagged his tail eagerly. Lucy reconsidered. She supposed she could take him along for the ride to the farm and drop him off at the house on her way to the meeting.

"You win, just this once," she said, opening the door.

A blast of cold air hit her, and she quickly shut the door, almost bumping Kudo's nose.

"Oops. Just a minute—I've got to get my coat zipped."

She slapped her hat on her head and pulled on her gloves.

"Now we can go," she told the dog, holding the door for him.

Kudo ran ahead of her to the car and waited by the rear hatch. As soon as she lifted it, he jumped in and stood in the cargo area wagging his tail and smiling.

"We're just going for a little ride," she warned him as she started the engine. In the rearview mirror she could see him grinning at her, his big pink tongue lolling out of the side of his mouth.

What a doofus, she thought. Though not quite so much of a fool as Jack O'Hara, who actually thought he could bribe Ted to support the casino. Maybe that sort of thing happened in the world of big business, but it certainly didn't happen at the *Pennysaver*.

As she drove along, she wondered if bribes were business as usual at Mulligan Construction. From what Howard White had said at the meeting, it seemed O'Hara was pretty important in the company. Hadn't he said O'Hara would be the next CEO? She had wanted to ask St. John Barth about him on Thanksgiving, when he'd mentioned he used to work for Mulligan Construction, but the opportunity had slipped by when the conversation took a different turn.

She glanced at the dashboard clock as she pulled into the yard at the farm and saw she was late; it was already ten past three. Brown and O'Hara would have to make their case for the casino quickly because she could only stay for a half hour at most if she was going to get to the meeting in time.

She debated what to do with Kudo. She would have liked to let him out of the car but she wasn't confident she could control him, even on the leash. It was cold and windy outside, but the sun was shining and the car would stay warm, so she decided to leave him.

"Be a good boy," she told him.

Kudo stared at her for a minute, almost as if he couldn't believe he was going to be left behind. Then he curled up in a ball for an afternoon nap.

As usual, there was an assortment of vehicles in the Browns' farmyard, but none of them looked like the kind of car O'Hara would drive. The shiny black pickup truck was Andy's, his wife drove the Caravan, and the battered Corolla with radio station stickers probably belonged to one of their kids. The motorcycle, she figured, could belong either to Andy or one of his boys, maybe even a farmhand.

Lucy wasn't sure if she should go to the house or the barn. There'd been mention of mulled cider, which seemed to indicate the house, but since the barn door was propped open, she thought she might as well check there before climbing the hill to the house.

After the bright, albeit waning, sunshine outside, it took a few minutes for her eyes to adjust to the dim light inside the barn. It was surprisingly warm, and she pulled off her beret and jammed it in her pocket.

"Over here!" yelled O'Hara, and she finally made him out standing by TomTom Turkey's pen.

As she got closer and her vision cleared, she was shocked to see he was wearing a leather motorcross suit.

"I took you for the kind of guy who drives a Lexus or a BMW," she said in a teasing tone.

"You'd be right," he said, smiling. "I've got a Lexus but I ride my bike whenever I can. It's great exercise and a lot more fun than sweating on a treadmill in some stinking gym."

"A lot more dangerous, too," said Lucy, thinking of the cyclist who had harassed her on the back road and wondering if it could possibly have been O'Hara. She thought of Bear Sykes and his cell phone but dismissed the thought. It seemed unlikely that O'Hara would be at Sykes's beck and call; it must have been one of the young toughs Ted had told her about. She relaxed.

"Where's Andy?" she asked, glancing uneasily at the turkey, who was pacing back and forth in his pen. "I don't think old TomTom here cares much one way or the other about the casino."

"That's where you're wrong," said O'Hara with mock seriousness. "Before you got here, he was telling me he loves to play blackjack."

"I think craps is more his style," said Lucy, wrinkling her nose.

"You may be right," agreed O'Hara, unrolling the plans and

laying them out on a stack of hay bales. The sun was sinking lower in the sky and it streamed through the high windows, lighting the entire area in a golden glow. "Andy had to make some phone calls but he said he'd be right over."

Lucy stepped closer, studying the blue-and-white diagram.

"This is what they call an elevation," O'Hara said. "It shows what the casino will look like from the southeast, actually the main entrance."

Lucy looked at the rounded awning, which was reminiscent of a long house. She noticed the carvings of a bear and turtle that stood on either side of the doorway. Her eyes followed the soaring lines of the hotel tower and she counted the rows of windows.

"Fourteen stories. It seems so big. Bigger than anything we've ever seen in Tinker's Cove."

"I know. But what would you rather have? A tall building like this or a sprawling complex covering acres of land?"

"I guess I never thought of it that way," said Lucy.

"This is so much more economical. It's energy efficient." O'Hara paused, looking at her. "You know, I'll never understand you country folk. You've got all this empty land—acres and acres of it—and you all act like one building is going to spoil it. What gives?"

Lucy shrugged. "People around here like it the way it is."

"I noticed." He tapped the plans with his finger. "You can't hold back progress, you know. Whether you like it or not, things are going to change in Tinker's Cove, with or without the casino. If the tribe gets federal recognition, the whole balance of power is going to change. It won't be Howard White and his buddies calling the shots anymore. And your boss Ted? He's awfully cocky for a guy whose entire livelihood is tied up in that rickety newspaper. I mean, think what one carelessly thrown match could do to that place."

Lucy's head jerked up and she stared at O'Hara. "Is that why you had me come here? To send a message to Ted that you're going to torch the *Pennysaver* if he doesn't support the casino?"

O'Hara had been getting the full force of the slanting sunlight; it was so bright it illuminated the dancing dust particles in the air. Beads of perspiration had formed on his upper lip and he wiped them away with his hand.

"You've got me wrong," said O'Hara, unzipping his jacket. "I just think people should think things through before they make big decisions."

"That's good advice for—" began Lucy, stammering to a halt as her eyes fell on the short black thread that dangled from the neck of his sweater. It should have held a button, a woven leather button just like the ones that remained.

"Well, for anyone," she continued brightly, hoping he hadn't noticed her staring. "It's just common sense," she babbled on, wondering if O'Hara's missing button was *the* missing button. "What my mother used to tell me: 'Think before you speak.'"

O'Hara nodded and leaned forward to pull out another plan, and she instinctively stepped back. He looked at her curiously.

"I think that, if you keep an open mind when you look at these plans, you'll have to agree the casino could be a real asset to the town. Look here. We've used a woodland theme. A brook with waterfalls actually runs through the gaming area and there will be recordings of birdsong. The furniture will be Adirondack style, like a lodge, right down to a gigantic fieldstone fireplace."

He tapped the plan with his finger, inviting Lucy to step

forward and take a closer look. She knew she should do it, but she couldn't make her feet move. All she could think about was that missing button.

"I know casinos aren't everybody's cup of tea," he said, sensing her discomfort. "Let me show you the shopping concourse. It's truly magnificent. It has a four-story waterfall."

As he spoke, Lucy came to a decision. She had to get out of there. She'd make up an excuse, a little white lie, and leave.

"You know," she said, making a show of checking her watch. "I just realized that I have to pick up my daughter from Brownies."

Damn it. If only she could take her eyes off that darn sweater. But no matter how hard she tried, her gaze kept returning to the sight of that dangling thread.

"I thought you said you had until four when the selectmen have their meeting." His eyes had become flat and his tone was insistent.

"I'm sorry. I just forgot about the scout meeting. I really do have to go," insisted Lucy, wishing she had never agreed to meet O'Hara.

"I only have a few more points to go over with you," he said firmly. "It won't take long."

Looking through the long barn, Lucy could see the door, still ajar. More than anything she wanted to go through it.

"I can't stay," she said. "I really have to pick up my daughter."

"Can't she wait for a few minutes?" His tone was unexpectedly vehement and it struck Lucy that O'Hara was a man used to getting his own way, a man who didn't like to be crossed.

"Ten minutes," she said, hoping he'd accept a compromise. Besides, she was probably just being silly. There was no sense jumping to conclusions. Lots of people wore those sweaters. What had Horowitz said? Every man in American had something with that kind of button in his closet. Furthermore, she knew they tended to fall off. How many times had she replaced the buttons on Bill's sport coat? Having a missing button wasn't a crime and it didn't mean O'Hara was a murderer. The sooner she went along with him, she told herself, the sooner she'd get out of there. Her best bet was to behave as normally as possible without giving him a hint of her suspicions. She could keep a poker face as well as anyone.

"How many stores in the shopping concourse?" she asked, trying to sound interested.

"Forty or so, ranging from high-end jewelry and fur boutiques to souvenirs and T-shirts."

"This is a much bigger project than I imagined," she said.

"Mulligan is one of the biggest construction companies in the Northeast," he boasted. "We only do big projects."

"Really?" Lucy decided to lay on the flattery. "And you're in line to be the next CEO?"

"I don't know where Howard White gets off saying stuff like that." He glanced at TomTom, who was still regarding them suspiciously from his pen. "One thing I've learned in business is never to count your chickens, or your turkeys, before they're hatched. There are plenty of foxes sniffing around, believe me."

"From what Howard said, it sounded like a sure thing."

"No way. I've got a lot of competition for the job." He looked at the plans. "Of course, if I can make a go of this thing it would give me a real advantage." He paused and smiled smugly. "You see, this casino project is my baby."

"What do you mean? Didn't the Metinnicuts hire you?"

"No way. It was my idea," he said. "You see, I've known

Andy for a long time. We went to college together. When he told me the local tribe was trying to get federal recognition, I approached Bear Sykes. He hadn't even thought of a casino until I mentioned it. I mean, of course they'd thought of it, but they hadn't come to any decision."

Lucy nodded. "From what Ellie told me they were mostly interested in maintaining their heritage and establishing a cultural identity."

"Whoa," said O'Hara, holding up his hands in protest. "If I hear those words one more time—I mean, what do they want? We've got bears and turtles and babbling brooks and fucking birdsongs, pardon my French. But that wasn't enough, not for Mr. Nolan. It wasn't enough that this casino can generate enough money for the entire tribe to go live in Tahiti if they want, for God's sake, but he's nitpicking every little thing. Talk about bad timing. Just when we need to grease the wheels he comes in throwing sand around. That guy made a big mistake when he tangled with me."

O'Hara suddenly realized he'd said too much. "Not that I had anything to do with his death."

"Of course not," said Lucy, backing away from him. "That never crossed my mind."

O'Hara's eyes were fixed on something in the corner. Lucy followed his gaze and recognized a maul—an oversize mallet with a steel head used to force a wedge through a log to split it into firewood.

"Of course, I'm not shedding any tears for him," said O'Hara, picking up the maul and checking its heft. "I guess you could call it a lucky break."

Lucy had split plenty of wood in the days when they'd heated their house with a woodstove, and she knew to the ounce exactly how heavy a maul was. She had once dropped one on her foot, which had turned black-and-blue for weeks. She didn't even want to think about the damage one could cause if it were used as a weapon. She looked toward the door, estimating the distance. If she made a run for it, would she make it? Not unless O'Hara was distracted, she decided.

"I've always believed you make your own luck," said Lucy, nervously backing up against the turkey pen and reaching in her coat pocket. Behind her, she could hear TomTom making throaty noises. "Things seem to be going pretty well for you. You wouldn't want to do anything foolish."

"One thing I know," he said, stepping toward her. "You don't get ahead by being indecisive—you can't be afraid to take risks."

He started to lift the maul and Lucy knew he planned to kill her, just as he'd killed Curt Nolan. She edged away from him and reached deeper in her pocket, finally finding what she was looking for: the red beret she had stuffed there earlier. She pulled it out, waving it and tossing it straight at O'Hara.

He instinctively ducked and grabbed for it, giving Lucy an opportunity to unlatch the gate of TomTom's pen.

Enraged by the sight of the red beret in O'Hara's hand, the huge bird went straight for his supposed rival. Caught off balance by the unexpected attack, O'Hara went flying and landed on his seat in a pile of straw.

TomTom cocked his head, blinked his eyes and decided he'd been so successful at cutting this guy down to size that he might as well finish him off. He puffed out his chest, spread his tail, and renewed his attack.

Lucy didn't wait to watch. She started to run for the door but stopped in her tracks when it flew open and Kudo ran in, followed by Barney Culpepper.

"Hold it right there!" bellowed Barney, reaching for his gun.

O'Hara froze, holding the maul at shoulder height and keeping a wary eye on the turkey. TomTom, however, was no longer interested in attacking him. He was checking out a new opponent: Kudo, who had faced off opposite him, growling.

"You're under arrest," Barney told O'Hara. "Put the maul down and put your hands behind your back."

"What's the charge?" demanded O'Hara, cocky as ever.

"Mistreating an animal will do for starters,'" said Barney, snapping on the cuffs.

Her knees shaking, Lucy stroked Kudo's thick ruff. He wagged his tail, then jumped at TomTom, sending the turkey scurrying for the safety of his pen. Lucy fastened the catch with trembling hands. Then she collapsed on her knees, burying her nose in the dog's fur and hugging him.

He tolerated this embarrassing display for a few seconds, then pulled away, cocking his head and pricking up his ears.

"You're right," said Lucy. "It's time to get out of here."

CHAPTER 22

L ucy had just put Kudo in the car when she heard sirens. So did the Browns, who began pouring out of the house and streaming down the hill to the barnyard. *About time*, thought Lucy, slamming down the hatch. *Where were you when I needed you?*

Andy led the group, marching up to Barney and demanding, "What's going on?"

Marian Brown stood a few steps behind him, wiping her hands on her apron and keeping an eye on the kids.

"I'm making an arrest," said Barney, lifting off his cap and running his hand through his brush cut before replacing it.

Andy peered in the back of the cruiser, then raised his eyebrows in shock when he recognized Jack O'Hara.

"There must be some mistake!" he declared. "That's Jack!"

"Excuse me," said Marian, stepping beside her husband, "but what possible reason could you have for arresting Mr. O'Hara?"

"Well, somehow I think it's for more than attempting to assault a turkey," said Barney as a couple of state police cars spun into the driveway with their lights flashing.

Barney went to confer with the new arrivals, leaving Lucy with the Browns.

"Do you know what's going on?" asked Andy.

"I'm not sure," said Lucy, "but I think your friend killed Curt Nolan."

Marian and Andy exchanged glances. Then Marian bustled off, shooing the kids back into the house. Andy hitched up his overalls and studied Lucy.

"Are you the one who came up with this bright idea?" he asked, hooking his thumbs in the straps of his overalls and looking down at her.

"It wasn't me," said Lucy, watching as Barney returned to the cruiser and drove off with O'Hara, followed by one of the state police cars.

"O'Hara asked me out here to show me the plans—at least that's what he said, but things got a little out of hand." She shuddered and looked at Andy. "What were you all doing? I must have been in the barn with him for half an hour. Didn't you notice you had company?"

Andy's face got a little red and he gave his overalls another hitch. "The boys and me were watching TV, one of them talk shows. It was about moms who steal their daughters' boyfriends." He grinned. "It got pretty wild there—pulling hair, fighting. They had to pull a couple of 'em apart." He shook his head. "They shouldn't allow stuff like that on TV."

Maybe you shouldn't watch it, thought Lucy as Lieutenant Horowitz approached them.

"I think we've got everything under control here," he told Andy. "Thanks for your cooperation."

"No problem," said Andy. "Do you mind telling—"

"I'm afraid I can't say anything right now," Horowitz told

him. "Now if you don't mind, I have a few questions for Mrs. Stone."

Andy stood his ground for a moment, then realized he was being dismissed. He shrugged and went back to the house, leaving them alone.

Lucy took a deep breath and looked up at the sky, which was orangey from the setting sun.

"I thought we had an understanding," said Horowitz, scolding her. "I thought you were going to stay out of this."

"I was. I did," answered Lucy quickly. "Honest."

Horowitz spoke slowly. "O'Hara's a dangerous man."

"You don't have to tell me," said Lucy indignantly. "He was going to bash my brains out with a maul."

"I don't doubt it for a minute," said Horowitz, fixing his pale gray eyes on hers. "Once we started talking to people at Mulligan Construction, he became our top suspect. Nolan wasn't the first, you know. O'Hara was involved in the disappearance of a secretary, but there wasn't enough evidence to charge him. We got a lot of information from a former employee who was planning to move here."

"St. John Barth?" asked Lucy.

Horowitz looked at her curiously. "You know him?"

"My husband is restoring a house for the Barths, but they changed their minds. They want to sell it."

"Barth didn't want to be anywhere near O'Hara," said Horowitz by way of explanation. "Barth knew too much about O'Hara."

Lucy screwed up her mouth. She couldn't believe she'd had Barth at her dinner table the day of the murder and he'd had the answer. If only she'd asked him.

"Is something the matter?" Horowitz sounded concerned.

Lucy shook her head. "I never suspected him, not for a minute." She shivered, thinking what a close call she'd had. "Is that why Barney came? He knew O'Hara was here?"

"Not exactly. Your boss called. I guess your conversation with O'Hara was recorded somehow on the message system. When he found out you were meeting O'Hara he was worried about your safety. It seems O'Hara had threatened him earlier today."

Lucy shook her head. "I can't believe I was so stupid. O'Hara wanted me to take another look at the casino plans. He said I should keep an open mind."

"You never suspected he had killed Nolan?"

"No. I had my suspicions," she paused, "about somebody else."

"Ah." Horowitz put his long fingers together. "So I guess I was right and you were wrong."

Lucy grimaced. "I guess."

"I hope you'll keep that in mind in the future," he said. "Some things are best left to the professionals. Now go back home to your family and count your blessings, Mrs. Stone. You were very lucky today, you know."

"I know," said Lucy.

She managed a little smile and he gave her a nod. Then he started across the yard to his car.

Lucy watched him go for a moment, then called out, "Lieutenant! Just thought I'd let you know there's a button missing from O'Hara's sweater—not that it means anything, of course, but it's worth checking out."

"Thank you," he said, giving her a salute.

Lucy took a last look at the sky, now a deep purplish blue, and opened the car door. Kudo was waiting for her.

"Extra rations for you tonight," she told him. "A whole can of turkey and giblets."

She had no sooner spoken than she could have sworn she heard a distant protesting gobble from TomTom in the barn.

"Did you hear anything?" she asked Kudo as she started the car.

There was no answer from the cargo area, but she did hear him lick his chops.

CHAPTER 23

It was a beautiful spring morning. Lucy had to admit that; who could argue with a cloudless blue sky, flowering apple trees and gorgeous, lush lilac bushes covered with blossoms that bobbed in the warm breeze? It was the sort of day that lifted your spirits, put a smile on your face and a bounce in your step.

Nevertheless, her heart was heavy as she drove the familiar route to Andy Brown's farm. Today the ground-breaking ceremony for the new casino was to take place and she was covering it for the newspaper. Even though she knew the casino would bring jobs and money to Tinker's Cove, she hated to see the quiet countryside she loved become the site of a gleaming monument to greed and avarice. They called it entertainment but she knew better; gambling was simply another way to separate a fool from his money. Money that would be better spent on shoes for the children and groceries and mortgage payments.

Looking back over the last few months, Lucy could hardly believe how smoothly the casino project had progressed. One by one the expected obstacles had toppled. The Bureau of Indian Affairs had recently revised its policy on tribal recognition and had granted the Metinnicut people tribal status in record time. The state legislature, where both Democrats and Republicans were eager for increased tax revenue, had voted to approve the casino with little discussion. Faced with what appeared to be an unstoppable juggernaut, the members of the Tinker's Cove Planning Board had been unwilling to risk embroiling the town in expensive court appeals and promptly issued the necessary approval. In a matter of months the casino project had gone from a set of paper plans to reality.

She supposed the project's success would have assured Jack O'Hara the job he wanted so much that he was willing to kill for it. Perhaps he was taking some satisfaction from the fact that the casino would be built, from whatever section of the hereafter he was presently occupying. O'Hara hadn't been willing to face a trial and the likelihood of spending the rest of his life in jail. Instead, he had managed a spectacular escape and had been shot by pursuing police officers. "Suicide by cop," they called it, but Lucy suspected O'Hara was betting he could get away.

As Horowitz had told her, it was St. John Barth who fingered O'Hara in the first place. He had been the last person to see the missing secretary alive, getting in O'Hara's car, but although he'd told the police, they had never been able to make a case against O'Hara. Barth had left the company, figuring it would be prudent to get as far away from O'Hara as he could. As he had explained to Bill, when O'Hara had turned up in Tinker's Cove, he didn't think he could risk an encounter. So he and Clarice had decided to sell the house. Now, with O'Hara out of the picture, the Barths had moved in and St. John was working on a true-crime book about his former nemesis.

The thought made Lucy smile as she parked the car and climbed out, checking to be sure she had her camera and notebook. As she made her way through the crowded parking lot to the pumpkin field where the casino was to be built, she saw the crowd was divided into several groups.

Holding center stage was Sandy Dunlap, dressed in a red power suit and sporting a chic new hairdo, backed by Mulligan Construction executives and town officials sympathetic to the project. Rumor was she was considering a run for the state legislature, and Lucy had no doubt she'd win. As Ted had pointed out so often, Sandy was a terrific campaigner, but she didn't have a clue what to do once she got in office.

The Brown family was also there in force, all dressed in their Sunday best. Lucy wondered if they would stay on in the farm house, next to the casino, or if they'd take the money and settle somewhere else, someplace where there wasn't a tacky casino spoiling the landscape.

Also standing with Sandy and beaming approval were a group from the Business and Professional Women's Association of Tinker's Cove led by Franny Small. This newly formed group was having a definite impact on town politics, well out of proportion to its small size.

Last, but not least among the group gathered around the town officials, were Bear Sykes and the Metinnicut people, dressed in traditional Native American clothing decorated with fringe, beads, and feathers.

Another group was also waiting for the ceremony to begin, but these people had grim expressions on their faces and had arranged themselves in front of a Mulligan Construction bulldozer. Jonathan Franke was there, holding a placard that read, *Bet on the environment*, and so was Fred Rumford, holding a traditional deerskin drum. Ellie was absent, Lucy noticed, speculating that she would have found herself in an awkward position, having to choose between her loyalty to the tribe and her relationship with Jonathan.

There was a squeal from the microphone as Sandy began speaking and thanked everyone for coming.

"This project has not been without controversy," she continued, getting a few chuckles from the crowd, "but change is always controversial. Today we are embarking on a new adventure, which we hope will bring unprecedented prosperity to our community— to our whole community."

Everyone, except the protesters, applauded. They remained stubbornly in place, in front of the bulldozer.

Sandy raised her hand and the machine roared into life, she lowered her hand and it began rumbling forward, making the first cut in the field. The protesters stood their ground until the last minute. Then they scattered for safety to the sidelines, where they stood in a ragged row. Fred Rumford began beating his drum slowly, as if for a dirge.

Lucy had snapped some pictures and was moving among the crowd, collecting quotes, when it suddenly became much quieter. The slow drumbeats continued but the bulldozer had stopped and was idling in the middle of the field. The operator had jumped down and could be seen on his knees, pawing at the dirt.

Rumford passed his drum over to Franke, who continued the slow beat, and ran out to join the bulldozer operator. He, too, knelt and began gently brushing away at the soil. When he stood up his solemn expression had been replaced with a huge smile.

"We have archaeological remains," he exclaimed, and the protesters erupted into joyful cheers.

"What does that mean?" asked Sandy, looking puzzled.

"That means everything stops. Right now. We have to call the state archaeologist, who will determine if the site is historically valuable and should be preserved."

A little worried furrow appeared between Sandy's brows.

"You can't do that!" exclaimed Andy Brown. "This is my land and I say we're going ahead." He tapped the bulldozer operator on his shoulder. "You, get back up on the machine. Let's go."

The fellow shook his head. "Sorry. No can do." He tilted his head toward Rumford. "He's right. It's a state law. We have to wait for the archaeologist."

"How long will that take?" demanded Andy impatiently.

The fellow shrugged. "A couple of weeks maybe."

"And then we can go ahead with the casino, right?"

"Wrong." It was Rumford, looking as if he'd stumbled on the Holy Grail. "These are human remains, very old remains. And Metinnicut pot shards. If I'm right, and I'm sure I am, this is a gravesite dating from 1400 or earlier."

"So what? There's stuff like that all over the farm. Arrowheads, bits of this and that—I don't know what all."

"There are?" Rumford could hardly contain his delight. "All over, you say?"

"Yeah. What of it?"

"This is a priceless archaeological resource!" Rumford was bouncing on his toes. "It can't be touched! It's one of a kind! It will have to be excavated and researched! Do you know how rare this is? It's fantastic! It's what I've been waiting for my entire life."

"What about the casino?" insisted Brown.

"There's no question about that. You'll have to find another site for the casino."

Brown glared at him angrily, then stomped off to confer with the Mulligan executives.

Bear Sykes approached Rumford. "You say these are the remains of my ancestors?"

"I'd bet my life on it," said Rumford. "Heck, I'm going to stake my career on it. This land holds a wealth of information about the Metinnicut people."

Sykes nodded. "It is good," he said and began clapping his hands and singing a traditional chant. He was soon joined by other members of the tribe, and Franke picked up the beat on his drum. Someone produced a tightly knotted bundle of sage leaves and lighted it; fragrant smoke rose heavenward.

Lucy took a deep breath and savored the sharp scent of the burning herbs. She surveyed the field filled with friends and neighors and looked beyond to the budding trees that rimmed the field. She looked up at the blue sky, where a single dark cloud had formed directly overhead blocking the sun. Then she thought of Curt Nolan.

She remembered the day he died, how his sightless eyes had looked up at the sky. Today, if he was up there, perched on that cloud and looking down on the human comedy in Andy Brown's pumpkin field, he must surely be smiling. As she watched, a gleam of bright light broke through the cloud. It split apart and the sun shone brightly once again.

A *Lucy Stone* Thanksgiving

Lucy Stone has cooked the same Thanksgiving dinner for years. In fact, it's the same dinner she remembers her mother and grandmother cooking when she was a little girl. Lucy has inherited her mother's china, and her grandmother's crystal and linen, and uses them to set the table. She takes great pleasure in taking them out for the holidays—she even enjoys ironing the linen tablecloth and napkins!

The menu is simple: New England home cooking based on recipes from *The Fannie Farmer Cookbook*. Lucy has the eleventh edition, which was published in 1965, and doesn't think much of the newer versions.

For a centerpiece, Lucy arranges colorful fall leaves on her best white damask tablecloth and piles fresh fruit and vegetables on top. The arrangement varies from year to year, depending upon what's available, but she likes to use apples, pears, and Concord or Fox grapes, punctuated with tiny pumpkins and squash. She doesn't use tropical fruits such as oranges and bananas, believing that only native-grown New England produce is appropriate for Thanksgiving. A scattering of mixed nuts in their shells completes the arrangement, which the family nibbles on after the meal. When the children were younger, Bill used to make little boats out of the walnut shells, continuing a tradition from his own childhood.

Five kernels of dried corn are placed at each place setting. That was the daily ration allowed to each of the Pilgrims during their first difficult winter in Plymouth Colony, and it is a reminder of the hardship they endured so they could enjoy the freedom we take for granted today.

Appetizer

Lucy tends to agree with her mother, who always maintained appetizers were too much trouble and only spoiled people's appetites, anyway. Sometimes, though, she does serve shrimp or oysters before dinner.

Shrimp are served chilled, on ice, with cocktail sauce and lemon slices.

Oysters are served raw, on the half shell, also with cocktail sauce.

Soup

What? And make more dishes to wash?

Main Course

Roast turkey with bread stuffing (Sensitive about her weight, Lucy now mixes chicken broth, instead of water and butter, with either Pepperidge Farm or Arnold stuffing.)

Giblet gravy

Mashed potatoes

Sweet potatoes or yams (the canned kind, heated in the oven while she makes the gravy)

Creamed onions (white onions from a jar in white sauce)

Petite peas (frozen, not canned)

Condiments (These are served in crystal dishes Lucy inherited from her grandmother.)

Cranberry sauce (whole berry)

Celery with pimento-stuffed olives

Sweet pickle mix (the kind with cauliflower and tiny onions)

Dessert

Mince pie (Lucy always uses a jar of Grandmother's brand mincemeat.)

Apple pie (Macintosh or Cortland apples)

Pumpkin pie (A good way to use up pumpkins left over from Halloween)

Coffee, fruit, and nuts

Please turn the page
for an exciting sneak peek of
Leslie Meier's
newest Lucy Stone mystery

WEDDING DAY MURDER

now on sale at bookstores everywhere!

Lucy felt a little odd as she drove off in the Subaru later that day to the shower, the wrapped Pyrex bowls set carefully on the passenger seat. The Fourth of July had always been a family holiday with a cookout followed by fireworks, but this year Elizabeth and Toby had made plans with their friends, and Lucy had been invited to the shower.

Left with only the two younger girls, Bill had accepted an invitation to the Orensteins' barbecue. Lucy knew they'd have a good time, but she still felt a little guilty about going to the shower all by herself.

On the other hand, she admitted to herself, wild horses couldn't have kept her away. Sue needed her moral support—that went without saying—but this was also an opportunity to see Thelma in action. Lucy couldn't begin to imagine what she had planned for the shower. Anything could happen. Entertainment by Chippendales? Siegfried and Roy and assorted feline companions? The Rolling Stones, dropping by to play an unplugged private concert? Nothing seemed too outrageous for Thelma, given her access to her son's money and her willingness to spend it.

As she drove, she cast a nervous eye on the sky where clouds were gathering. The spell of fine weather they'd been enjoying was finally coming to an end; thunderstorms had been forecast and she hoped they'd hold off until after the fireworks.

When Lucy pulled into the parking lot at the harbor, the Davitz's yacht was brightly lit with Christmas lights, even the gangplank was outlined in twinkling white lights. As she drew closer, she could hear the buzz of conversation and the tinkle of piano music. For a moment, she felt like pinching herself. The warm night air, the music, the graceful figures on the deck—she felt as if she had wandered into *The Great Gatsby*.

Stepping on board the *Sea Witch*, she was met by a uniformed steward, who welcomed her and relieved her of her gift, placing it with others on a nearby table. She then made her way to the open deck on the stern, where the guests were gathered, and looked for her hostess.

She didn't find Thelma, but she did see Sue and Sidra and hurried right over, embracing Sidra and giving her a big hug.

"It's wonderful to see you—and such a happy occasion. You know we all wish you so much happiness."

"It's nice to see you, too, Aunt Lucy," replied Sidra.

Lucy studied her, realizing again just how much she resembled her mother. She had Sue's neat, petite body and her straight, glossy hair. Her face was softer and plumper than her mother's; where Sue's lean features made her striking, Sidra was pretty, even beautiful.

"You look wonderful—a beautiful bride," said Lucy. "I can't get over how much you look like your mother."

"That's the last thing she wants to hear," said Sue, an edge to her voice.

"Nonsense. I could've done a lot worse." Sidra sounded as if she were going through the motions, repeating platitudes, thought Lucy, watching as she turned to greet another guest.

"C'mon. I'll show you where the bar is," Sue offered.

"Where's Thelma? I haven't had a chance to say hi."

"She was here a minute ago." Sue shrugged. "Must have flown off on her broomstick."

Lucy didn't like the sound of this. She wondered if the mother and daughter reunion hadn't gone quite the way Sue wanted.

"You seem a little upset," she said. "What's going on?"

"I'll have a gin and tonic, light on the tonic," said Sue, stepping up to the bar. "Lucy, what'll you have?"

"White wine."

As soon as the drinks were set before them, Sue tossed hers back in one long swallow and replaced the glass. "I'll have another."

Lucy took her hand and realized she was trembling.

"Hold on a minute—tell me what's wrong."

"I'm a wreck. My God, I need another drink."

Lucy glanced at the bartender, who had raised a questioning eyebrow.

"Okay," she said, nodding. "But then you have to tell me what's wrong."

Lucy picked up the fresh drink before Sue could grab it and led her to a quiet corner, next to the bar. "Talk," she said, handing her the drink.

Sue took a quavery breath. "The gun—you know, the one I hid—is gone."

This was the last thing Lucy expected to hear.

"Do you think Sid found it?"

"Who else?"

"Did you ask him about it?"

Sue looked at her as if she were crazy. "I didn't tell him I hid it, so how could I tell him it was gone."

"I think you need to talk to him about this."

"No." Sue was adamant. Her glass, Lucy noticed, was again empty.

"Now, what are you two doing conspiring in the corners?" demanded Thelma, descending on them in a dress comprised of layers and layers of fluttery chiffon accessorized with ropes and ropes of twinkling stones.

Diamonds? wondered Lucy, embarrassed to be found by her hostess behaving so unsociably.

"Such a lovely party. . . ." began Lucy, only to be interrupted by Sue.

"We were just getting drinks," she said, turning her back on Thelma and marching to the bar.

Lucy tried to cover her friends' rudeness. "Is Ron going to be here tonight?"

It was the wrong thing to say.

"He was supposed to be, but he hasn't shown up yet." Thelma was clearly annoyed, but she gave a little chuckle. "Isn't that just like a man?"

Unbidden, an image of Ron appeared to Lucy. He was clutching his chest, which was bleeding, and Sid was standing over him, holding a smoking gun. Lucy blinked, and found herself staring at Thelma's raccoon eyes.

"Just like a man," repeated Lucy.

"Well, I hope he gets here in time to open the presents," said Thelma, bustling off to welcome a new arrival.

Lucy turned her attention to Sue, who was feeling the effects of her drinks.

"Come on. Let's join the party," she said, taking Sue by the elbow.

"Letsh no'," said Sue, leaning heavily on her arm.

As Lucy led her back to the deck, Lucy wondered how many drinks she'd had. This wasn't like Sue, who rarely drank more than a glass of white wine at a time. Lucy looked for a chair, noticing that the party had divided into two camps: a cluster of women in pastel dresses represented the home team while a group dressed almost identically in black sleeveless shifts seemed to be the New Yorkers. Lucy decided to cross the great divide and led Sue to a seat by the New York crowd.

"You must be one of the bridesmaids," she said, extending a hand to a very thin girl with very long hair. "I'm Lucy Stone, an old friend of the family."

"How nice," said the girl, turning around and tossing her hair in Lucy's face.

"That's Susanna. She works with Sidra," said Sue. "C'mon. Let's go talk to Rachel and Pam."

Seeing that the New Yorkers had closed ranks around Sidra, Lucy followed Sue's unsteady progress to the other side of the boat. There, Rachel Goodman and Ted's wife Pam were chatting with Phyllis.

"You can say what you want about Thelma," said Rachel in a low voice. "But the woman sure knows how to throw a party."

"Look at these shrimp." Phyllis held up a skewer. "They're huge."

"And these little crab cakes—delish!" added Pam.

"Good idea," said Lucy, thinking that Sue could use some solid food.

"Not hungry," said Sue. "Thirshy."

Lucy shook her head and Pam, taking in the situation, grabbed Sue's other arm.

"C'mon, Sue. Let's take a turn 'round the buffet table."

Between the two of them they got Sue to the table, but when Lucy let go of her arm to reach for a plate, Sue wriggled away and disappeared into the crowd.

"We tried," said Pam. "How much has she had?"

"Too much," said Lucy. "Should I have the bartender cut her off?"

"Not the way she is now. She'd just raise a ruckus. With luck she'll find a quiet spot and pass out."

"And if not," said Lucy, "she'll raise holy hell." She studied the lavish buffet and came to a decision. "Whatever happens, I'll probably need nourishment."

"That's the spirit," said Pam. "Oooh, these stuffed mushrooms are fabulous."

"Mmm," agreed Lucy.

"It's time for the gifts," announced Thelma, trotting around in her high heels and waving her arms, in effect, performing an odd little dance of the seven veils in her layered dress. "Everyone, take a seat."

It took a few minutes for the group to get settled, forming

a sort of circle around Sidra. There was still no sign of Ron, and Lucy didn't blame him. He would have been the only man present and certainly would have felt rather awkward. Thelma clapped and a steward appeared, carrying a tray of gifts. He was followed by another, and another, until the pile of wrapped presents set before Sidra towered above her.

"Oh, my goodness," exclaimed the bride-to-be, as a little color rose in her cheeks. "This is too much. It's embarrassing."

"At least she has the decency to blush," observed Phyllis, a touch of vinegar in her voice. "Where's Sue?"

"Sleeping it off, I hope," said Lucy. She was worried about Sue, but didn't feel she could absent herself from the group without being conspicuous.

"Now, who's this from?" Sidra had plucked a large box from the pile and was opening the card. "From Susanna. I know this is going to be lovely."

"Who is Susanna?" hissed Pam.

"One of the WIBs," replied Rachel. "Women-in-Black."

Sidra was pulling the gift from waves of tissue paper, revealing a Cuisinart. Everybody oohed.

"Oh, you shouldn't have. Thank you so much. . . ."

Sidra was interrupted by Molly Thacher, her old high school friend. "Now, Sidra, what did you do with the bow?"

Sidra fumbled with the discarded wrapping and found the bow.

"What do you want with it?"

"Why, she's going to make a hat—just like they did at my baby shower," said Carrie Swift, Chuck Swift's wife. "They made me the cutest hat by taping all the bows to a paper plate."

"Oh," said Sidra, with a conspicuous lack of enthusiasm.

"I'll make the hat, if you just give me a paper plate," offered Molly.

"Too bad. No paper plates," said one of the WIBs, throwing her hands in the air.

Molly and Carrie shared a glance.

"Next present," announced the third WIB, passing a huge box to Sidra.

There were more oohs and aahs when this gift—a crystal punch bowl—was revealed.

"Oh, Lily! It isn't Waterford, is it?"

Lily smiled demurely and nodded.

"You darling! You shouldn't have!"

"Darn tootin' she shouldn't have," muttered Phyllis. "What's Sidra going to do with a white elephant like that?"

Lucy shrugged and bit her tongue. She wasn't going to tell Phyllis how much that particular white elephant had cost.

"Now, what could this be?"

Sidra was holding up a flat little package, simply wrapped in tissue paper and white curling ribbon.

"Oh—that's mine!" exclaimed Molly.

All eyes were on Sidra as she unwrapped the gift: four handwoven potholders in violent shades of purple and pink.

"What are . . ." began one WIB.

"Like you make in camp . . ." volunteered the second WIB.

"On a little loom!" finished the third, dissolving into helpless giggles.

"I made them myself," volunteered Molly, puzzled at the reaction to her gift. "I used your favorite colors. Remember, in eighth grade, you said you were going to have an all-pink house?"

"Really, you shouldn't have," exclaimed Sidra. From her tone, it seemed clear she wasn't pleased to be reminded of her childhood excesses.

"No expense spared!" hooted the first WIB.

"One hundred percent synthetic!" added another.

"Your favorite colors!" screamed the third.

"Well, I think they're very pretty," said Carrie, patting Molly's hand.

Molly's head was bowed and Lucy hoped she wasn't crying. They're not worth your tears, she wanted to tell her.

"Ah—a present from Kat . . . I bet it's going to be naughty," said Sidra, as she untied the bow and lifted the top off the next box. When she saw what was inside, she shrieked.

"What could it be?" wondered Pam aloud.

"A sexy nightie?" guessed Lucy.

"Not quite," said Rachel dryly, as Sidra held up a black leather mask, a whip and a pair of gloves.

"It's the whole outfit," volunteered Kat. "Just in case Ron gets out of hand."

The women on the boat were silent. Even Thelma seemed at a loss for words, choosing instead to fan herself with a napkin.

"What size do these come in anyway?" asked one of the WIBs.

"Mean, meaner and meanest," replied Kat, sending Sidra and the other WIBs into gales of laughter.

Lucy decided to take advantage of the moment to slip away and look for Sue. She found her, predictably, at the bar. Perched on a stool, she was telling the bartender all about her troubles.

"Jusht don' reck, reckanize my own daughter," said Sue, shaking her head sadly. "The li'l girl I raised wouldn't ack like thish."

"How's it going?" asked Lucy, taking the seat beside her.

"Know tha' movie—'*Vasion of the Body Sna-snashhers?* Thass wha's happened. They've snashed Sidra. She looksh like Sidra and talksh like Sidra, but she's not."

From what Lucy had seen, she thought Sue might be on to something. "Did you talk to her about the wedding plans?"

Sue nodded and drained the last of her drink.

"She sez whatever Thelma wansh is fine with her—doesn't want to alee—aleenate her mother." Sue hiccuped. "In-law." She passed her drink to the bartender. "Fill 'er up."

In response to his glance, Lucy mouthed the word

"tonic." He nodded in understanding and made the drink without adding any gin.

Sue took a swallow and Lucy held her breath.

"Mmm good," said Sue.

"C'mon," said Lucy, standing up. "Let's go up to the top deck and get a good spot for the fireworks. They'll be starting soon."

"Goo' idea."

Sue wasn't too steady on her feet, but Lucy managed to get her up the stairs and out into the fresh air. From below, they could hear the women's voices as Sidra worked her way through the pile of presents, but they had the upper deck to themselves. Lucy led Sue to a pair of deck chairs by the railing and they sat down, looking out over the harbor. A crowd had gathered in the parking lot and on the hills around the harbor, but Lucy and Sue couldn't see them from where they sat. A few boats bobbed about, filled with people waiting for the fireworks to start, but for the most part the harbor was dark and peaceful. The water gleamed black with silver reflections from the lights on the boats. Anytime now the fireworks would start.

Lucy noticed Sue's head drooping. At last, she was finally drifting off. Sitting beside her. Lucy took a moment to reflect. She could imagine how she would feel if Elizabeth behaved as Sidra had and how horrified she would be if her college friends turned out to be like the WIBs. Lucy clucked her tongue, watching as a single rocket rose screaming into the night sky and exploded in a burst of light, a blossom of fiery sparks that bloomed and faded.

Soon the sky was filled with exploding fireworks and the party moved up to the upper deck, crowding around the railing facing the harbor.

Sue woke and, guessing that her greenish pallor was not the reflection of the fireworks, Lucy helped her up and led her downstairs. Unsure where the head was located, Lucy steered her toward the railing, just in case.

"Don' fee-el goo'," said Sue.

"Look at the fireworks," urged Lucy, hoping to distract her.

Sue clutched the railing and leaned over. Here we go, thought Lucy, but she was wrong. Sue was pointing to the water.

"Whaash tha?"

Lucy looked down and saw something white.

"A reflection?"

"No." Sue leaned over farther and Lucy grabbed the back of her dress.

"Whoa, there. You're going to fall in."

"Thas wha' happened. Somebody fell in."

Lucy looked again. Sue was right. Whatever was floating there did resemble a human shape.

"It's probably garbage or something," said Lucy, looking up as a giant rocket exploded overhead, filling the sky with light. In the distance, she heard a boat motor start up and felt the yacht rock slightly under her feet, as the wake hit.

"Not garbage." Sue tugged her sleeve. "Look."

Lucy looked and saw the white form now had arms and legs and a head, all floating a few inches below the surface of the water. Another wave came and the body rolled over. Even in the dim light, Lucy was sure it was Ron. The recognition hit her like a tidal wave and she found herself gripping the railing with every bit of her strength.

Sue moaned. "I'm gonna be sick."

Please turn the page for an exciting sneak peek of
Leslie Meier's newest Lucy Stone mystery
ST. PATRICK'S DAY MURDER!

CHAPTER ONE

Maybe it was global warming, maybe it was simply a warmer winter than usual, but it seemed awfully early for the snow to be melting. It was only the last day of January, and in the little coastal town of Tinker's Cove, Maine, that usually meant at least two more months of ice and snow. Instead, the sidewalks and roads were clear, and the snow cover was definitely retreating, revealing the occasional clump of snowdrops and, in sheltered nooks with southern exposures, a few bright green spikes of daffodil leaves that were prematurely poking through the earth.

You could almost believe that spring was in the air, thought Lucy Stone, part-time reporter for the town's weekly newspaper, the *Pennysaver*. She wasn't sure how she felt about it. Part of her believed it was too good to be true, probably an indicator of future disasters, but right now the sun was shining and birds were chirping and it was a great day to be alive. So lovely, in fact, that she decided to walk the three or four blocks to the harbor, where she had an appointment to interview the new harbormaster, Harry Crawford.

As she walked down Main Street, she heard the steady drip of snow melting off the roofs. She felt a gentle breeze against her face, lifting the hair that escaped from her beret, and she unfastened the top button of her winter coat. Quite a few people were out and about, taking advantage of the unseasonably fine weather to run some errands, and everyone seemed eager to exchange greetings. "Nice day, innit?" and "Wonderful weather, just wonderful," they said, casting suspicious eyes at the sky. Only the letter carrier Wilf Lundgren, who she met at the corner of Sea Street, voiced what everyone was thinking. "Too good to be true," he said, with a knowing nod. "Can't last."

Well, it probably wouldn't, thought Lucy. Nothing did. But that didn't mean she couldn't enjoy it in the meantime. Her steps speeded up as she negotiated the hill leading down to the harbor, where the ice pack was beginning to break up. All the boats had been pulled from the water months ago and now rested on racks in the parking lot, shrouded with tarps or shiny white plastic shrink-wrap. The gulls were gone—they didn't hang around where there was no food—but a couple of crows were flying in circles above her head, cawing at each other.

"The quintessential New England sound," someone had called it, she remembered, but she couldn't remember who. It was true, though. There was something about their raspy cries that seemed to capture all the harsh, unyielding nature of the landscape. And the people who lived here, she thought, with a wry smile.

Harry Crawford, the new harbormaster, was an exception. He wasn't old and crusty like so many of the locals; he was young and brimming with enthusiasm for his job. He greeted Lucy warmly, holding open the door to his waterfront office, which was about the same size as a highway tollbooth. It was toasty inside, thanks to the sun streaming through the windows, which gave him a 360-degree view of the harbor and parking lot. Today he hadn't even switched on the small electric heater.

"Hi, Lucy. Make yourself comfortable," he said, pulling out the only chair for her to sit on. He leaned against the half wall, arms folded across his chest, staring out at the water. It was something people here did, she thought. They followed the water like a sunflower follows the sun, keeping a watchful eye out for signs that the placid, sleeping giant that lay on the doorstep might be waking and brewing up a storm.

"Thanks, Harry," she said, sitting down and pulling off her gloves. She dug around in her bag and fished out a notebook and pen. "So tell me about the Waterways Committee's plans for the harbor."

"Here, here," he said, leaning over her shoulder to unroll the plan and spread it out on the desk. "They're going to add thirty more slips, and at over three thousand dollars a season, it adds up to nearly a hundred thousand dollars for the town."

"If you can rent them," said Lucy.

"Oh, we can. We've got a waiting list." He shaded his eyes with his hand and looked past her, out toward the water. "And that's another good thing. A lot of folks have been on that list for years, and there's been a lot of bad feeling about it. You know, people are not really using their slips, but hanging on to them for their kids, stuff like that. But now we ought to be able to satisfy everyone."

Lucy nodded. She knew there was a lot of resentment toward those who had slips from those who didn't. It was a nuisance to have to ferry yourself and your stuff and your crew out to a mooring in a dinghy. With a slip, you could just walk along the dock to the boat, untie it, and sail off. "So you think this will make everybody happy?" she asked. "What about environmental issues? I understand there will be some dredging."

He didn't answer. His gaze was riveted on something outside that had caught his attention. "Sorry, Lucy. There's something I gotta check on," he said, taking his jacket off a hook.

Lucy turned and looked outside, where a flock of gulls and crows had congregated at the end of the pier. "What's going on?" she asked.

"The ice is breaking up. Something's probably come to the surface."

From the excited cries of the gulls, who were now arriving from all directions, she knew it must be something they considered a meal. A feast, in fact.

"Like a pilot whale?"

"Could be. Maybe a sea turtle, a dolphin even. Could be anything."

"I'd better come," she said, with a groan, reluctantly pulling a camera out of her bag.

"I wouldn't if I were you," he said, shaking his head. "Whatever it is, it's not going to be pretty, not this time of year. It could've been dead for months."

"Oh, I'm used to it," sighed Lucy, who had tasted plenty of bile photographing everything from slimy, half-rotted giant squid tentacles caught in fishing nets to bloated whale carcasses that washed up on the beach.

"Trust me. The stench alone . . ."

She was already beginning to feel queasy. "You've convinced me," she said, guiltily replacing her camera. Any photo she took would probably be too disgusting to print, she rationalized, and she could call him later in the day and find out what it was. Meanwhile, her interest had been caught by a handful of people gathered outside the Bilge, on the landward side of the parking lot. Tucked in the basement beneath a block of stores that fronted Main Street, the Bilge was a Tinker's Cove landmark—and a steady source of news. It was the very opposite of Hemingway's "clean, well-lighted place," but that didn't bother the fishermen who packed the place. It may have been a dark and dingy dive, but the beer was cheap, and Old Dan never turned a paying customer away, not even if he was straight off the boat and stank of lobster bait.

Lucy checked her watch as she crossed the parking lot and discovered it was only a little past ten o'clock. *Kind of early to start drinking,* she thought, but the three men standing in front of the Bilge apparently thought otherwise.

"It's never been closed like this before," said one. He was about fifty, stout, with white hair combed straight back from a ruddy face.

"Old Dan's like clockwork. You could set your watch by it. The Bilge opens at ten o'clock. No earlier. No later," said another, a thin man with wire-rimmed glasses.

"He closed once for a couple of weeks, maybe five or six years ago," said the third, a young guy with long hair caught in a ponytail, who Lucy knew played guitar with a local rock band, the Claws. "He went to Florida that time, for a visit. But he left a sign."

"What's up? Is the Bilge closed?" she asked.

They all turned and stared at her. Women usually avoided the Bilge, where they weren't exactly welcome. A lot of fishermen still clung to the old-fashioned notion that women were bad luck on a boat—and in general.

"I'm Lucy Stone, from the *Pennysaver*," she said. "If the Bilge has really closed, that's big news."

"It's been shut tight for three days now," said the guy with the ponytail.

"Do you mind telling me your name?" she asked, opening her notebook. "It's Dave, right? You're with the Claws?"

"Dave Reilly," he said, giving her a dazzling, dimpled smile.

Ah, to be on the fair side of thirty once more, she thought, admiring Dave's fair hair, bronzed skin, full lips, and white teeth. *He must be quite a hit with the girls*, she decided, reminding herself that she had a job to do. "Has anybody seen Old Dan around town?" she asked.

"Come to think of it, no," said the guy with glasses.

"And your name is?" she replied.

"Brian Donahue."

"Do you think something happened to him?" she asked the stout guy, who was cupping his hands around his eyes and trying to see through the small window set in the door.

"Whaddya see, Frank?" inquired Dave. He turned to Lucy. "That's Frank Cahill. You'd never know it, but he plays the organ at the church."

"Is he inside? Did he have a heart attack or something?" asked Brian.

Frank shook his head. "Can't see nothing wrong. It looks the same as always."

"Same as always, except we're not inside," said Brian.

"Hey, maybe we're in some sort of alternate universe. You know what I mean. We're really in the Bilge in the real world, having our morning pick-me-up just like usual, but we're also in this parallel world, where we're in the parking lot," said Dave.

The other two looked at each other. "You better stick to

beer, boy," said Frank, with a shake of his head. "Them drugs do a job on your brain."

"What am I supposed to do?" replied the rocker. "It's not my fault if Old Dan is closed, is it? A guy's gotta have something. Know what I mean?"

"You could try staying sober," said Lucy.

All three looked at her as if she were crazy.

"Or find another bar," she added.

"The others don't open 'til noon," said Brian. "Town bylaw."

"Old Dan has a special dispensation?" she asked.

The others laughed. "You could say that," said Dave, with a bit of an edge in his voice. "He sure doesn't play by the same rules as the rest of us."

"Special permission. That's good," said Brian.

"Yeah, like from the pope," said Frank, slapping his thigh. "I'll have to tell that one to Father Ed." He checked his watch. "Come to think of it, I wonder where he is? He usually stops in around now."

My goodness, thought Lucy, echoing her great-grandmother who had been a staunch member of the Woman's Christian Temperance Union. She knew there was a lot of drinking in Tinker's Cove, especially in the winter, when the boats sat idle. Some joker had even printed up bumper stickers proclaiming: "Tinker's Cove: A quaint little drinking village with a fishing problem," when government regulators had started placing tight restrictions on what kind of fish and how much of it they could catch and when they could catch it. She'd laughed when she first saw the sticker on a battered old pickup truck. After all, she wasn't above pouring herself a glass of wine to sip while she cooked supper. She certainly wasn't a teetotaler, but her Puritan soul certainly didn't approve of drinking in the morning.

The laughter stopped, however, when they heard a siren blast, and the birds at the end of the pier rose in a cloud, then settled back down.

"Something washed up," said Lucy, by way of explanation. "Probably a pilot whale."

The others nodded, listening as the siren grew louder and a police car sped into the parking lot, screeching to a halt at the end of the pier. The birds rose again, and this time they flapped off, settling on the roof of the fish-packing shed.

"I've got a bad feeling about this," said Dave. "Real bad."

He took off, running across the parking lot, followed by Brian and Frank. Lucy stood for a minute, watching them and considering the facts. First, Old Dan was missing, and second, a carcass had turned up in the harbor. She hurried after them but was stopped with the others at the dock by Harry, who wasn't allowing anyone to pass. At the end of the pier, she could see her friend Officer Barney Culpepper peering down into the icy water.

"I know Barney," she told Harry as she pulled her camera out of her bag. "He won't mind."

"He said I shouldn't let anybody by," insisted Harry, tilting his head in Barney's direction.

Lucy raised the camera and looked through the viewfinder, snapping a photo of Barney staring down into the water. From the official way he was standing, she knew this was no marine creature that had washed up. "I guess it's not a pilot whale?" she asked, checking the image in the little screen.

Harry shook his head.

"It's a person, right?" said Dave. "It's Old Dan, isn't it?"

Lucy's fingers tightened on the camera. There was a big difference between jumping to a conclusion and learning it was true, a big difference between an unidentified body and one with a name you knew.

"I'm not supposed to say," said Harry.

"You don't have to," said Brian. "It's pretty obvious. The Bilge has been closed for days, and there's been no sign of him. He must've fallen in or something."

"Took a long walk off a short pier," said Dave, with a wry grin. "Can't say I'm surprised."

"He was known to enjoy a tipple," said Frank. He eyed the Bilge. "He'll be missed."

"What a horrible way to go," said Lucy, shivering and fingering her camera. "In the cold and dark and all alone."

"Maybe he wasn't alone," said Dave, raising an eyebrow.

"What do you mean?" asked Lucy. "Do you think somebody pushed him in?"

"Might have," said Frank. "He made a few enemies in his time."

Dave nodded. "You had to watch him. He wasn't above taking advantage, especially if you'd had a few and weren't thinking too hard."

Something in his tone made Lucy wonder if he was speaking from personal experience.

"And he wasn't exactly quick to pay his bills," said Brian, sounding resentful.

Another siren could be heard in the distance.

"So I guess he won't be missed," said Lucy.

"No, I won't miss the old bastard," said Frank. "But I'm sure gonna miss the Bilge."

The others nodded in agreement as a state police cruiser peeled into the parking lot, followed by the white medical examiner's van.

"The place didn't look like much," said Brian.

"But the beer was the cheapest around," said Dave.

"Where else could you get a beer for a buck twenty-five?" asked Frank.

The three shook their heads mournfully, united in grief.

Two of her four kids may be out of the nest, but Lucy knows only too well that mothering is a lifetime commitment. At least she gets to kick back and enjoy a fancy Mother's Day brunch with her brood—that is, before the festivities are interrupted by a nasty scene courtesy of Barbara Hume and Tina Nowak. Opposites in every way, the only thing these mean moms have in common is the need to best each other at every turn, using their teenage daughters as pawns in elaborate games of one-upsmanship . . .

The hostilities only escalate when Bar and Tina team up to host an after-prom party for local teens. Lucy—persuaded to participate so she can keep an eye on her own daughter, Sara—has a front row seat for the fireworks. But even after witnessing the women's claw-sharpening rituals, she never expects to see actual blood spilled—until Tina is shot dead on the public tennis court, right in front of Lucy.

Having witnessed Tina's death, Lucy naturally expects to cover it for the *Pennysaver*, but when her boss snatches the story, she's relegated to backing him up instead of taking the lead. It's an exercise in frustration, especially since Lucy can shake neither the image of Tina's last moments nor the suspicion that the evidence against prime suspect Bar isn't as cut and dried as it seems . . .

Lucy is determined to unravel the close-knit knot of suspects, even if she doesn't get the byline. But when the threads threaten to entangle one of her own, Lucy will come face to face with a killer who has a thing or two to learn about motherly love . . .

**Please turn the page for an exciting sneak peek at
Leslie Meier's
MOTHER'S DAY MURDER,
coming in April 2009!**

CHAPTER ONE

The photo on the front page of the Sunday paper was familiar. NO MOTHER'S DAY FOR CORINNE'S MOM read the headline about the plump, sad-eyed woman holding a photo of her pretty teenage daughter. Lucy Stone didn't have to read the story; as a reporter for the weekly *Pennysaver* newspaper, she knew all about it. Corinne Appleton, who had a summer job working as a counselor at the town recreation program in nearby Shiloh, disappeared minutes after her mother dropped her off at the park. The story had been front page news for weeks, then had gradually slipped to page three and finally the second section as other stories demanded attention. But now, ten months later, Corinne was still missing.

"How come you're looking so glum?" demanded her husband, Bill, as he entered the room. "Aren't you enjoying Mother's Day?"

Lucy quickly flipped over the paper, hiding Joanne Appleton's reproachful face.

"My mother always said Mother's Day was invented by the greeting card companies to boost sales," she said, beginning the struggle to get into a pair of control-top panty hose.

"I always heard it was a creation of the necktie manufacturers," complained Bill, who often declared he never regretted giving up suits and ties and Wall Street for the T-shirts and jeans he wore as a restoration carpenter in the little Maine town of Tinker's Cove. "I finally found this in the coat closet downstairs," he said, holding up a rather crumpled tie, the only one he possessed.

"If you think a tie is torture you ought to try panty hose," said Lucy, who usually wore jeans and running shoes, practical attire for her job. Today she was squeezing into heels and a suit for a Mother's Day brunch at the fancy Queen Victoria Inn. "I don't want to seem ungrateful, but I liked it better when the kids gave me homemade cards and plants for the garden."

"And I'd cook breakfast and you'd get to eat it in bed."

"Eventually," laughed Lucy. "I'd be starving by the time it actually arrived."

"That's because they had to pick the pansies and make the placemat and decorate the napkin," said Bill. "It was quite a production. And then they'd fight over who got to carry the tray." He looked across the bed at his wife, who was standing in front of her dresser, putting on a pair of earrings. "Those were the days," he said, crossing the room and slipping his arms around her waist and nuzzling her neck.

His beard, now speckled with gray, tickled and Lucy smiled. "Those days are over," she said. "Our little nest is almost empty."

It was true. Only Sara, a high school freshman, and Zoe, in fifth grade, remained at home. Toby, their oldest, lived with his wife Molly and their son, eight-week-old Patrick, on neighboring Prudence Path. Elizabeth, their oldest daughter, was a senior at Chamberlain College in Boston.

"Can you believe we're grandparents?" continued Lucy, tickling Bill's ear.

"You're still pretty hot," said Bill, appreciatively eyeing her trim figure and cap of glossy dark hair.

"It's a battle," sighed Lucy, leaning forward to smooth on her age-defying make-up.

Bill grabbed her hips and pressed against her but Lucy wiggled free. "We'll be late," she said, reaching for her lipstick. "Besides, now that I'm actually in the panty hose there's no chance they're coming off."

Bill sighed and headed for the door.

"But I appreciate the gesture," she added.

Out in the hallway Bill was knocking on the girls' bedroom doors. "Bus leaves in five minutes," he said. She heard him go downstairs, followed by the clatter of the girls in their dressy shoes.

Lucy was the last to join the group in the kitchen. Bill was handsome in his all-purpose navy blazer, the girls adorable in flowery dresses that bared their arms and shoulders. They'd freeze, but there was no point telling them; they'd been planning what to wear for weeks, ever since Toby came up with the idea of treating his wife and mother to the Mother's Day brunch. "It's Molly's first Mother's Day," he said. "We should do something special."

Unspoken, Lucy suspected, was his concern for Molly, who was making a slow recovery from a difficult pregnancy that ended abruptly on St. Patrick's Day, several weeks earlier than expected. Little Patrick hadn't appreciated his sudden entry into the world and was a cranky and fussy baby, demanding all his exhausted mother's attention. Lucy helped as much as she could with household chores and meals, but only Molly could breastfeed the hungry little fellow, who demanded a meal every couple of hours, day and night. Toby did his best to help, too, but he was putting in long hours on the boat, getting ready for lobster season.

The new parents were already seated when they arrived at the inn's sunny dining room. Patrick was propped in a baby seat between them, sound asleep.

"What an angel," cooed Lucy, stroking his downy cheek. Even in his sleep his lips made little nursing motions.

"More like a barracuda," complained Molly. She was still pudgy from her pregnancy. Her face was splotchy and she needed a haircut. Nevertheless, she'd made an effort, and although she was still wearing maternity pants, she'd topped them with a pretty pastel sweater. Seeing her, Lucy was reminded of the terrifying days after Toby's birth, when she was afraid of dropping him on his head or sticking him with a diaper pin or starving him or overfeeding him and thereby proving her incompetence as a mother.

"The first three months are the hardest," said Lucy. "But you're obviously doing something right. He looks great."

"He's much too skinny," said Molly. "Even though I nurse him constantly, I don't think he's getting enough."

Lucy sat beside Molly and took her hand. "He just looks skinny to you, believe me," she said. "Look at those little creases on his wrists. He's positively chubby."

"That's what I've been telling you," chimed in Toby.

"He's the cutest baby I've ever seen," declared Zoe. "When will he be old enough to play?"

"Around six months," said Sara, causing everyone at the table to look at her in surprise. "What?" she responded, defensively. "I took that babysitting course, remember?"

"I remember, I'm just surprised you do," said a familiar voice.

Lucy turned around and saw Elizabeth, city chic in tight black jeans, stilettos, and streaked hair. "I thought you were in Boston!" Lucy exclaimed, jumping up to hug her daughter.

"I took the bus. I couldn't miss brunch at the Queen Vic," she said, taking the last seat. "I used to work here, remember? Today they're waiting on me!"

"Well, now that we're all here," announced Bill, "let's hit the buffet."

It was really a moment to savor, thought Lucy, when she returned with a plateful of favorite foods: fruit salad with melon and berries, eggs Benedict, smoked salmon, and a croissant. And that was just to start. The buffet featured a raw bar with shrimp and oysters, stuffed chicken breast, ham, roast beef sliced to order, vegetable medleys and salads, plus a lavish tiered display of desserts set up in the middle of the elegant dining room. But while the food was delicious, there was only so much a body could eat. It was spending time with her family, especially Elizabeth, whom she didn't see that often, and the new baby, which was most precious to her.

Seeing them like this, with clean faces, and dressed in their best clothes and minding their manners, was priceless. She couldn't help but be proud of them. Toby with his broad shoulders and easy smile, Elizabeth in her sophisticated clothes and city haircut, Sara who had shed her baby fat and emerged as a graceful will o' the wisp, and Zoe wit her sweet, round face and big blue eyes. And they didn't just look good, they were good citizens. Toby was recognized by the other fishermen as a hard worker and a capable seaman, Elizabeth not only had top grades but had been chosen by her college to be a resident advisor, Sara was an honor student and cheerleader who also volunteered at the local animal shelter, and Zoe was the delight of her teachers and a keen member of the youth soccer team.

She looked across the table at Bill, who was about to eat an enormous piece of sausage, and smiled at him. She was a good mother, but she couldn't have done it without him.

"What are you smiling about?" he asked, spearing a piece of bacon with his fork.

"I'm just happy—it's really special to be here with you all."

"I can't believe the baby is sleeping," said Molly "I was afraid he'd scream his head off. This is special."

Toby made eye contact with his father and, receiving a nod, pulled two pink envelopes out of his jacket. "Dad and I wanted to make it even more special," he began, "so we got these for you."

Lucy opened the thick envelope, which was lined with glossy ink paper, and withdrew a card printed with raised letters: PURE BLISS. Opening it she found a gift certificate entitling her to a facial, body wrap, massage, manicure and pedicure at the fabulous new spa everybody was talking about that had recently opened at the ritzy Salt Aire Resort and Spa.

"You shouldn't have," she said. She was about to add that the gift was too expensive but bit her tongue just in time. This present, this Mother's Day, wasn't about her. It was for Molly, and she realized that her gift certificate came with a string attached: to make sure Molly got to the spa. "This will be fun, won't it, Molly? A whole day of pampering."

"I can't leave the baby for a whole day," she said, shaking her head.

"Sure you can," said Toby. "I'll take care of him."

Sara chimed in. "We'll help, too, won't we, Zoe?"

"I can't wait," agreed Zoe.

"You can't feed him . . ."

"They can, if you pump in advance," said Lucy. "And you won't be gone for a whole day, especially if we tell them to put us on the fast track."

"Well," she said, sighing, "it does sound fabulous."

"I can't wait. Let's book our appoint—" began Lucy, but she was interrupted in mid-sentence by a strident, complaining voice that cut through the hum of conversation and the tinkle of silverware to silence the entire room.

"This is unacceptable, simply unacceptable. When I made the reservation I specifically requested the table in the corner with two windows."

Lucy recognized Barbara Hume, who was standing in the doorway with her husband, Bart, and her sixteen-year-old daughter, Ashley. Today, as usual, the family projected an image of perfection. Bart, actually Dr. Barton Higginson Hume, was a noted cardiac surgeon. Tall and reedy, he towered over his petite wife, Barbara, who preferred to be called Bar, "just like Mrs. Bush, the *first* Mrs. Bush," and never seemed to have a single shellacked hair out of place. Today she was trim as ever, in a pale green suit and bone pumps with a matching bag. Ashley was standing behind her parents, and even though she was perfectly turned out in a pink pleated miniskirt and matching jacket, she was slouching awkwardly with her toes turned in.

"I demand to see Jasper," continued Bar, her voice growing even louder and more authoritative. Everyone in the room turned to watch as the inn's longtime maitre d' hurried over.

"Is there a problem?" he asked.

"I'll say there's a problem. I was promised that the corner

table, the one with the two windows," said Bar, raising a perfectly manicured hand and pointing with her pink-tipped finger, "would be reserved for us."

Lucy also recognized the family occupying the table, the Nowaks, who were making a point of ignoring the fuss. At least Tina was. She was a large, sporty woman, and was shoveling fork-fuls of food, intent on getting her money's worth out of the buffet. Her husband, Lenny, a slight, serious man with a mop of curly gray hair who wore oversized tortoiseshell eyeglasses, was staring at his plate and pushing his food around with his fork, looking distinctly uncomfortable. In contrast, their sixteen-year-old daughter, Heather, was staring contemptuously at Bar, just as you might expect from a talented figure skater who competed regularly and wasn't afraid of a challenge.

"It's a family tradition," continued Bar, in a voice that carried to the farthest corners of the room. "We come here every year for Mother's Day and we always sit at that table."

Jasper cleared his voice and folded his hands. "I am so sorry. There must have been some confusion. We have some new staff members from the Ukraine . . ."

"The person I spoke to was not Ukrainian. She spoke perfect English."

"I regret the mistake," continued Jasper, "but as you can see the table is occupied. I will be happy to sat you someplace else."

"I did not reserve a table 'someplace else,'" snapped Bar. "I demand that you move those Nowaks from the table that should have been reserved for us and reseat them." Bar glared at Tina. "Frankly, I wouldn't be surprised if *somebody* hadn't done this on purpose, just to slight me."

If she was hoping to get a response from Tina, she was disappointed.

Bart, however, cleared this throat, perhaps signaling his wife to cease and desist. If he thought such a subtle sign would calm Bar, he was mistaken.

She snapped her head around to face him, eyes ablaze. "Darling," she began, in a tone that was hardly loving, "perhaps you should slip the maitre d' a little something so we can get the table we want?"

At the Nowaks' table, Tina's face reddened, but she continued to concentrate on her food. Her husband, Lenny, looked as if he were ready to abandon ship and vacate the table. He half rose from his chair but, receiving a sharp glance from Tina, sat back down. Heather was smirking, evidently finding the entire episode just another example of parental foolishness.

Jasper assumed a painted expression. "That will not be necessary," he said. "Now, since it is impossible . . ."

"Nothing's impossible," declared Bar, eyes blazing, "since you've gone to the trouble of importing all these Ukrainians— temporary workers, I presume, who will be returning to their native villages at the end of the summer?"

"Absolutely," said Jasper, with a nod. "They all have temporary work visas."

"You'd better see they do. The country's already got twelve million illegal aliens, you know, and we don't need any more. Especially since most of them don't even bother to learn English."

"We screen our temporary workers very carefully and I can assure you they all speak English."

"Well, that's something. Now why don't you put them to work and have them reseat *those* people," she pointed at the Nowaks, "so we can have *our* table."

Jasper's professional veneer of patience was wearing thin.

"We cannot disturb the other diners," he said. "I'll be happy to seat you at another table."

"Come along, Bar," said Bart, taking his wife by the elbow. "How about that table over there? It's by a window, too."

"But it's not the corner," replied Bar. "It's not *our* table."

Bart was firm. "It's a window, and I'm hungry."

"Oh, all right," she said with a sigh, dramatically rolling her eyes. "I don't want to make a fuss."

"Right, Mom," muttered Ashley, sarcastically, as the group was ushered past the desired corner table.

Tina waited until Bar was behind her chair and then she spoke to her husband. "Don't you think it was rude of Bar to make such a fuss?" she asked, in a loud whisper. "Especially for someone who thinks she's the next Emily Post."

Bar pretended not to hear the comment but seemed to flinch slightly as she followed Japer to the small window table adjacent to the Stones' large round one. Jasper made an elaborate show of pulling out chairs for Bar and Ashley and even placed napkins on their laps with a graceful flourish and snapped his fingers to attract the water boy's attention. He was filling their glasses when Bar took her revenge.

"You know," she began, placing her hand on her husband's arm and leaning toward him, speaking in a low tone that nevertheless carried across the room, "sometimes when I'm target shooting I imagine Tina Nowak's face on the target." She giggled and smoothed her napkin. "It's a surefure way to get a bull's eye."